The Wolf of Kisimul Castle

Highland Isles Series

HEATHER
USA TODAY BESTSELLING AUTHOR
McCOLLUM

This book is a work of fiction. Names, characters, places, and incidents are the product of the author's imagination or are used fictitiously. Any resemblance to actual events, locales, or persons, living or dead, is coincidental.

Entangled Publishing, LLC
644 Shrewsbury Commons Ave
STE 181
Shrewsbury, PA 17361
rights@entangledpublishing.com

Scandalous is an imprint of Entangled Publishing, LLC.

Edited by Alethea Spiridon
Cover design by Erin Dameron-Hill
Cover art from DepositPhotos and Period Images

Manufactured in the United States of America

First Edition August 2017

This book is dedicated to my friend Marsha and all the service dogs she trains.

You train dogs for the blind. You interpret for the deaf. You teach with heart and patience. You are steadfast in your faith. You love with your whole self.

I am honored to be one of your oldest friends. You are beautiful.

Chapter One

Kilchoan Castle—West Coast of Scottish Highlands
August 1523

Mairi Maclean stared at the reflection of her friend in the polished glass. "Why would my groom send someone else to kiss me before our wedding?" she asked.

Ava Maclean, Mairi's sister-in-law, laughed. "It was actually Tor's idea last night over too many whiskies. Geoff slurred something about thinking you didn't want to marry anyone, especially him. So your brother—"

"Your husband," Mairi returned, throwing the blame of Tor's foolish idea back on Ava.

Ava grinned. "Tor said that Geoff should send his most handsome friend to kiss you before the wedding. If you still walk down the aisle to Geoff after that, then you really do want to wed him."

"Drunken plans should not be made the night before weddings," Mairi said, twisting in her seat. "Do ye think Geoff will do it? Send someone to kiss me?" The idea was ludicrous.

Ava shrugged. "But if you're wondering about the marriage at all, you might want to refuse it." Her face grew serious. "Mairi, Tor said you don't have to wed the new MacInnes chief to help the Maclean clan. Just being at Kilchoan Castle again must…" She looked around the small room. "It must bring back horrible memories of your first marriage here."

Mairi had wed the elderly Fergus MacInnes, at her father's request, to strengthen the ties between their clans. While her husband was away on raids against other clans or English regiments, his son, Normond, had made life miserable for Mairi as he stalked her. The castle at Kilchoan had become a prison, forcing Mairi into the role of hiding mouse to avoid rape. But now there was a new chief in charge of the MacInnes of Kilchoan, and Mairi was once again marrying to secure an alliance with the Maclean neighbors.

"Which is why I told Geoff I'd be sleeping in a different room from the chief's." Too many ghosts in that room down the hall.

Ava fixed a few curls intertwined with the pink roses crowning Mairi's head. She sighed. "I don't know if I could go back to Somerset where my bad memories live."

"Memories can't hurt ye, if ye push them down deep enough," Mairi murmured. She took a deep breath and released it. "I will go through with the wedding, but this is the last time I will ever say vows. If this husband dies, I'll just become an old maid and spin wool alone in a cottage at Aros Castle. And I'll take in kittens, aye, kittens."

Ava *tsk*ed. "You're only twenty-three years old, and there's no reason that Geoff MacInnes will die before you are both old and gray. You two could fall in love and be blissfully happy."

Mairi stared into the reflection of her own eyes. Could others pick out the disappointment hidden in the grayish green? It didn't matter. Determination, to be an asset to her family, overrode her childhood dream of foolish love. "'Tis better to guard one's heart, for it is easily battered."

"True," Ava said. "But what good is a heart if you keep it locked up? Sometimes the walls that protect can imprison."

Mairi smiled wryly. "Ye sound like an old sage."

"Really, Mairi. Even if something dreadful happens to Geoff, you must leave yourself open to other possibilities. Where there is life, there is hope. Surely you'd want to marry to have children." She glanced at the angel sleeping in the wooden cradle, her two-month-old daughter, Hazel. "They are a blessing."

"One can have a child without wedding," Mairi said, looking up from under lowered lashes.

Ava met her gaze, her smile chiseled down to seriousness. "I was born illegitimately. It can be done, but it is easier for you and the child if you have a father around. I don't know what I'd do without Tor helping me."

Mairi's brother was an exceptional father and regularly walked around the castle blurry-eyed from taking turns with Ava when Hazel fussed through the night.

"I think Geoff MacInnes could make a fine father and husband," Ava said. "He's young, handsome, and strong."

"At least he doesn't leave food in his beard," Mairi murmured as she stood to smooth the green fabric of her full skirt where it flared out from her narrow waist. Her first husband had worn his meal half the time.

"Knock, knock," called Ava's half sister, Grace Ellington, as she walked into the room.

"Shhh," Ava said and indicated the sleeping babe. A look of apology collapsed Grace's smile, quickly to be replaced by a new one as she walked over to Mairi.

"You look lovely," Grace whispered.

"You can talk normally," Ava said. "Just don't shout. She

was up most of last night again."

"Maybe you need to keep her awake during the day," Grace suggested. "We could poke her," she said with a teasing smile.

"Humph," Ava said, "Some godmother and auntie you are."

"You know that I love little Hazel with all my heart," Grace said, bending over the cradle to inhale. She turned her face up to Ava. "And she smells delicious." She looked at Mairi. "I just love sweet baby smell."

Ava walked around Mairi. "I think you are complete." She smiled broadly. "You look beautiful."

"Just make sure to smile," Grace said. "A happy woman is radiant."

Mairi turned to the polished glass. The dress was green with pink roses embroidered down the V-shaped stomacher to match the fresh roses in her crown. The sleeves were fitted to the elbows where they flared out into points of fine gauze. Gold braid lined the square neckline and stomacher. The full skirts enhanced her small waist, the ribbons cinching it in the back. Her wavy hair had been left to flow freely about her shoulders. Ava had pinched her cheeks, but the blush couldn't hide the freckles that spotted across her nose. Geoff had met her before. He knew what he was getting, in temperament and in freckles.

She forced her lips into a smile and leaned toward the polished glass. Radiant? Hmmm… *I am happy. I am happy.* If she thought it enough, it would be true. Right?

"Ava and I need to go to the chapel," Grace said and gave Mairi's hand a squeeze. "Ooh, your hand is bloody freezing." She rubbed it between her own hands.

"Let's leave the foul talk tucked inside today, Grace." Ava said and crossed to pick up Hazel from the cradle, snuggling her against a shoulder. The sweet girl's little mouth opened and closed as if she suckled in her dreams.

"Sorry," Grace said, but didn't look repentant, bringing out a genuine smile on Mairi. "It's all the warriors around me up here in Scotland."

Grace walked out with a little wave, and Ava looked back at Mairi. "Geoff's man will come retrieve you," she whispered over Hazel's tucked head. "And if we don't see you at the chapel, we'll know Tor's foolish idea was, in actuality, quite excellent."

Mairi rolled her eyes.

"What do you mean, not see her at the chapel?" Grace asked from the hall.

The door clicked shut behind her friends, and Mairi turned to the window overlooking the courtyard below. It was summertime, but the herbs hadn't been tended, and they looked scraggly amongst the stones lining a walkway. Two running hounds and a shorter mixed breed stood tethered to a tree. They strained at their ropes, and Mairi didn't see any water source nearby. Did Geoff know his hounds were thirsty and held captive? She frowned.

The door behind her opened, and she turned. "We must first take water down…to the…courtyard." Her words trailed off at the sight before her. *Ballocks*. Geoff had sent a dark-haired, handsome giant to kiss her.

Tall and broad, his shoulders and chest tapered down to a narrow waist. Legs braced, as if for battle, he stood with a sword in hand, the weight making his arm bulge, the muscle straining against the linen of his tunic. His body took up the entire entryway.

"May I enter?" he asked, his voice hushed and deep.

"Aye, come in."

He shut the door with a soft *click*. Mairi's heartbeat pulsed into a gallop, and she watched his dark brows slant inward over serious eyes as he searched the room. Wavy hair matched a cropped beard covering a strong jaw. And his lips... Mairi wet her own and swallowed against the dryness of her mouth. They were lush, sensuous, and absolutely perfect for kissing. When his gaze rested on her, Mairi inhaled and squared her shoulders.

"I doubt it will sway me, but do what ye've been tasked to do," she said. Her words held indifference, which was a complete farce. She dared any woman to encounter a man of such raw manliness without being affected by the idea of kissing him.

He crossed to the window without a word and looked out at the courtyard, his eyes scanning beyond. "Where is everyone?" he asked.

"At the chapel, I assume," she said, stepping closer. He probably smelled of sweat or ale. She inhaled. Nay. She smelled pine and the sea and fresh air on him.

He turned, and she rubbed her nose to hide the action of sniffing him. His gaze dropped to her as if her nearness surprised him. "We will go," he said.

Mairi sighed. "I won't have Geoff wondering if I would have failed his test, so go ahead." She let her eyes flutter shut and waited.

"Go ahead?" he repeated, and she blinked open.

"Aye," she said, starting to feel foolish. "Kiss me, if ye're going to. Otherwise take me to the chapel."

The only change in the man's devilishly handsome face was a slight rise in his brows, his clear blue-gray eyes widening the smallest amount. Those damnably tempting lips opened and closed, and his gaze drifted to the shut door before returning to her. He stared at her, as if he were delving into her thoughts.

The idea shook Mairi, and she frowned. "Well, if ye're not—"

The man wrapped his hand around her arm, slowly

reeling her in with constant, gentle pressure until she had to tip her head back to see his face. He radiated authority and determination, as if he could order the mountains to move, yet chose to hold her instead. Her heart hammered in her chest as he set his hand on her cheek.

"A kiss, and then we go," he murmured, moving his thumb across her jaw. She had time for only a quick inhale as he descended.

Mairi had expected a bruising press of his mouth like Geoff had given her when he'd asked her to wed. But this man's kiss was gentle and warm. With slight pressure, he tipped her head to seal their lips together, moving against her as if tasting an aged whisky. Heat flowed down through Mairi, wiping away all rational thought. Her knees numbed, but the man seemed to accept her weight easily as he held her against his hard body. His height made him loom over her, but Mairi felt safely surrounded by power instead of fearful. Her fingers reached behind his head to feather through his wavy hair. They were still woven in the dark mass when he gently pulled back, ending the most sensuous kiss Mairi had ever experienced. What bloody foolishness was Geoff thinking?

Her traitorous body begged for more, but she stepped back, hands to her flushed skin above her low neckline. The man adjusted himself through his kilt, proving that he too had been affected by the kiss.

"Who are ye?" she asked.

His inhale seemed to help him gain his senses, and he returned to look out the window at the courtyard. "Your escort."

"I mean your name," she said. Could she really go through with wedding Geoff now that she knew such kisses existed? *Damn Geoff.*

The man turned back to her, an intense hardness to his features. "Alec."

Alec? She didn't know the name. Hadn't she met all Geoff's men at Kilchoan?

Without a word, he grabbed her hand, pulling her toward the door.

"Wait," she said and grabbed the bouquet of pink roses from off the bed as they passed. Although, the word meant more than a simple pause to collect her favorite flowers. Because hadn't she just failed Geoff's test? She dug in her heels, jerking back. "I said wait."

He turned to her. "There's no time."

She huffed. "Something like this can't be rushed. I mean, do ye live here? Why haven't I seen ye before? I don't know if I can—"

Her words cut off as his hands encircled her waist. In a fluid motion, as if she weighed no more than a suckling pig, he lifted her, setting her over his shoulder.

"God's ballocks," Mairi cried out and thrashed him on the back with her bouquet, scattering pink petals. "Put me down."

But he didn't comply. Instead, he strode with purpose out through the decorated, vacant, great hall. Her outstretched hand hit the tower of spiced cakes sitting on a table by the exit into the courtyard. Arching upward, she watched them topple. With it came the realization that she was not being taken to the chapel.

"I said put me down." She sucked in sporadic inhales as he carried her slung over one massive shoulder. He pulled his sword as they neared the dogs and lowered her feet to the ground. With a furious look, he raised his sword with the hand that wasn't anchoring her to him. For an instant Mairi wondered if he'd slaughter the dogs, but he sliced through their ropes, freeing them.

"If ye don't walk, I will carry ye," he said.

"Who the bloody hell are ye?" she asked, her rose crown hanging before her eyes. She slapped it back and quickened her steps to prevent him from dragging her. On the other side of the garden gate, in the thick wall surrounding Kilchoan, sat two men on horses in a dense stand of young trees. They wore green plaids, making them hard to spot. A white horse with roses in its mane stood to the side of the pebbled road next to an unconscious man tied to the trunk of an oak. This was definitely not a foolish prank or loyalty test.

She turned to Alec, a thousand questions on her tongue. What was happening? Who was he? "Why did ye kiss me?" fell from her mouth. Of all the questions, she'd chosen the most foolish of them all.

"Ye kissed her?" the warrior with red hair asked, his eyebrow rising high.

The other man scrunched his face. "That wasn't part of the plan."

"The plan changed," Alec said.

"But the plan never changes," red hair said, scratching his chin. "Unless it involves dogs." As if on cue, the three freed dogs ran up to the horses, tails wagging. Some watchdogs they were.

"I can't believe he bloody kissed her," the other man said, a grin spreading across his lips.

Without another word, the large warrior hoisted her up onto his black horse and climbed behind her. He pulled her up against his hard chest. "I have a right to know who is stealing me away," Mairi said, twisting to peer up into his face. A glint sharpened his steely blue-gray eyes. "Who are ye?" she whispered.

Without warning he clicked his tongue, and his horse took off, making her turn forward to grasp the pommel. His lips, the ones that had made her question meeting Geoff at the end of the aisle, came up next to her ear. "I am Alec MacNeil, and ye are Mairi Maclean MacInnes…my new wife."

Chapter Two

Alec had to admit that the idea of wedding the old bastard's widow was growing on him. He knew Mairi MacInnes was young, and she was renowned for her temper and quick wit, but no one had told him that her kisses could sear a man on contact. From her lush curves that had pressed against him, to the intriguing sprinkle of freckles across her narrow nose, and her bonny hazel eyes, everything about her piqued his interest.

"And there was no one there with her?" Kenneth asked, looking behind them as they followed the path they'd ridden in on from the shore. Finally, they'd had a turn of luck. Abducting his enemy's widow was proving much easier than Alec had anticipated.

"I am most certainly not marrying ye," Mairi said. "I'm marrying Geoff MacInnes or I'm..." She stopped in mid sputter, her bouquet clutched in her hands, smashed against the saddle horn. "Or I'm raising kittens." Her last words came in a near shout, prompting Kenneth to toss him a clean rag.

Alec tried to ignore the soft floral scent coming from her

skin and the roses in her hair as he pulled her back to work the rag between her lips. "Then until ye wed me, ye are my prisoner," he said. Mairi fought back with her rose bouquet that had become a thorny mace, twisting to glare at him as she hit him about the head.

"She's a right vicious lady," Kenneth said with the hint of a grin and reached over to yank the bouquet from her hand, tossing it far back into a briar patch. "She drew your blood." He brushed his own cheek to show Alec where a thorn had stung him.

"The hounds are following," Alec's best friend, Ian MacLeod said from up ahead where the dogs dodged the horses.

"MacInnes had them tied in the yard without provisions. I can see their bones and the smaller one has welts on her back. He deserves to lose them," he said, tightening his hold on the slippery woman before him. He leaned closer. "If ye don't sit still, I'll tie ye, stomach down, across the saddle. I'd rather not see Sköll kick your bonny head when he gallops."

Mairi didn't seem to care if she were kicked in the head or not, and he had to tighten his hold on her. Alec pressed forward in the saddle, making Sköll pick up his speed in a smooth canter through the green forest, quite different from the treeless, rolling landscape of Barra Isle. The multitude of tracks from wedding guests would hide their own in the soft loam.

The four of them made swift time to the shore where two other MacNeils waited with the ferry that would take them out to the anchored three-masted *Sea Wolf*. Living on a distant island, surrounded by the angry North Atlantic, required at least one swift, strong vessel that could carry horses, men, and cargo, such as a twisting she-serpent. Alec had two galleons.

If it hadn't been urgent to board before the wedding guests followed, he'd have stopped to tie her hands together. Luckily, years of training with heavy weapons against bloodthirsty raiders had given him the agility and strength to deal with one surprisingly fierce female who smelled of roses. He snorted, yanking a short rope from his belt to wrap around her hands. "Cease, woman," he ordered. She glared back, pulling in air through her pert nose. Maybe she couldn't breathe easily. He untied the gag.

"Ye free dogs, but bind women?" she asked, inhaling deep draughts of air.

"Aye on the dogs. Not usually on the women," he answered, hauling her down off the horse.

"More dogs?" the leader of his oarsmen, Daniel, called as the three hounds followed the horses on board the ferry to their ship.

"They chose to follow," Alec said.

"Unlike me, ye bloody beast," Mairi spat as he pulled her with him toward the bow of the small vessel, giving the three horses and dogs more room.

The oarsmen, loyal warriors from Barra, wore frowns. Revenge was grim work. They picked up a rhythm, slicing through the waves toward the *Sea Wolf*, the sturdy sails ready to rise as soon as they boarded. If their luck continued, the MacInnes would wait for a good while, thinking the bride merely delayed, before seeking her out and finding their man asleep with a bump on his head. Alec's jaw relaxed, the tension lessening across his shoulders just thinking of the surprise the new MacInnes chief would suffer when he realized his bride was gone. And what a lovely bride at that.

Alec glanced at the proud woman leaning forward at the rail, her chin tipped upward, face into the sea wind. Even with his enemy dead, retribution felt satisfying. "An eye for an eye," he murmured, looking back out toward the low hump of land in the far distance. *A bride for a bride.*

• • •

Mairi pressed against the hull of the large sailing ship where she sat, watching the crew lead the horses and dogs off. The three-hour sail across the Atlantic had been cold despite the summer month, and she huddled out of the wind, arms wrapped around her knees. Luckily the wedding costume had many layers, so only her arms had suffered. She'd refused the blanket the MacNeil arsehole had offered her.

"Time to go," Alec said as he strode up to her.

"Go where?"

He stared down at her, his legs braced like a man used to the feel of a ship beneath his feet. "That depends on ye."

She pushed all the mix of annoyance and fury and discomfort she felt into one slicing glare. Yet he didn't look away, which just made her angrier. She pulled back her lips to speak through her teeth. "I. Will. Not. Marry. Ye."

His one brow rose as if he were humored. "Then ye go to the dungeon. Either ye can walk off my ship with dignity, or I can throw ye over my shoulder. 'Tis your choice, lass."

"Ye son of a pock-marked whore."

"So, ye've met my mother? She goes by Sister Muriel of Iona Abbey now." They stared at each other for several heartbeats. "Ye choose over the shoulder then," he said and took a step toward her.

"Don't touch me," Mairi said and propelled herself upward, her hands still bound.

The sardonic grin that had lurked around his lips faded. "Unlike some Highland chiefs, I don't touch a lass without her consent." He pivoted and walked toward the gangplank.

With a huff, Mairi followed, stepping gingerly down the plank, trying not to fall into the sea. The island they were tethered to must have deep water frontage for a ship this size to moor right to it. She glanced outward at a village across the water. Thatched cottages ran along a road that snaked away into gently rolling hills.

She followed Alec MacNeil along the rocky path that ran beside the massive castle wall jutting high into the sky. Green moss grew in the gray rocks stacked upward. Seaweed wavered just under the water where white barnacles pocked the rocks. A prickle of deep unease spread across her upper back and shoulders. "Where am I?" she asked.

"Your new home, Mairi MacInnes," Alec said and stopped before a barred door that swung inward. "Kisimul Castle."

The name dropped like a boulder into her stomach, and she turned back to the sea before her. Kisimul Castle. The only stronghold in Scotland never to have been breached because of its situation on a rock island in the middle of Castle Bay off the Isle of Barra. The massive fortress had its own fresh water well dug down through the center. Water and vast stores of food made the castle immune to sieges. Surrounded by ocean, Kisimul was truly an unbreachable prison.

He waited until she turned back to him. "Have ye changed your mind? We can go above if ye consent to wed," he said.

"Never," Mairi said, swallowing as she neared the door opening through the rock wall on the back of the castle. A shield, emblazoned with a wolf's head, sat mounted over it, lips pulled back in a toothy snarl. Her heart thudded hard as she ducked under the low door arch into the dark corridor. Ever since her entrapment, during her first disastrous marriage at Kilchoan, tight spaces had become nightmarish.

She forced herself to breathe evenly. Kisimul Castle had been erected nearly a century ago, withstanding strong Atlantic storms without toppling. Surely the rocks above her head would stay put. They stopped before a barred cell, and Alec opened the hinged door. "Your chambers."

She walked inside, and he locked it. "Will ye starve me then? Leaving me bound and without a way to protect myself?

Withholding water until I either die or agree to your terms?"

The wry grin came back to curve his lips. "Ye know very little about me, lass." He slid a dirk from his boot. With a flick of his hand, the blade flew between the bars to stab into a dirty pallet on the floor. He raised his chin toward the small barred window cut into the stone at the back. "If ye change your mind and wish to come above, call through the window. Someone will alert me."

Her glare made it quite clear that she would never call for him through the bloody window. She turned her back to him and waited until she heard his boots clip away. As soon as the door closed, Mairi hurried to the pallet. With the blade's tip held firmly, she sawed the rope across the upper blade until the strands snapped, freeing her hands. She rubbed her wrists as her gaze explored the small room. No vermin droppings littered the floor, thank the good Lord. The pallet was stained but didn't look wet. There was a privy hole in the corner and a chipped pitcher on a washing stand, bone-dry empty.

Mairi stood on tiptoe to see through the bars of the window. The opening was too small to allow her to pass even if she could get the bars off. Fingers curled around the iron, she held herself up to see a small courtyard, a blooming rosebush to one side. Summer grass flanked a pebbled path. At the far end, the three dogs that MacNeil had stolen from Kilchoan lapped at a bowl of food. Had the small one really been beaten like he told his man? Were the dogs Geoff's? Maybe a wedding guest had brought them along for the celebratory hunts afterward.

Footsteps on the pebbles made Mairi look to the far right where a boy walked. From his height, he looked to be about seven or eight years old. He kept close to the wall until he reached her window and knelt before it. The whisper of a gasp came from him when he realized she was staring back, only a foot away.

He blinked but didn't move away. "I am supposed to hate ye," he said after long seconds, sounding gruffer than his years warranted.

"Considering that ye are out there and I am trapped in here," Mairi said. "I guess that I'm supposed to hate ye, too."

His eyes opened wider, and he studied her.

"I am Mairi Maclean."

"Liar," he said. "Ye are Mairi MacInnes, widow to Fergus MacInnes."

"I have no loyalty to the MacInnes. When my husband was killed, I returned to Aros and took my family name again."

"Liar," he repeated with a petulant frown. "If ye aren't loyal to the MacInnes, why were ye about to marry another one?"

She opened her mouth to retort but realized she had no answer except that Geoff had asked her, which would make no sense to the child. "'Twas for strategy," she finally said. "Ye know my name. What's yours?"

The stubborn way the boy held his mouth, and the gray-blue in his eyes, made her think of Alec MacNeil. "Are ye his son? The man who stole me away?" she asked.

"I am Weylyn MacNeil," he said and narrowed his eyes. "Weylyn means son of the wolf."

"Ye best get along, before your father finds ye conversing with the enemy."

The boy sat back on his heels, looking over his shoulder toward the dogs. "Ye aren't his enemy," Weylyn said. He looked back at her before standing. "Ye're his prize."

"Weylyn," called a man as he walked into the courtyard, making the lad jump to his feet. "Come meet three new hounds. Your father wants ye to check them over."

The boy ran toward the dogs who were still licking the bowls. Mairi watched as he let each one smell his hands before running his fingers over their bodies like Mairi had seen her mother do when assessing a new patient. He spoke to the man called Ian, shaking his head, brown hair sticking out at odd angles. Did he have no mother or nurse to comb his wild hair?

Behind Mairi something clanged against the bars. She turned to see a girl, a bit older than the boy. She'd threaded a cup and wrapped cloth through the bars. "There's food and drink for ye," she said.

The girl was pretty and had the same features as the boy. Another of MacNeil's children? The girl frowned as she looked about the cell. "I'll bring ye a blanket." Turning, she traipsed off. Mairi picked up the small sack that held cheese, an apple, and smoked meat. She sniffed the cup and then swallowed the watered-down ale. Och, it tasted wonderful after her deep thirst.

Running back with a folded blanket in her arms, the girl stopped short of the bars. Cautiously she pushed the woven wool through.

"I am Mairi Maclean."

"Ye are Mairi MacInnes," the girl replied. *Good God, not again.*

Mairi picked up the blanket, shaking it out, and wrapped it around her shoulders. The cell was dank and cold. "Thank ye," Mairi said with a nod. "And who are ye?"

"Cinnia MacNeil."

"And does your father know ye're down here?"

"Aye. I'm ordered to care for ye like my brother takes care of the new hounds."

Mairi bit into the juicy apple. It wasn't a spiced wedding cake, but it was delicious. "Do ye have a nurse in the castle, a lady to care for ye?"

The girl's pretty face paled, her thin brows lowering. "Not since my mother died and her maid left."

Mairi lowered the apple from her lips. "I am sorry, about your mother." Mairi had been very fortunate to grow up with both of her parents. Her mother, Joan, was still vastly important to her life. What must she be thinking right now with her only daughter missing?

Without another word, the girl ran back up the corridor, leaving Mairi alone. The children knew why she was here, maybe even why their father had stolen her away from Kilchoan with the ludicrous order to marry him. He didn't even know her. All she knew about him was that he was kind to dogs, and despite her fighting against him, he hadn't bruised her. Already he was more honorable than her dead husband and his lecherous son.

Mairi finished her meal and wrapped herself up in the blanket. She would close her eyes and imagine she was outside instead of swallowed up in the monstrous rocks surrounding her. Darkness grew, and she slept fitfully on the lumpy pallet. Dreams of being chased kept her tossing, the devilishly handsome face of Alec MacNeil growing closer until she slowed and let him catch her.

Mairi jerked out of sleep. Something in the cell had moved. Yanking her knees under her, she pushed up, her eyes trying to penetrate the black. She blinked, but the slice of moonlight through the bars didn't reach far, leaving dense shadows in all the corners. The darkness made the space seem smaller, and Mairi swallowed against a whimper. It was like being locked in the chest again.

Breathing rapidly, Mairi waited, listening for another clue as to what lurked nearby. It could be a rat. Were there adders on tiny islands? She clutched the sharp blade Alec had left her as the sound of an animal's nails clicking on the cobblestone floor gave her a direction to watch.

"Go on," came a light whisper, followed by a small growl.

Mairi stood. "Who's there?"

Movement in the shadow by the bars shifted into the muted moonlight. It was a dog, its head and shoulders through the bars. With another shove from behind, the dog leaped all the way through, jogging right up to her. It barked once and danced around her skirts. It looked like one of Geoff's dogs, the small, thin one that Alec claimed to have welts on its back. Footsteps thudded away up the ramp.

Following Weylyn's example, Mairi held out a hand for the dog to sniff. It licked her fingers and shoved its head under her palm. She exhaled long. "So, ye're of a friendly nature." She stared through the dark where she was certain Weylyn had stood before running off. Did he think the dog would have attacked her? Or did he know the dog was kind? *And warm.*

"Come here." She patted the pallet, and the dog jumped up, curling into the blanket against her. Warm indeed, its slender body heated the space nicely. It would likely also keep rats or mice away. Whether the child meant it or not, he'd offered her something forbidden to prisoners. A friend.

Chapter Three

"Ye've got her," Ian MacLeod, Alec's second-in-command and best friend said.

"And ye kissed her," his cousin, Kenneth MacNeil said. "Which as far as I can tell, had nothing to do with the dogs."

Alec ignored his statement. It wasn't a question anyway, and he bloody hell didn't have an answer to any questions regarding Mairi's request for a kiss. She'd obviously thought he was someone else, but why would she have kissed someone other than her groom on her wedding day? Perhaps she didn't want to wed Geoff MacInnes. Her kiss had certainly pointed toward that, how she'd melted into him and met his lips fully. She was soft and full of curves and smelled of flowers. Like a newly sharpened claymore, she'd cut right through his discipline with her honest response and heat.

The three of them sat in the empty great hall at the long table. Cinnia had left the breakfast she'd prepared and fled to her room like she was wont to do since Joyce had died. Weylyn had grabbed a dark roll and mumbled something about seeing to the new dogs. "What are ye going to do with her?" Ian asked and drank from his ale cup, his brows lifting.

That was a question he could answer. "Make her marry me," Alec said. "I need a new lady of Kisimul." He ground his teeth against the burned edge of a chunk of cured ham. But he'd never complain. It would bruise his daughter's tender heart.

"She didn't seem too receptive to the notion," Kenneth said with a wry grin.

"Give her a week in the dungeon, and she'll come around," Alec said. "A lass likes a bed and a private jakes." He'd make certain she was fed and given warm clothes, but the lass needed to comply. Since his wife had been killed and her help had fled, the household had fallen apart. He needed a mother for his two children, and someone to direct maids and a cook. But more importantly, he needed revenge.

"Once she weds me, we will send word to her kin," he said. "And the MacInnes."

"She was set to marry one of them this morning," Kenneth said. "The new chief, Geoff MacInnes. He's not the son of Fergus MacInnes. Don't know where that bastard, Normond, is."

Ian snorted. "Now that's some wolfish luck," he said and nodded toward the large wolf crest over the cold hearth. "Catching her *before* she wed, else ye'd have to kill that MacInnes to make her a widow again."

Although perhaps that would have satiated his blood lust for revenge. When Alec had discovered that Fergus MacInnes was safe from his sword, by dying before he could reach him, Alec had vowed to seek revenge against his family. But with the constant raids from the MacDonalds of South and North Uist and continual advancement of English along the mainland, Alec had been unwilling to leave Barra Isle unprotected. Even though the island was small, its white sand beaches, fertile soil, and dense game populations made it exceedingly coveted by other clans. The Lord of the Isles had deeded the isle to the MacNeil clan nearly a century before, and Alec, the Chief MacNeil of Barra, was not about to give it up.

Alec stood. "I'm going into the village. Ian, ye can stay behind today."

Ian grunted, running a hand through his red hair. "Cinnia and Weylyn keep to themselves. They don't need me staying back."

"Weylyn's only seven and Cinnia is ten," Alec said, dismissing his friend's words as he tapped his leg, calling his two wolfhounds from their spot near the hearth. They leaped up to follow him, their large, shaggy bodies like gray rugs come to life. "A protector with more years than they combined must remain here."

Kenneth slapped Ian on the shoulder. "Years, not brains."

"I'll be telling Cinnia to give ye an extra helping of dinner this eve," Ian said, making Kenneth laugh.

Alec strode out of the keep, his wolfhounds following on either side of him. He paused to bend down to each one, rubbing around their eyes and scratching their heads. "Good pups," he murmured. "Time to meet some new friends." They followed him through the bailey and around to the courtyard where he trained his dogs.

Weylyn had taken the female dog to his room to meet his own dog, but the two males were lying in a spot of sun. They jumped up, trotting over. Alec stood back while the four dogs sniffed, growled, and quickly decided that Geri, his largest wolfhound, was the leader of the four. Raising the whistle he wore on a cord from his neck, Alec blew two short bursts. Immediately, Geri and Freki returned to flank him, allowing the two new dogs to come up to him.

Alec rubbed their thin coats, noting the protruding ribs. Yet their eyes danced and tails wagged. "Ye're friendly, aye," he said, bending to greet each one. "I think I might have a good home for ye."

Millie, the sixty-year-old woman just north of the village, needed a companion. Her hearing had faded to silence, and a dog could warn her of incoming raiders, possibly even keep them from coming into her cottage. He'd need to train the dogs first, but they seemed eager to please.

If only the MacInnes lass was similar. From his periphery, he saw the dungeon window cut into the base of the family quarters at the far end of the grassy yard. Did she still sleep? Or did she watch him now, cursing him with each breath? He could go down there, but it was imperative to make her feel alone, forgotten, if he had any hope to sway her. Years of working with his dogs had taught him that the threat of solitary exile was stronger than the threat of death for most living creatures.

Cinnia brought her a meal each day, but that was it. His discipline, which matched the stony strength of Kisimul, kept him from even looking directly at the window. Unless, of course, she called out. It had been only a night and day, though, and Mairi MacInnes seemed a much harder woman to tame.

"Go on," Alec said, releasing the two wolfhounds to run about the yard. He threw a thick stick from a pile he'd had his oarsman collect from the woods while waiting for them on Kilchoan. Barra had very few trees, so Alec found them for the dogs on other islands and the mainland. Freki, the female, collected the stick and trotted it back to Alec for another throw. Over and over he threw the stick for the small pack until their tongues lolled out of their panting mouths.

The wind shifted, spiraling down into the courtyard, and the faint smell of roses teased Alec's inhale. Surely it wasn't from Mairi. He glanced toward the window and spotted the rosebush growing along the left side. Of course. He pushed the smell and the feel of the woman, riding before him, from his mind. He was a disciplined warrior and had no time for damned roses and a foolish woman. His patience was legendary, with dogs, bickering clansmen, untrained warriors, and family.

He blew the high-pitched whistle twice, and the two new dogs followed his hounds to his side. Aye, they would learn quickly. Striding toward the arched exit into the bailey, one of the dogs barked. Over his shoulder, he saw one running to the dungeon window. He poked his nose inside.

"Come," he called and blew again, his tone like a firm bark without a hint of question, and the dog returned to follow him out of the courtyard. No visiting with the prisoner. Solitary exile would be Mairi MacInnes's existence until she agreed to wed.

• • •

Mairi held the dog's neck. "Nay," she whispered and held her breath as Alec turned to lead his four dogs away. Had he heard her dog bark, calling to one of Geoff's male dogs? If Alec knew she had the sweet pup, he'd probably take her away. Mairi clung to her, resting her cheek along her side. "Shhh, Daisy."

She peeked, her eyes level with the grass, but the courtyard was empty. Thank God. She exhaled, relaxing against the rough wall. "Damn man," she whispered, her forehead tense. She rubbed it. How could he be patient and kind to his dogs and steal away an innocent woman? The beasts seemed to love him. She'd always trusted the instincts of dogs, but they were wrong this time. Alec MacNeil was a devil.

Daisy licked the side of her face and squirmed until Mairi released her.

"She probably has to piss."

Mairi turned to the boy, one hand to her thumping heart. "Weylyn, ye need to announce yourself."

He frowned at her without a word, tapping his leg, and the thin dog pressed through the bars.

"Will ye bring her back?" Mairi asked.

"If Artemis wants to return, I'll let her."

"Her name is Daisy," Mairi said. "Thank ye for letting her in last night."

"Her name is Artemis after the goddess of the moon and wild animals. Da always names his dogs after Greek and Norse myths. His wolfhounds, Geri and Freki, are named after the wolves of the Norse god, Odin." As if he realized he was saying too much to a prisoner, he turned and stomped away. Daisy followed behind him, thin tail wagging.

Irritating, just like his father.

Mairi quickly used the exposed privy hole in the back corner of the cell, replacing the flat wooden cover as she heard footsteps coming down the slanted walkway. She combed fingers through her hair, the knots catching. The footsteps were light, not at all like the heavy boots of a stubborn scoundrel.

Mairi pulled the hair to her back, dividing it to braid, as she watched Cinnia set the wooden board of blackened bread and yellow cheese between the bars. "The porridge burned, so all I have is toast and cheese to give ye."

"Porridge can be tricky," Mairi said. "Ye must stir it constantly when the fire is hot."

Cinnia's unsure expression tightened into a vexed look. "I know now. I thought I'd seen cook just cover it and leave it."

"When the fire is very low."

She pointed at Mairi. "How do ye do that?"

"My hair?"

"Aye." Cinnia pulled her long tresses to the side, the tangles giving her a bushy look.

"First ye have to comb through it, which I've been trying to do with my fingers. It doesn't work as well."

Cinnia watched, her little mouth scrunching up. "If I bring ye a comb, will ye teach me to braid my hair?"

Mairi stopped, one eyebrow raised. "If ye bring me a privacy screen with the comb, I will."

The girl's little mouth pinched in thought. "There are some empty rooms now that everyone's left Kisimul." She pulled her thick hair to one side. "Agreed."

"Artemis," Weylyn called from the ramp as Daisy came running back down, her nails clicking on the stone to echo about the dungeon. With a wiggling back end, she squeezed through the bars. Weylyn halted at the bottom. "I guess she'll stay with ye. I have Ares to look after anyway. He's my dog."

Cinnia grabbed her brother's hand. "Come help me," she said, dragging him up the ramp.

By the time Mairi was done feeding herself and Daisy, Cinnia and Weylyn were carrying down a privacy screen painted with purple thistles.

"I don't think prisoners get to have privacy," Weylyn said as they slid the folded screen to Mairi through the bars.

"How is she supposed to use the privy out in the open?" Cinnia said, hands on her hips, which gave her a much older appearance. She huffed, making one of the curls framing her face pop upward. "It takes ye an hour to cuck, and that's in the privacy of your own room."

"Hold your tongue," he hissed.

Mairi set the screen around the privy hole, her heart light. Only one day in a dungeon, and already the simple things in life could make her smile.

"And here's the comb," Cinnia said. Instead of throwing it through, she held it between the bars so Mairi could take it. She had a comb for herself as well, which she used to rake through her terrible tangle of hair.

"Ease the comb through," Mairi said, showing her how to tease out the knots by holding the hair and picking lightly at the tangle. The girl was pretty, though dirty, with smudges on her forehead and black under her nails. When was the last time either of them had bathed? "Hair is easier to manage when it's clean," she commented.

"Ye brought her a privy screen and a comb so she'd teach ye to do your bloody hair?" Weylyn asked. "Wait until I tell Da."

Cinnia snapped around to glare. "And I'll tell him ye gave her Artemis, who now answers to Daisy." As if the dog understood the conversation, she stood on her hind legs, letting out a little bark before jumping onto the middle of the stained pallet.

"Bloody lasses," Weylyn grumbled and walked off, kicking a rock that struck the stone wall of the tunnel. Cinnia's confident smile told Mairi that they didn't have to worry about her brother.

• • •

Alec watched the small herd of sheep that two boys and a dog prodded down a pebbled path through the village. He tipped his head to the baker's wife as she handed him some fresh bread. "Ye taking care of those children up there in Kisimul?" she asked, her gaze shifting to his wolfhounds on either side of his horse.

"Aye. Cinnia is learning to cook, and Weylyn continues to help with training the dogs," Alec said. A few words to Ruth and the whole town would know. The only way to communicate quicker was to stand before the chapel and yell it out at midday.

"'Tis a shame there's no woman there to care for them," she said, hands on her wide hips. She clucked her tongue. "Joyce wouldn't want her household to run amuck." The woman must envision dogs tearing through the bedrooms and shitting about the great hall.

"I will endeavor to find another lady of Kisimul as soon as I can." Alec watched a pair of oxen pull barrels of wine from the dock. The mid-aged priest, Father Lassiter, stood haggling with the tradesman on God's price for his communion wine. With the way the man ran through it, Alec wondered if maybe the good pastor was doing more than just sampling the drink.

"Well, don't be treating the next lady like one of your bitches," Ruth said, reminding Alec that he had way too much to do to keep talking with the village gossip. "Ladies don't like to be kept on a leash. It's why all the women of Kisimul up and leave."

He turned back to look down at Ruth, his voice low. "Perhaps if I had leashed Joyce, she would be alive today." Would she still walk the halls of Kisimul, running his household, caring for their children? Or would she have left in another fashion? They had wed for alliances, not love, and although she seemed faithful, she hadn't seemed happy. And then, one day, she had left.

"Good day," he said and tipped his head as Ruth's lips pursed tight, and he tapped Sköll to get the horse moving. He needed to check on Millie, hunt for some game, and end the day in the village square, where he would sit to judge some complaints between villagers. An orderly day was a productive day.

Alec nodded to Kenneth on the way up the path into the hills. The two rode silently, keeping their bows nocked in case a stag jumped from a thicket. They caught two hares before halting in front of Millie's cottage. She stood in the yard, throwing feed to her chickens. She raised her hand in greeting, her weathered face creasing even more with her smile.

"Still strong," Kenneth said. "She must be getting up there in age."

"Don't let her see ye saying as much," Alec said about the woman who had been the only constant in his life. A friend of his father's and frequent visitor to Kisimul after he died, she had cared for Alec when his mother had deemed him old enough to rule the clan on his own and abandoned him for Iona's Abbey, leaving him alone. He'd been sixteen years old.

She didn't talk now, as if not being able to hear had stolen her words. Alec didn't like her living out here in solitude, but the stubborn woman refused to live at Kisimul. She wanted her freedom, she'd told him when he'd turned twenty, and he'd ferried her over to the village where she found this cottage. She visited for Christmastide but never stayed.

"All is well?" he asked and moved his fingers in their own language that they'd developed over the last year. She'd resisted at first, realizing quickly that some of the signs were ones he used to control his dogs. So, she'd created signs of her own and taught him. She could also read the movement of lips.

She nodded and ushered them inside, out of the constant wind that skirted the low hills of the western islands. The cottage smelled of stew, and she dished up two bowls immediately. Did she know that he and Kenneth were nearly starving from the burned rations they currently endured at Kisimul?

"Would ye come back to the castle with us?" he asked, using a mix of words and his finger signs. She shook her gray head. "Why not? The children are lonely." He didn't actually know if they were or not. They'd never complained, preferring to stay safely surrounded by the walls of Kisimul, especially after their mother had been slain going into the village.

Millie's fingers moved, and she poked him in the chest.

"What did she say?" Kenneth asked.

Alec sighed. "The usual."

Kenneth grinned at her. "Aww now, Alec's not lonely on Kisimul. He's got me and Ian and the children and a pack of dogs."

"Two, Kenneth. I have two dogs, not a pack."

"Right now ye have five, and Weylyn's got another."

Millie made the sign she used often, linked fingers to look like a chain. She was also reminding him that she wouldn't be locked up on Kisimul.

"Ye could come and go with a ferry," Alec said. "And have your own small boat."

Her lips turned wry, as if she didn't completely believe him. He placed his hand to his heart. "I promise."

"Tell her we would pay her to cook for us," Kenneth said, scraping the last bits of stew out of his bowl with a crust of bread.

In the end, Alec left Millie again at her small cottage. She'd protected him after his mother left, and yet she wouldn't let him protect her in her old age. Highly frustrating. But unlike dogs, who could be ordered by the alpha male, Millie made decisions for herself. Hopefully she would take in the two MacInnes dogs once he trained them. Alec would leave them there, anyway, and Millie's soft heart wouldn't allow them to starve. She'd take them in eventually, and they would protect her if she wouldn't let Alec.

Kenneth and he hunted, bringing down one red deer that would feed the five of them and the six dogs currently living in Kisimul. Millie had sent them away with two loaves of bread to add to the one Alec had purchased from Ruth. He settled two disputes in the village square: the first about a herd of sheep that one farmer wanted to move across a valley where others grazed, and the second was a punishment given to three foolish boys who would build Millie a wall in recompense for taking a small boat into the bay without permission.

Alec stood as the people dispersed, stretching his shoulders in the late afternoon sun. The day had followed his plan. Just as it should, for he, Alec MacNeil, was the Wolf of Kisimul, the one who kept order on Barra, the one responsible for the lives before him. His discipline, planning, and strategy would rebuild the confidence of his people after the MacInnes had stolen their security.

Father Lassiter stood up from the steps of the chapel and ambled over. He fiddled with the large cross he wore around his neck. "A blessing to have ye exceedingly wise in the way of judgment," he said, nodding to Alec.

"Small issues are easy to judge wisely, but thank ye, Father." He strode toward Kenneth where he loaded cut peat on a sled tied to their two horses.

Father Lassiter walked quickly to stay next to him, his face growing red with exertion. "Son, have ye thought about the judgment ye should make against the MacInnes for their foulness? It's been ten long months since the savage deed."

When had Alec not thought about revenge? He'd walked the empty halls of Kisimul night after night while making plans to seek retribution. "Aye," he answered, not looking to the priest.

"The village is behind ye, Alec," he said, placing a staying hand on his arm. Alec stopped so he wouldn't drag the man. "Fergus MacInnes is likely burning in Hell right now, but the MacNeils support a war against the MacInnes. I thought ye should know."

Alec had kept his plans to seek revenge on Clan MacInnes a secret to all but the few men who'd helped him retrieve Mairi, and he'd made sure they were men he could trust to keep their mouths shut. He preferred a united Scotland, where the clans could join together to defeat the larger beast, King Henry and his English forces. Until he ascertained that Fergus MacInnes had the support of his clan against the MacNeils, he would seek revenge on only the bastard's house. Alec was a patient man and had sought answers before acting. But answers were few, no matter how many people on the isles he questioned.

"Ye've earned the ear of the village," Alec said in response.

"'Tis good they are trusting ye now." The priest had arrived on Barra the previous year, having been assigned by the Catholic Church to replace the elderly priest who had shepherded his parish for fifty years before dying peacefully in his bed.

Father Lassiter smiled. "Aye. It's taken many months."

"Excuse me, Father," Alec said, nodding to the man and grabbing a sack of grain that he'd had milled into flour. *Humph. More bread for Cinnia to burn.*

He glanced up as he heard feminine laughter. Several lasses stared, the dark-haired one smiling coyly. Kenneth leaned back against his horse's side with a grin. "Ye could just wed one of the town lasses. It's been nearly a year since Joyce's death. One of the lasses from the village would come back to Kisimul, take care of your children and cook for us." He crossed his arms and tipped his chin toward the young women. "Just pick one and love her so well she won't care about a curse."

Alec lowered the flour onto a wooden sled tied to Sköll and walked back toward Kenneth. "There is no curse, and I have a wife back at Kisimul," he said under his breath. A lovely, rose-scented wife with a delicate sprinkling of freckles over her nose and a body shaped with soft curves.

Kenneth snorted. "Ye have a locked-up she-wolf in the dungeon. There's a big difference, and if ye don't know that, the last ten months have taken more of your brain than we thought."

"My brain is sound. Exile, with a good dose of discomfort, will make Mairi MacInnes agree. I've a solid plan, and it will go as I've ordered it." It would work if he could just win against his nagging desire to go see her. He must keep his mind off Mairi MacInnes.

"Solid plan, huh?" Kenneth asked, pushing away from his horse to look out toward the bay, his brows gathering. "Does your plan involve the castle being on fire?"

Chapter Four

"I thought Da was going to strangle ye," Weylyn said from his stool at the bottom of the ramp.

Cinnia paced along the small dungeon corridor, face in her hands. "There was grease off the bacon." She stopped in front of Mairi, who stood on the other side of the iron bars from her. "It caught on fire, and then the fire caught the baskets that our cook used for biscuits." She threw her hands wide. "Suddenly the whole kitchen was a flaming oven."

"Ye're not burned, are ye?" Mairi asked.

Cinnia shook her head, tears in her eyes. "Ian dragged me out, and Da showed up with Kenneth shortly after. The three of them put out the fire before it could spread to the upper kitchen or any other buildings, but the lower kitchen is scorched."

Weylyn kicked the wall in an annoyingly even rhythm. "Aye, and now I have to help her clean it, even though I wasn't there."

"Family helps family, Weylyn," Mairi said. Her heart hurt for the girl. She knew how it felt to be a disappointment. It was a hollow feeling between your heart and your bowels. A hole, which half the time she wished to disappear into and half the time desperately wanted to fill with duty. Was that why she'd said yes to Geoff when he'd asked her to marry him?

It wasn't the work to clean the kitchen that brought tears to the girl's eyes. It was the disappointment from her father. "Did he say anything to ye?" Mairi asked, her fingers curling around the cold iron bars. If she could reach Cinnia, she'd hug her.

"Nay," Cinnia said. "He gave me his silent stare."

Weylyn stopped kicking and shook his head. "The stare is the worst."

Mairi sighed, leaning her forehead into the space between the bars. "My da used to yell all the time, but sometimes I think that's better than silence."

Cinnia nodded vehemently.

"Our da doesn't yell," Weylyn said. "Except in battle. He orders people around a lot because he's the chief, but he never loses his patience."

So, the man was as disciplined as he seemed when she watched him work with the dogs in the courtyard. "Come here," Mairi said and grasped Cinnia's hands through the bars. She rubbed the girl's knuckles with her thumbs and dipped her head to catch her sad gaze. "I am glad ye weren't harmed. I'm sure your father loves ye. Sometimes men have a hard time showing it."

Although, who was she to say anything kind about the monster who'd stolen her and locked her up. The one who'd kissed her so passionately that she'd dreamed of him, his muscled arms wrapping around her, his lips kissing down her neck. Stupid, traitorous dreams.

She forced a smile for the girl. "Ye need to learn to cook. Something simple and delicious."

"How? I know nothing, and there's no one to teach me. Not even lessons to read."

Mairi straightened up. "I will teach ye." She wasn't the best cook, but she knew a few simple recipes that Cinnia could master. "Let's start with stew, no grease involved." She looked up at the boy. "Weylyn, fetch us a pot."

"Why should I help ye? Ye're our prisoner."

"I might also be the one to fill your stomach tonight," Mairi countered, hands on her hips as she stared him down. The boy was lazy, as young boys often were when they weren't trying to prove themselves to someone. But even a lazy boy knew it was better not to be hungry.

"Humph, she's got a mean stare, too," he said to Cinnia, but headed up the ramp, a scowl on his face.

Hope filled the young girl's eyes. "Thank ye."

"We lasses need to stick together," Mairi said, scratching Daisy on the head.

• • •

"They gobbled it all up," Cinnia said, her smile wide as she squeezed Mairi's hands through the bars. "Just like the stew, the baked fish, and the roast goose." It had been nearly a week of daily lessons from Mairi, and Cinnia was doing exceptionally well considering Mairi was stuck in the dungeon and unable to teach her in the kitchen.

"Ian saw me reading a book and told Da that he thought I'd found a cook's journal." The girl bounced high on the toes of her slippers and let go to spin around. "I didn't correct him."

Daisy's nails clicked on the ramp as she ran down, jumping up to dance on her back legs with Cinnia, making the girl laugh. "Off," Weylyn scolded the dog as he followed, his arms full of chain links.

"Does no one notice ye bringing things down here?"

Mairi asked, glancing at the articles she'd been collecting in her cell over the last few days. Weylyn hefted the set of chains through the bars to pool on the stone floor, his payment for Mairi mending a pile of his clothes.

"There's no one about to notice," Cinnia said and picked up the folded pile of bedclothes, including a set of velvet drapes to hang around the bed that Mairi would suspend from the chains. "Da goes into the village every day, leaving Ian or Kenneth to watch us. Ian's easier to avoid as he just works with the dogs or cleans the livestock pens. Kenneth spends time in the great hall, so we have to make a showing there."

"Sometimes he teaches me with the practice sword," Weylyn said.

"Not as much as Mairi's been training ye with her *sgian dubh*," Cinnia said and handed the bedclothes through to Mairi.

Was it wrong to teach the children of one's enemy how to wield a short but lethal *sgian dubh*, like the one Alec had left her that first day? Cinnia would never use it against her, and even Weylyn was warming up to her with every lesson. It wasn't Mairi's fault that their father spent more time with his dogs than his children. The poor bairns definitely needed care and were very grateful for Mairi's attention and lessons, bringing her various furnishings from the empty bedrooms.

With their help, Mairi had created a suitably comfortable bedroom behind bars. They'd brought wood, nails, and a hammer for Mairi to fashion a table. A thick rug now covered a large area of the cold floor, and Mairi slept on a clean mattress that they'd managed to stuff between the bars. Daisy would watch on as if perplexed about why they couldn't slide in and out like her.

Thank goodness for the dog, who nuzzled up to her during the night. She was a nice distraction from the ever-present ghost of Alec MacNeil and his damnably kissable mouth and her own idiocy in letting herself be captured. By the fifth morning of watching Alec train his dogs through her window, Mairi had stopped berating Alec MacNeil and started blaming herself for her predicament. How could she have been so thoroughly fooled when he'd come to her room at Kilchoan? Enough to kiss him and then not alert someone, anyone, before he stuffed the gag in her mouth. She deserved to be imprisoned for being an idiot.

A wet nose pushed against her cheek, and Mairi realized she'd set her head in her hands.

"Are ye angry again?" Weylyn asked and passed a fresh flask of water for Daisy through the bars.

Mairi stood and poured the water into the bowl. "It's hard not to be angry when stuck sitting behind bars," she said and scooted the table under the iron loops to hook the chains around her bed.

"Ye're actually standing," Weylyn said, grinning.

She grunted, standing on the table to attach the chain to the ceiling. "And stinking in this dress." She'd removed the stomacher after the first night, but the dress kept her warm in the dampness of the dungeon. Thank goodness it was summer or she'd surely freeze down here.

"I can get ye some clean clothes," Cinnia said. "And we could heat some water for ye."

Mairi smiled at her, pointing her finger. "And for that I will teach ye to make berry tarts."

"Berry tarts?" Weylyn's eyes grew round. "We'll heat the water right now."

• • •

"I could have added a bit more sugar," Cinnia said as she watched the three men chewing her bilberry tarts.

"Nay," Kenneth said, the purple juice sitting on his bottom

lips. "'Tis perfect. Where did ye learn to make them?"

Ian pointed at her, swallowing. "That book had the recipe, didn't it?"

Alec watched his pretty daughter blush and look down at her clasped fingers. With two braids coiled around her head, she looked very much like her mother. The lass must miss her. "Cinnia," he said, waving her over. She perched on his knee, making her seem younger and further away from leaving Kisimul one day. "These are delicious. I think ye may have a talent for cooking. Ye'll be such a help around here." That was, until she left. Everyone left Kisimul. He shoved the dark thought away.

His daughter's smile lit her whole face. "I need practice." Her smile faded. "Just not with bacon."

"I'll teach ye the right way to handle grease," Ian said, grabbing another of the tarts. "'Tis my fault for not watching ye closer." He slumped forward, chewing slower as if guilt soured the sweet pastry.

Bloody hell, he should feel guilt, Alec thought, but said nothing more than he already had after the kitchen fire. He'd nearly lost his daughter, and Ian hadn't suffered enough yet from scaring years off Alec's life.

"What do ye think of your sister's baking?" Kenneth asked Weylyn.

The lad sat back, rubbing his stomach that already held three of the berry treats. "'Tis the start of something wonderful." He smiled, making the two warriors laugh heartily.

Kenneth looked to Alec. "Ye should send one down to the MacInnes lass. Maybe she's ready to hear ye out, and a tart might tempt her after a week of discomfort and loneliness."

Tempt her? Hadn't that been what she'd thought of Alec when he'd shown up in her room at Kilchoan? That he was there to entice her with a kiss? Could she possibly know how that kiss had led to a week of temptation for him?

That damn kiss. One breach in discipline, and he'd paid for it with unwanted dreams of Mairi MacInnes. Those soft, honeyed lips; silky waves of golden hair; warm, smooth skin. Last night he'd even dreamed that she'd let him trace the spaces between the fairy-kiss freckles across her nose and cheeks. It had taken every bit of his restraint to stay away from her for the week. Seven days of making himself continue his routine, rowing to Barra, so he wouldn't break his plan by going down to see her. He'd spent extra time each morning in the back courtyard outside her window, willing her to call out for release. Surely by now she must be ready to do about anything to free herself from the dismal, lonely dungeon.

Cinnia scooted off his knee, her smile gone. "Ye should make her wait another day," she said. "It's only been a week."

Alec studied her, raising one eyebrow at his suddenly anxious daughter. She was usually of a forgiving nature, never wanting him to discipline the dogs with temporary exile from the pack. "Do ye wish me to keep her locked down there longer?" Even though Cinnia hadn't said it, she'd been angry with his plan to capture Fergus MacInnes's widow. Yet now she seemed content in keeping Mairi locked below.

"I… Perhaps just a bit longer," Cinnia said, her gaze shifting to Weylyn, who pushed up straight.

"A few more days might make her more receptive to your offer, Father," Weylyn said, his face too serious for that of a seven-year-old boy.

Something was going on between the two of them. Kenneth and Ian had lost their smiles, having picked up on the tension. Children weren't good at hiding their worry or guilt. Ian opened his mouth, but Alec was quick to signal him to stay silent.

Alec reclined back in his chair, crossing his arms as if settling in for the night. "I will take your advisement under consideration." He looked to his son. "And how is Artemis doing? I haven't seen her about."

"Well," Weylyn said, shrugging his stiff shoulders. "She likes Ares. They play a lot, and I exercise her while ye are away during the day." He propped his lips upward into an anxious grin.

Alec nodded. Aye, the boy was nervous. His eyes shifted to Cinnia, who busied herself with arranging the two remaining tarts on the plate. Kenneth looked pointedly between the siblings, his eyes wide, but Alec gave a small shake of his head.

"I'll want to see Artemis tomorrow then," Alec said. "See if she's put on some healthy weight with proper food and care."

"Aye, sir," Weylyn said.

Alec stood, stretching. "Ye two should go up to bed. Dawn comes early in the summer. And Cinnia…"

"Aye?"

"Thank ye for the fine food. Your mother would be very proud."

She gave him a sad smile and took Weylyn's hand. Since their mother died, they'd been sharing Cinnia's bed. The hollow feel of loneliness, which Alec had carried as an only child, ensconced at Kisimul, was so familiar that it was like a forgotten gouge on an old tree with the bark growing up around it. It was good his children had each other.

As soon as the sound of Weylyn's boots faded on the steps, Ian stood. "Those two are up to something."

"What have they been doing during the day?" Alec asked, grabbing the last two tarts as he stood.

"They spend time here in the hall," Kenneth said. "I haven't seen the dog except a few times when Weylyn took her out to the courtyard."

"I see them about now and then," Ian said. "But I'm oft busy keeping the animals alive."

"I think we need to watch them closer," Kenneth said.

"Even when they aren't in the kitchen."

He nodded to Kenneth and Ian. "See ye in the morn."

"Ye're going down there, aren't ye?" Ian said.

"Absolutely." Alec grabbed the wrapped tarts and lit a taper from the coals in the hearth.

Pushing silently through the door to the dungeons, he was thankful he'd oiled the hinges after depositing the lass down there. He stepped lightly along the declining, stone ramp and paused when he spotted a glow from up ahead. Had the children given Mairi a candle and flint to keep away the heavy darkness? Could that be why they looked guilty? It was a humane gesture that he should have considered. He'd thank the children in the morning for their forethought.

Alec blew out his own candle and treaded silently down the ramp. Would she be sitting on the mattress or pacing? Or standing at the window, waiting for the sunrise and his appearance to finally ask for her release?

A low growl stopped Alec, his gaze shifting to penetrate the deep shadows. An animal? What animal would be free on Kisimul? Only a dog. The growl came again, closer and closer, until he could see the shadowed outline of Artemis. Her tail wagged when she realized it was he, and she ran up the ramp with clicking nails. What was Weylyn's new dog doing down here?

"Daisy? Come, girl." Mairi's voice was relaxed, without strain or fear or even a gruffness that comes with disuse. And who the hell was Daisy?

The wide ramp downward opened up into the dungeon with its single cell. Most of it was still in shadows, but Alec's gaze was drawn to the illumination behind what looked like a painted privacy screen in the far corner. The dog ran ahead of Alec, pressing and wiggling until she slid through the narrow bars.

"Good girl," Mairi said from behind the screen.

Alec could plainly see the woman's silhouette with the bright light behind her. Slender legs and arms moved as she turned, shaking out a garment, which she set over her head to float down over her form. He inhaled and caught the faint smell of roses.

The silhouette picked up something from a chair. A comb? As she raked through her long hair, he could hear her contented inhale. A soft hum issued from her lips, the notes following a gentle cadence that reminded him of a child's song.

Alec watched in stony shock as the dog trotted out from the screen. His eyes, having adjusted to the darkness, followed Artemis as she leaped up onto…a suspended bed, surrounded by thick drapes. He stepped forward and blinked hard to clear his vision. Blankets and pillows adorned the platform, creating a nest of luxury. His gaze moved about the space. Was that a thick rug across the floor? And a table? How in hell did she acquire a table when Alec was the only one with a key to the cell? His hand pressed against his pocket that hung from his belt and felt the iron key through the leather. *Mo chreach!* She wasn't uncomfortable, counting the bloody minutes until she could beg him for her release.

Anger flared through Alec, but his stalwart discipline kept him still as a statue. The light flared brighter as Mairi stepped from behind the screen. Like an angel, her hair flowed around her shoulders, not frizzed with dirt but combed into waves of silk. She didn't wear her muddied gown, but a clean shift, edged across her full bosom with lace. Her lips opened and closed on the notes of a whispered song. Toes ensconced in slippers, she tread across the woven rug toward her bed and set the oil lamp on the table. As if sensing his gaze, she froze and turned on her slippers toward the bars.

He stared at her, finding his voice. It rasped out against the silence permeating the dungeon. "What the bloody hell is all this?"

Chapter Five

Mairi jumped, peering into the dense shadows, a hand to her chest. Her heart thumped against it. "God's ballocks, MacNeil, ye nearly scared the life out of me. And then what would ye have to bargain with? A dead woman."

He came to the bars, his hand wrapping around the thick iron. "Ye have a bloody bedroom set up in my dungeon." The volume of his voice had grown to fill the rock-enclosed space.

Her hands slid down to perch on her hips. "When left alone, I'm more resourceful than ye anticipated." He'd figure out soon enough that Weylyn and Cinnia had been helping his prisoner, but Mairi wouldn't throw them to the wolf, even if he was their father.

"Unless ye are a witch and conjured the contents of one of Kisimul's better bedchambers, ye've had help."

Mairi sat down on the edge of her swinging bed to scratch the dog's head. "Daisy's fetched everything I need."

"Daisy? What the hell does that name symbolize?"

"That she's sweet like a pretty flower."

"Artemis is sweet?" His words came with numb

incredulity, and she noticed that the knuckles of his hand had turned white with his grip.

"Nay, *Daisy* is sweet," she said, scratching the happy dog's back.

Alec shook his head and grabbed the iron bars as if he could wrestle them apart. "Ye had more help than a little dog. How the hell did ye get all of this through these bars?"

She smiled, her lips tight, and continued to pet Daisy. He couldn't force her to talk, and as long as he stayed outside the damn bars, she was safe from his anger.

With a huff of disgust Alec yanked his hands off the bars, stretching them to clasp behind his head as he pivoted and paced two steps away, only to return, his face hard. "The children helped ye, didn't they?"

Her smile dimmed to a frown. She hadn't considered all the repercussions when she bargained with them for her comfort. "Don't ye touch them," she seethed, sliding off the bed to stand. "'Tis your fault for leaving them unattended." Daisy jumped off the bed, circling Mairi as she traipsed across the space to stand directly in front of him. She grabbed the bars. "Cinnia could have been burned in that fire, killed. While ye spend your days God only knows where, leaving one dimwitted soldier to watch two creative, intelligent, energetic children." His angry face matched her own, but she continued without pause.

"They came to me, filthy, with dirty, ripped clothes and tangled hair. A girl desperate to please her father with her cooking but not given any direction. A little boy wanting to become a warrior without anyone to give him practice and instruction. Left to themselves, it's no fault of theirs if they sought out help from the only source left open to them."

They stared into each other's faces for several heartbeats, Mairi fighting the urge to grab the man by the shirt to shake him. She noticed a slight twitch in one of his eyes. He opened his lips, those damnable lips that drew her in.

"Ye taught Cinnia to cook? The stew. The tarts tonight. From down here?"

"She's determined to be an asset to ye here in this prison ye call a castle. I used that and tricked her into bringing me things. Same with Weylyn. Do not blame them." She squinted her eyes at him. "I'm wily, MacNeil. They didn't stand a chance unguarded around me."

"If they had followed my orders to leave ye be, they'd not have allowed ye to sway them toward treason."

Treason? The word twisted Mairi's stomach. Could the man who'd kissed her so gently in Kilchoan, locking her up without delivering a single bruise to her skin, be so cruel as to treat his own children like traitors? "Do not harm them," she said. "'Tis completely your fault for leaving them uncared for. Do ye have so little love for your own offspring? Giving what feeling ye have to beasts instead?" She pressed her cheeks against the cool iron bars. "Not a nurse or their mother to care for them."

His face came closer. "Their mother was murdered, her throat slit for no reason save that she was the wife of The MacNeil of Barra Isle. In a bloody attempt to prove Kisimul is not impenetrable."

Mairi's breath wrapped into a boulder, making her unable to swallow or speak as she watched Alec's face harden into barely controlled fury. She knew that the children's mother was dead, but hadn't wanted to press them for details on the matter.

"They came to the castle to kill her?" she whispered.

"Nay. She went to the village, without my permission, and your husband took the opportunity."

She stepped back, a hand to her heart. "Fergus MacInnes killed your wife."

The look on his face was answer enough. Mairi had

known Fergus was a bastard, leaving her with his lecherous son despite her telling him Normond was stalking her. But to kill an innocent woman…

"I…" She forced herself to breathe past the tightness in her chest. "Am very sorry. He was a cruel man, without common decency."

Alec didn't move, but something softened in his glare. "Ye hold no loyalty to your husband?"

"Not when he deserves none," she answered.

She watched Alec's nostrils flare on an inhale. "Did he harm ye?"

Mairi blinked. Memories, which she'd stomped down inside, fought to surface. "Most of the time he ignored me. It was his son who left his mark." She tipped her head to the side. "And how about Alec MacNeil? Do ye harm women and children?" She let the side of her lips turn up at the corner at the ridiculousness of her question. "Ah wait, ye do harm women. By locking them up. Do ye harm children then?"

"Do my children act beaten?" Alec asked. "Terrorized with the idea of disobeying me? Remaining silent and hiding in shadows?"

Since children didn't usually disobey so completely as to furnish a bedroom for a prisoner, without past transgressions, Mairi guessed that they'd gotten away with much in the past. "No," she said. "But they need someone to guide them, more than a warrior who would rather be riding and hunting with his chief than remaining behind to care for them."

"Wed me, and they will be yours to guide," he said.

Her smile soured. He wouldn't beat Cinnia and Weylyn, but he'd use them to bargain with. "Let me out of here, and I will act as the children's nursemaid here at Kisimul." He stared silently at her. "I will teach Cinnia to cook, mend their clothes, keep them clean and out of trouble while ye are gone. I can teach Weylyn to care for the animals penned here."

"Ye would stay?" he asked.

She huffed. "From what I know of this castle, if ye don't take me away, I have no choice but to stay until ye decide I can go." She stepped up to the bars, wrapping her fingers around them. "What are ye going to do with me?"

"My plan has not changed," he said low and inhaled a full breath.

"I will not wed ye, Alec MacNeil," she said just as low. "I've offered ye a compromise, and I suggest ye take it. And when my clan tracks me down, ye will give me back."

"So ye can wed another MacInnes?"

Mairi's stomach twisted into nausea, but she tipped her chin higher. "Whatever I do will be because I wish it, not because some man decrees it."

She waited, but Alec revealed nothing of his thoughts. Without another word, he turned and traipsed up the cobblestone ramp out of the dungeon. Mairi opened her mouth but didn't call out. Would he forbid the children from coming down? Would he halt her food until she conceded?

She swallowed and bent to pick up Daisy. Would Alec take the dog away? Mairi felt the first stirrings of panic since she'd been locked in there a week ago. She kissed the dog's head as she turned out the lamp and felt her way to their bed. It might be their last night to warm each other. She blinked against the ache of tears and pulled Daisy into her under the blankets. Bloody Alec MacNeil. Even without violence, he could absolutely harm her.

• • •

Alec strode through the great hall, his boots cracking on the flat stone. He signaled to his wolfhounds to stay and ignored Ian as he pushed out through the front doors of the keep to the courtyard. A bloody bedroom. In his dungeon!

Anger and frustration balled up inside him, making him yearn to battle something. He drew his sword, and, since there was no one but Ian and Kenneth to witness his lack of discipline, he swung it before him at the shadows, in practiced arcs and thrusts. The moon beamed just over the edge of the wall into the bailey, giving him light. His boots crunched in the pebbled dirt, loud in the silence of night. His muscles flexed and bunched, growing warm with the effort. He welcomed the familiar heat to bleed off his anger.

Ian stood in the doorway. A shadow near the kitchen sharpened into Kenneth as he walked out. "Lo there," he called. "I take it she didn't say she'd marry ye."

Alec sliced his steel through the cool night air, making a whistle in the wind. His cousin skirted the bailey to join Ian by the door to the main hall.

A bloody bedroom, luxurious enough for a princess. This whole week wasted. *Swing. Thrust.* A whole week of staying away from her, depriving her of comfort when she was up to the top of her silky head in comfort. No exile to sway her. No wishes for a private privy.

He walked up to a sack stuffed with straw that they often used for training. He stabbed the end of his blade into it, twisting to yank it back out. Groomed, clean, and sweet smelling. *Damn roses.*

"Did ye not take down the tart?" Kenneth asked.

"Shut up," Ian warned. "When was the last time ye saw Alec lose his reason?"

Alec held his sword, the tip pointed to the stars. Had Mairi MacInnes taken his reason? *Bloody damned hell!*

He should have checked on Mairi earlier, should have sent his men down to feed her, not Cinnia. He should have convinced a nursemaid to remain at Kisimul to watch the children after Joyce was killed. *Everyone leaves Kisimul.*

"Mo chreach," he cursed and lowered his sword, shunting

it back into the scabbard at his side. What should he do now? Remove all the luxurious trappings and feed her slop? Forbid the children to talk to her? He slammed his hand against a row of buckets hanging against the wall of the horse barn and looked up at the stars overhead. He breathed in through his nose until his chest felt like it could burst on the fresh air. How many times had he stood here alone, staring up at the stars, asking God what he should do now? More than he could count. And besides, he doubted God would force a woman to wed him.

Alec released a gust of breath. Ian and Kenneth parted to let him pass as he trudged back into the keep. Should he turn into the ruffian Mairi thought him to be? *Kiss her again.* The thought filtered up through the crush of possible schemes. *Och*, but she'd certainly despise him then.

Alec grabbed his ale cup off the long table. It was nearly empty. *Damnation.* He didn't even have a kitchen maid or housekeeper to see to simple things like provisions while he rode the land around the village, seeing to his people, protecting them with his reputation and his sword.

Ian and Kenneth watched him in silence. Alec threw himself into a chair by the cold hearth and looked around the sparse hall with its few lit sconces. It was the same hall he'd seen his whole life, first as a child, then as a young chief, ruled by his mother and then left to rule on his own. Untried and untaught. Had he committed the same crime with his own children? Without Millie helping him as a lad, he might have set the kitchen on fire, too. Although he wouldn't have carried a whole bloody bedroom down to a prisoner.

His gaze roamed the tan plaster that coated the granite of the walls. Cold and hard, the stone made the castle unaffected by arrow shot and even cannon from passing ships. Kisimul was an impenetrable shell in a warring world. It was built to protect and repel the enemy. Why then was it practically abandoned?

Kenneth leaned into Ian's ear and whispered something, but Alec ignored them to study his home. Dirt marred the stone floor, webs among the rafters, and spots on the glass window panes. Currently, his dungeon looked in better shape. The only decoration in the great hall was one tapestry covering the far wall, its threads weaving the shaggy coat of a wolf, a lone wolf who stared outward, challenging him to care about something other than revenge.

Ian walked over to lean into the wall opposite him. "Are ye going to tell us what happened down there?"

"Or is it too horrible to utter?" Kenneth asked in a tone that bordered between jest and true worry that his cousin had gone insane and massacred the lass.

Alec snorted, driving his hand into his pocket to fish out the iron key to Mairi's cell. He tossed it to Kenneth, who caught it out of the air. "Unlock her cell in the morning."

"Ye're letting her go?" Ian asked, his brows shooting up.

Alec met his friend's gaze. "From her cell, aye, but not from Kisimul."

Chapter Six

"Holy shite," came a man's voice, making Mairi sit up amongst the bedclothes behind her velvet curtains. Daisy growled low, popping up and jumping from the suspended bed, her nails clicking on the floor. She barked between growls.

Mairi poked her head out of the curtains. The gray dawn light showed one of Alec's men at the door. "Artemis?" he said. "What are ye doing down here?" He peered into the cell. "Living quite the comfy life, from the looks of it."

"Daisy," Mairi called, and the dog ran back, hopping on her back legs to be scooped into the bed. This might be the last time she would get to hug the pup. She looked into the dog's brown eyes and kissed her snout, rubbing her ears.

Outside the curtains, Mairi heard the scrape of metal in the iron lock. He was opening her cell? Her heart thumped, and she jammed her hand under the pillow for the dagger Alec had given her on the first day.

Blade wrapped tightly in her fingers, Mairi climbed to her knees and looked out the curtains once more. The man had dark hair and wore a smile. "Hello," he said and gave a little bow. She remembered him from the clearing outside Kilchoan. "I am Kenneth MacNeil, Alec's cousin. His father was my mother's brother."

"What are ye here for?" she asked, only too aware that she was wearing a smock behind the curtains.

"Just to open the door. Chief's orders." His gaze moved about the cell, and he let loose a snorted chuckle. "No wonder," he mumbled and rubbed his forehead.

"Did he give any other orders?" she asked.

"Nay. I figured ye two decided what ye're to do last night. Would ye like my assistance?"

"Can ye sail me off this bloody rock?" she asked.

"Woe lass, Kisimul is much more than a rock."

"Fine," she said. "Can ye sail me off this beautiful island topped with a castle of bloody splendor?"

He laughed. "Nay. That was the only other order Alec gave. Ye'll be staying on Kisimul. But ye might want to go see Weylyn and Cinnia. I'm guessing they had a hand in this." He nodded to the furnishings. "And they're pacing up in the hall as if they're awaiting orders to the front line in a battle against the English."

God's teeth. Had Alec yelled at them? Certainly, he must have had words with them. "I will be right up as soon as I dress."

He nodded, crossed his arms, and leaned back against the wall.

"Which I will do when ye go away."

"Oh, aye. Certainly," he said, jumping forward and turning to head back up the ramp.

Mairi hurried behind the screen where Daisy hopped playfully around her. "The day is full of surprises," she said and washed her face and teeth, raking the comb through her hair. She threw over her head the simple blue gown Cinnia had brought. It cinched easily in the back. She shoved her toes into the slippers that matched and secured the knife in the pocket. The door barely squeaked as she pushed through it.

Plucking the key from a nail in the wall to tuck inside her pocket, she bent to pick up the cloth that Alec had dropped the night before and flipped it open. Tarts. He'd come down to bring her tarts? "Come along," she said to Daisy, and they hurried up the stone ramp. It led to a door that opened easily, silently. No wonder Alec had been able to surprise her last night.

Daisy followed as Mairi continued along a passage toward a lit room. Sunlight. Her legs quickened. "Weylyn. Cinnia," she called as she ran into the hall.

The children stood before a cold hearth, and Kenneth sat at a table situated down the center of the room. Cinnia ran to her, throwing herself into Mairi's arms. "We had no idea what he was going to do to ye. He was frightfully angry."

Weylyn halted his run to a more sedate trot, stopping behind Cinnia. "It doesn't look like he beat ye," he said, his smile teasing and genuine.

Mairi looked the lad up and down. "Ye neither."

Cinnia huffed. "Da doesn't beat anyone, unless ye face him in battle. Says it's the responsibility of the mighty not to harm those weaker than they. But he could have frightened ye terribly."

Mairi smiled. "Do I look easily frightened?"

Kenneth chuckled from his spot. "I'd say not." He nodded to the children. "Ye have a job to do today. Make that dungeon look like a dungeon again."

Mairi's smile faded. "Am I to return to it tonight?"

Kenneth tilted his head, his smile wry. "I don't think he's decided yet." With a quick bow, he headed out into the clear morning. Daisy followed him.

"I won't let him," Cinnia whispered, her sweet face pinched.

Weylyn crossed his arms. "He may put us down there with her."

Cinnia tugged his arm. "We should get started."

"I'll be right along," Mairi said. She poured herself some cool milk from a pitcher and tried one of the slightly smashed tarts she'd carried up. Cinnia had done a fine job. She chewed as she turned in a circle to survey the medium-sized great hall. It was not as big as Kilchoan or her home on the Isle of Mull. Sparsely furnished, with only one tapestry of a wolf and a coat of arms over the hearth. Without a fire and the sound of voices, it appeared abandoned.

"Perhaps it needs a woman's touch," came a voice from above.

Mairi twisted around to see Alec standing at the top of a set of stairs built into the wall. Arms crossed, he looked like a warrior king perusing his domain.

"It needs a broom for certain," she said and hoped she hadn't jumped when he'd spoken. He couldn't see her frantically beating heart through her chest, and she was determined to keep her composure and her temper, if possible. "Do ye not employ any staff?"

He unfolded his arms and came down the steps. "I did, but they all fled when Joyce was murdered." He walked to the table and picked up the other tart, his gaze remaining on her.

"But she wasn't killed here," Mairi said, remembering his explanation last night.

"Nay, but they think Kisimul is cursed." He shrugged his powerful shoulders. "Whispers have abounded since I was a boy, before, actually. How the castle is a gateway to Hell through the well." He pointed to a small room off the hall where a door stood half open. "The water is fresh and good. It comes from below the seawater, but they think it is unnatural." He lowered into a backed chair at the head of the table, looking quite chief-like with his strong features and intelligent eyes.

"They blame the castle for your wife's death?" Mairi asked. She took a seat several chairs down from Alec.

"They blame MacInnes for my wife's death," he countered. "The villagers blame the castle for allowing the evil to pervade Barra Isle, bringing the MacInnes here."

"That doesn't make sense," she said.

"Superstition doesn't stem from sense. It comes from fear." He leaned forward. "My grandfather's wife died on Kisimul, birthing my father. My father brought my mother here, and she miscarried every daughter growing within her, I think four in total.

"When I was born, my mother refused to try to have more bairns because of the evilness of this place. My father died shortly afterward in battle, and she had Kisimul blessed by a priest. She even had a chapel built here and dedicated it to St. Anne, the patron saint of women. 'Tis two doors down from this hall." He pointed toward the door leading into a narrow bailey. "My mother remained on Kisimul only until I was sixteen when she left to take holy vows at Iona."

"Ye lived here the entire time?" she asked, glancing about the tomb-like interior.

"Aye. 'Tis the place for The MacNeil. Therefore, it is my home. It wasn't always this quiet. I wed Joyce Mackenzie when I was a score and two. She brought a cook, several maids, and her mare. But when she was killed, they returned to Clan Mackenzie. Without a woman on Kisimul to appease St. Anne, perhaps, evil is thought to run rampant in it."

"They ignored your orders to stay?"

"I gave no orders. Kisimul is not a prison, despite your recent sojourn in my dungeon. This is a place of safety. No cannon nor arrow can penetrate to the innermost buildings. The access is only by water, which gives those of us defending it the highest point. Never in history has anyone been able to take her."

"And yet no one wants to live here," Mairi whispered. She rubbed her arms through the thin material of her gown. "It is lonely here. It's only ye and the children?"

"My army resides in the village, easily called up. I visit and train with them daily. But it is only my cousin, Kenneth, whom ye met, and my most loyal friend, Ian MacLeod, who live here with my small family, and of course, ye now."

Her gaze snapped to him. "I am still a prisoner?"

He pushed the chair back. "In a way, though ye are free to roam about, care for my wild and naughty children as ye suggested last night."

She stood, too, crossing her arms. "Will ye keep me here forever, then?"

He came close, but Mairi refused to back up. He was at least as tall as her brother, Tor, the muscles of his arms apparent through his shirt. Power radiated from him with each step, his gray-blue eyes boring into her own. As if the tapestry behind him had come to life, Mairi felt stalked by the wolf.

Stopping before her, he slowly inhaled through his nose. "Roses." She held her breath as he touched one of the curls framing her face. "Do ye always smell of them, lass?"

"I asked," she said, keeping her teeth set, as if she could cage her temper by clenching her jaw. "Do ye intend to keep me prisoner here forever?"

He let the curl go. The slightest of grins touched his mouth. "Until ye wed me. Then ye will just be the lady of Kisimul."

His simple words, spoken without a hint of tender emotion, was the spark flung into Mairi's brittle temper. Fists clenching, she pressed her foot back and snapped it forward. *"Pòg mo thòin,"* she yelled as she kicked toward his shin.

Before she could make contact, Alec sidestepped, catching her foot. Damn skirts made her too slow. He raised one eyebrow. "I'm certain yer arse is lovely, but I will wait until after the ceremony to kiss it," he said, referring to her favorite curse.

She tried to wrench her foot away, but he held tight for a second before dropping it. "Do ye always do whatever ye feel like doing?" he asked with a shake of his head. "Let everyone know exactly what ye're thinking?"

She narrowed her eyes. "Do ye know what I'm thinking right now?"

"From the sharpness of your eyes and the way your fingers are clutched along your skirt, I'd say ye have my *singh dubh* hidden there."

The blasted man hadn't forgotten that he'd given it to her. Biting back the string of curses on her tongue, Mairi spun away and strode toward the dungeon where the children were. They were much less infuriating than their father, and they could take her on a tour of this water-surrounded, cursed gate to Hell.

• • •

Undisciplined and stubborn. Mairi MacInnes was not any closer to wedding him than she was a week ago. Joyce had been quiet, docile even, although those qualities bred secrets like sneaking away to the village by herself. If she'd asked him, he'd have said no since there were visitors on the island and the MacLeods of Lewis had been seen riding down through MacDonald territory just north of Barra. But she hadn't asked him and had taken a boat across alone.

"Heel," Alec said and tapped his leg as the two other dogs from the MacInnes ran up beside him. Once they fell in line, he clicked his tongue and fed them each a small piece of cooked venison. Artemis ran up, begging for hers.

"Your mistress has already ruined ye," Alec said and

pushed her arse to the grass. "Sit." She bounced right back up. He did it again. "Sit." Three more times, each one as patient as the last, he used the word and pushed her arse down. When she stayed for several seconds, he clicked his tongue and fed her a piece of venison.

"What kind of name is Daisy? There's absolutely nothing noble about it." He scratched the dog's head and walked along the courtyard. The window to the dungeon sat near the rosebush at the far wall. He could hear the children chattering as they worked below. Occasionally Mairi's voice chimed in, making him pause. When she wasn't hissing with anger, her voice was rather beautiful. It matched her face and hair, and the rose smell she exuded. In the hall, he'd wanted to kiss her again, if only to stop her vicious tongue. What would it be like to release her passion, when it wasn't tainted with anger?

He tapped his leg to get the other two dogs to fall in line. Dogs were much easier to deal with than women. Trainable, loyal, trustworthy. Though they certainly didn't smell like roses.

"Alec," Ian called as he walked through the lower kitchen into the courtyard. He didn't speak until he stepped close, and he kept his voice low. "A ship is moored off the south side of Barra. I led a group of warriors to meet two men rowing to shore."

"Who are they?" Alec asked, but as Ian's eyes shifted to the dungeon window, he knew.

Ian met his gaze. "'Tis Tor Maclean and Cullen Duffie of Mull and Islay. They've come to find Mairi."

Chapter Seven

"Can ye give me a tour of the castle?" Mairi asked as she helped Cinnia and Weylyn carry the rug they'd rolled up from the dungeon floor.

They'd left the suspended bed with the old mattress and the privacy screen and table that Mairi had built. The basics of civility. If Alec needed to lock up horrible monsters, then he could remove the rest himself.

"Certainly," Cinnia said and led the way down the corridor above the great hall, where two doors stood open, showing dusty bedrooms. They placed the rug in a midsized room with a tiled hearth at one end and a bed against the wall where they'd rehung the drapes.

"This shall probably be your room," Weylyn said. "It was our mother's."

So, Alec hadn't shared a room with his former wife. Interesting.

Mairi studied the children. "Ye must miss her terribly."

Cinnia nodded while Weylyn crossed his arms, looking down at his boots. "She didn't spend a lot of time with us, but we know she loved us," Cinnia said. "She was sad a lot of the time."

"When ye aren't frowning over Da, ye're much happier than she was," Weylyn said.

Mairi studied them. "I am not here to take her place, ye know."

"Da said ye were," Cinnia said, her voice stiff. "It's been almost a year since she died. It's taken Da that much time to figure out his revenge."

Mairi sat on the edge of the freshly made bed. "Ye know who I was married to before."

"Aye," Weylyn said. "The bloody bastard, Fergus MacInnes, of Kilchoan."

Mairi watched Cinnia's face pinch. "Our *seanmhair* said ye had nothing to do with the MacInnes's sins. That ye could never have chosen to wed someone so old and foul."

"Your grandmother is here?" she asked. "I thought she was a nun on Iona."

"Not our real *seanmhair*," Weylyn said, his brows scrunched low. "Millie. She came to help Da when his mother left him alone here. She lives outside the village on Barra now." He sniffed. "She heard Da's plan to take ye, retribution for the mother we lost." He looked down at his feet, his shoulders rounded in a child's attempt to keep raw emotions inside. He shrugged. "She said we should not hate ye, even though I still thought we should, ye being a MacInnes and all."

"Millie didn't hear or say anything," Cinnia said and looked at Mairi. "She can't hear, so she reads the way a person's lips move. And she chooses not to speak, using her fingers and hands to tell us things."

"Like the signals Da uses with the dogs," Weylyn added.

"Don't let Millie see ye say that," Cinnia said. "She'll ignore ye for a year, and we won't get her soft bread." Cinnia turned back to Mairi. "And secondly, I certainly don't hate ye." Her eyes welled up. "Ye didn't kill our mother."

Mairi felt tears press behind her own eyes and inhaled to keep them in place. She looked between the children, Weylyn with his fleeting eyes and frown and Cinnia barely holding onto her sorrow. "First," Mairi said, sitting straighter on the bed, "I would love to meet your *seanmhair*, Millie. She sounds quite clever, because she is right. I did not choose to wed Fergus MacInnes. And I did not know anything about his plans, foul or otherwise." She paused. "I suppose that was second."

She shook her head and looked to Weylyn. "Thirdly, I do not consider myself a MacInnes but a Maclean."

He nodded and filled his chest with air. "I'm glad Millie was right."

"About me not supporting Fergus MacInnes?"

"Nay. About ye being someone to break the curse," he answered.

"The curse of Kisimul?" she asked.

"Aye, the one that makes no one want to live on Kisimul with us," Cinnia said.

A movement by the door caught Cinnia's gaze, and her eyes opened wide. Alec MacNeil stood there, hands braced on either side of the doorframe. His brows were lowered, giving him a menacing look. Like a mother bear, Mairi stepped closer to Cinnia.

"I think that's enough talk of superstitious foolishness," he said, his gaze falling on her. Was he speaking to her? He didn't know her at all if he thought she wasn't going to ask questions.

"Aye, Da," Cinnia said. "We're done moving things up. Can this be Mairi's room?"

What an outlandish situation. Mairi opened her lips and closed them again, completely lost on what to say next. Would he say it was her choice if she preferred the dungeon as an unwed woman or this room wed to him? Did he think the presence of his children would stop her from throwing the water pitcher at his head? She waited.

"If she wishes," he said, eyes steady and his grip relaxing. He lowered his arms. "Ian, Kenneth, and I are headed to the village. I think the weather is turning, thus, ye need to stay indoors. I don't want waves to wash ye into the sea." He pinned them with a fierce gaze. "Follow my orders this time."

"Aye, Da," they both said, glancing downward. Guilt sat heavy in the bend of their shoulders.

He tipped his head to Mairi, turned on his heel, and strode away, his tread soundless.

"Does he always sneak around here?" Mairi asked.

Weylyn's stern frown turned into a grin. "He moves silently because he's a wolf. He's loud only when he's ripping out the throat of his enemies." He clenched his hand, so his fingers looked like teeth biting into someone.

"Weylyn," Cinnia said in a huff. "Don't make up vicious tales."

His eyes opened wide in innocence. "'Tis true. I heard Ian talking about it. Scares the shite right out of the English or the MacLeods of Uist when they raid."

Mairi planted her feet on the floor and stood. "Perhaps it is time for my tour. I've sat in small rooms far too long."

• • •

Alec could see Mairi's features in her brother as he approached alongside his friend. Tor Maclean wore his sword and frown as if walking into battle.

"MacNeil," he said. "I am Tor Maclean, the chief of the Macleans of Mull, and this is Cullen Duffie, chief of the MacDonalds of Islay. We are searching for my sister, Mairi Maclean. She was stolen."

"Not Mairi MacInnes? Wife to the bastard who raided our island, killing unprovoked?" Alec said, his voice low. If the two drew swords, they'd be completely outnumbered. Ian and Kenneth flanked Alec with his two wolfhounds, and his men walked quietly behind the two, forming a semicircle.

"Fergus MacInnes is dead," Maclean said. "And my sister had nothing to do with his atrocities." He exhaled. "I am sorry to hear about your wife."

Alec stared into Maclean's eyes. He was called the Beast of Aros, and something about the intensity in his gaze made Alec think that, under different circumstances, he would like Tor Maclean. "I am sorry to hear that your sister is missing."

"She's not been seen on Barra Isle?" Cullen Duffie asked. He narrowed his eyes as if searching Alec, but if he thought to read anything into Alec's stance or movements, he'd find nothing. Alec had spent a lifetime hiding his actual emotions and thoughts, first from a disapproving mother, then from a ridiculously superstitious clan, and finally from a wife who believed in curses enough to abandon her own children to sneak off Kisimul alone.

Alec met Duffie's hard gaze without a single blink. "Nay. Ask my men or any of the villagers. Your missing lady has not set foot on Barra." Alec knew the two who had rowed Mairi across from Kilchoan and the four others who had manned the ship to sail them home would never tell a soul what they'd seen, not even their own families. They were loyal MacNeils, each one of them. Even though he'd slept on Kisimul, he'd come ashore most days of his life, training and growing up with them.

"We will do that," Duffie said and finally looked away, his gaze perusing the village square. "We will stay the night and move up your coast to Eriskay and South Uist tomorrow."

"Ruth MacNeil, the baker's wife, lets a room above her shop," Kenneth said and pointed behind the two.

"How about Kisimul?" Maclean asked, looking out over the water. "We would visit it before we journey on."

Alec crossed his arms. "No one goes to Kisimul."

"Ye do," Maclean said.

"It is the seat for clan MacNeil. Only my children and I reside there."

"And his second in command and cousin," Kenneth added, pointing to himself and Ian. "'Tis a cursed isle in the bay."

"Yet ye leave your children there alone?" Duffie asked, also turning his eyes toward the water.

"I don't believe in curses," Alec said. "But I also know how to keep my family safe. Kisimul is impenetrable. I've already lost their mother. I will not lose them. No one goes there."

"There is someone on top of your wall," Maclean said, taking long steps toward the docks for a better look.

Alec's stomach tightened as his hand grasped the hilt of his sword. "Stay indoors" had apparently not been specific enough. With a nod to his men, they followed Maclean and Duffie toward the water line. He looked up to Kisimul's wall walk and saw golden hair caught by the wind. But the castle was far away, and no features were detectable on the woman standing there; her head was the only part visible. Alec let Maclean and Duffie study the figure at length. When Alec reached them, he stopped.

"My daughter, Cinnia," he said.

"Or the ghost of Kisimul," Kenneth said next to him.

Alec scoffed. "I will tell Cinnia tonight that ye thought she was a spirit." Alec knew that Maclean stared at his sister and not Cinnia, for her hair was too golden in the muted sun to be his daughter's. Alec uncrossed his arms and let them fall to his sides, a signal to others that he was not in the leastways anxious or hiding something. It worked with stray canines.

Would it work with two suspicious Highlanders?

"Ye have a son also," Maclean said, his eyes watching until Mairi moved around the corner to step inside a tower.

"Aye. He's only seven summers, and not yet hit his growing years, so 'tis hard to see him above the wall. No doubt he's following behind his sister."

Cullen Duffie looked between Alec and the now vacant Kisimul walk that ran the wall. His face grim, he turned to Tor Maclean. "Let us find a room. We can continue north."

"Do ye have reason to think someone took your sister up here to the Western Isles?" Alec asked. They'd been quite careful about leaving no indications of who they were.

Tor Maclean gazed directly back at Alec while Duffie's gaze followed a small herd of village dogs, chased by two laughing MacNeil lads. "Three of Geoff MacInnes's hounds were cut from their tethers when Mairi was taken. We found their paw prints along the northwest shoreline, along with horse prints. Anyone able to bring horses by boat would have a ship able to handle the crossing to these isles."

"Interesting," Alec said. "Bandits wouldn't take the time to steal dogs. And faithful canines won't just follow someone away from their home unless they were mistreated there. Perhaps your sister decided she was safer to leave."

"It was Mairi's wedding day," Duffie said. "She wouldn't have left, and she wasn't mistreated. 'Twas her choice to marry. And who would snatch away a lass on her wedding day but someone who was at war with the MacInnes?"

"Aye," Alec said. "I and the MacNeil clan of Barra are at war with the family of Fergus MacInnes, but it will extend to the rest of the clan if I discover others were involved in my wife's murder." He glanced at the midsized ship in the harbor. Had anyone on the ship seen Mairi walking the roofline? "If MacInnes hides upon your ship, tell him that none of his clan is welcome here."

Alec strode away, with Ian and Kenneth flanking him, his wolfhounds jogging behind. Gravel crunched under their boots as they headed toward the church. "Watch them," Alec said. "If they try to signal or return to their ship, get me. We'll return to Kisimul before them."

"Ye best marry her soon, before her kin figures out she's here," Ian said.

Kenneth dropped the weight of his hand on Alec's shoulder. "Kiss her again, man. She's certainly kissable looking." He grinned, his brows raised, and veered off the path with Ian.

Alec narrowed a glare at Kenneth's back and continued toward Father Lassiter, where he swept the front steps to the small church. "Any news or needs for intercession, Father?" Alec asked the wiry man.

He cocked his head toward Maclean and Duffie, who spoke with Ruth at the bakery before she ushered them inside. "Just those two looking around like we're as guilty as the devil."

Alec crossed his arms and watched the two Highlanders. "There's a bit of the devil in all of us, Father. That's why we need ye here."

The only reason those two were staying on Barra Isle was to ask the villagers if they'd seen Mairi. Luckily, Alec hadn't brought the new dogs over yet, in case they had a description. What would that be? Did Geoff tell them to look for canines with their ribs showing through their skin and welts on the young bitch's back?

A man who treated his dogs that way would likely treat his wife the same. Mairi should thank him for stealing her away. Could another kiss convince her of that? He snorted. Doubtful.

• • •

Mairi sat in the narrow rocking chair before the fire she'd built in the stone hearth. Daisy lay at her feet, both having feasted on freshly caught haddock, which Mairi had taught Cinnia and Weylyn how to clean, season, and fry. They'd also learned to bake fresh bread without burning it. 'Twas a good day for the children and the small pack of dogs that followed them around. Despite the lack of people on Kisimul, the dogs certainly made the place less lonely.

A knock at the door halted Mairi's rocking as her heart sped up. She'd been eating below when the dogs alerted them to Alec's homecoming. Bidding the children good night, she'd retired before he came inside.

"Aye," she said, rocking once more. The door was barred from the inside, so there was no worry of someone barging in. Daisy sniffed at the crack under it, tail wagging.

"I would speak with ye," Alec's deep voice came through the wood.

"Go ahead!"

"Not through a door."

Mairi huffed and stood, walking over. She placed her hand there and breathed deeply. Alec wasn't her dead husband's abusive son, yet the feel of the heavy wood beneath her hand reminded her of another time when she was imprisoned, hiding behind a wooden bar over a door. Subduing a tinge of panic, she lifted and let the bar fall. When Alec didn't push into the room, she pulled it open. Daisy rushed past his legs and down the stairs after the voices below.

Alec stood with his legs braced apart, one hand on the doorframe, his stare studying her face. "May I enter?"

She swept her arm aside. "'Tis your bloody castle, and I am but a lowly prisoner."

He walked in, shutting the door behind him. "I do not enter where I'm not wanted."

"Ye entered my room at Kilchoan," she said.

"I believe ye beckoned me in."

She blew air from her cheeks. "I didn't know who ye were. Had I known, I wouldn't be a prisoner here."

"Think ye could have stopped me from taking ye to Kisimul?" he asked, crossing to the fire. He squatted low to poke it with the iron stick.

"Certainly."

He looked over his shoulder, one eyebrow raised.

"Or I at least would have screamed loud enough to make your ears bleed. And ye'd surely have suffered bruises."

He stood and leaned back against the wall, resting his arm on the shallow mantel. Good Lord, he looked rugged and fine relaxing there, a grin turning up his mouth. "Ye're a right bloodthirsty bride."

He may be the handsomest man she'd ever seen, but he was still a scoundrel for stealing her. She huffed. "Bride? Ha! Prisoner."

"Ye've been treated very well for a prisoner. Perhaps I should rectify that."

She took a step back. "If ye try to lock me in that cell again, ye'll feel my blade, MacNeil."

"No need for cells or blades if ye wed me," he answered, meeting her step with one of his own.

"And then what? I marry ye, and ye let me leave? Go back to my home on Aros?"

He paused his advance, studying her. "Ye would like to return to Aros on the Isle of Mull? Not Kilchoan?"

"I've told ye, I do not consider myself a MacInnes."

"But ye were about to wed a second one."

She opened her mouth and closed it twice before talking. "My duty…" She cleared her throat and tipped her chin higher. "As daughter and then sister to the Maclean of Aros, was to form alliances with our neighbors by wedding into another clan's family."

He frowned. "Your brother, Tor Maclean, made ye wed into the MacInnes clan."

"Nay. My father did. Well, he asked me to. I could have refused, but then I would be a burden to my family, not an asset. When Geoff MacInnes asked me again to wed within their clan, Tor said I did not have to. But I would be an asset, not a burden."

"Ye could be an asset to the Macleans by wedding The MacNeil of Barra," he said, watching her closely.

She stepped up to him, her eyes narrowed. "If ye hadn't noticed, MacNeil, I do not like being forced to comply. A woman wants to have a choice in the matter."

"Will ye wed with me?" he asked, not breaking the bond of their stubborn gazes.

She concentrated on not blinking. "Asking me while I'm trapped in your bloody castle isn't asking me." She could just make out a long white scar running under his close-cropped beard. It ran the length of his jaw. His face was angular and beautiful in its intensity. His piercing eyes made her heart hammer too quickly. Did he ever smile with joy or did his lips only slant with a sardonic grin?

"I am patient," he said.

She scoffed. "Ye're also brittle, stubborn, and if ye blow that damn whistle for me to come, I'll shove it down your throat."

The edges of his mouth turned upward. "Noted. Now it's my turn."

"Your turn?"

"Aye. Mairi Maclean. Ye are undisciplined, stubborn, and rash."

"Rash? Undisciplined? How would ye even know any of that? Ye've been away from me most of the last week." Of course, he was right. Her mother and brother had both called her rash and undisciplined, but the blasted devil had no right to call her such without knowing who she was.

"Ye kissed me when ye were about to wed another," he answered. "That is rash and undisciplined."

Mairi clamped her teeth and sucked air in through her nose. "I was told that a man was coming to tempt me, by my betrothed, to see if after I kissed him I would still want to marry Geoff."

He quirked an eyebrow. "Quite risky of him. Did the kiss work?"

"What? Nay," she yelled but felt her face heat. The man couldn't possibly know that she'd considered calling off the wedding when he released her from that kiss.

"So, if I was to…kiss ye again, that wouldn't change your mind about wedding me?"

"Absolutely not," she said, crossing her arms. It took strength of will not to let her gaze drop to his sensual mouth. Like a starving dog with a meaty bone waving in front of her, she felt the pull. Was she so lonely that she would throw herself into the arms of her enemy? Even if those arms were warm and gentle, wrought of power and stone-hardened muscle?

He stepped forward. "Are ye certain?"

"Aye." She opened her eyes wide, her heart thumping behind her breast. "Ye don't frighten me with threats of persuading kisses, MacNeil."

He touched a curl along her cheek, his hand brushing her face. Mairi stood as still as a marble statue, mutiny on her lips, despite the itch of her fingers to touch him. Aye, it was loneliness that weakened her resolve.

"I don't suppose ye ever get frightened, Mairi Maclean." His words were low, rough, like the prickle of his cropped beard must feel sliding along her skin.

Mairi remained rooted to the floor. If she backed away, Alec would take it as some sort of victory.

He brought his hand downward, touching her bottom

lip with his thumb, and her breath caught. "Ye are brave and disordered," he said. "But the softest, most beautiful creature I've ever met."

His words wrapped around her more firmly than chains. Beautiful? She'd never been called beautiful by a man.

He leaned in, eyes on her as if waiting to see if she would turn away. But she didn't, wouldn't. If he wished to see if he could affect her with a kiss, then dammit, she would meet his challenge with one of her own.

Chapter Eight

Alec's mouth touched her lips, and he inhaled the fresh sea rose scent of her. She slanted, opening immediately. He'd expected cold and distant. Instead the woman was kissing him back, her fingers curling into his shirt at his shoulders as she molded herself in to him. She was all curves and heat, and tasted slightly of honeyed ale. Her hands worked up to circle behind his head, nails raking through his hair, battering his restraint.

He crushed her to him, leaning over to taste her deeply. She was more intoxicating than whisky. Thoughts of strategy melted away as erotic fire beat with each thrum of his heart. *More*. He wanted more of Mairi Maclean.

A noise hummed from the back of her throat, much like a moan, making him grow rigid beneath his kilt. Holding her with one arm, his other hand roamed down her back, pressing her lovely, rounded arse against him. His body demanded he strip her bare, and she wasn't helping. It was as if she'd given in to the carnal heat flaring between them, the one he'd tried to ignore from the moment of their first kiss.

She rubbed her pelvis against his length, driving him wild with want. He groaned, lifting her until only her toes touched the floor. The bed was only two steps away. Cold logic beat against the inferno coursing through Alec's body. Nay. This was wrong. She considered herself his prisoner with no ability to escape him. Would he add ravishment to stealing away a woman who he was realizing was innocent?

Alec's hands came to Mairi's shoulders. With one last taste, he broke the kiss. She panted, her large eyes dark, as if she too had let the kiss sweep away her good sense. Lips still damp, Mairi rubbed them closed against each other. "Go ahead," she said, still breathless, but her eyes clearing of the frantic passion between them. She swallowed and wiped a hand over her mouth. "Ask me to marry ye now." She stepped back, crossing her arms, her answer obvious.

Alec adjusted himself and watched her gaze drop to his kilt. Her eyes rose when he crossed his arms to mimic her stance. "Ye can kiss a man like that and still love another?" he said, his words cutting. Were all women disloyal? Joyce had kissed him, but then left without a word. His mother had said she loved her son, but then abandoned him to Kisimul.

"I never said I was in love with Geoff MacInnes," Mairi said, blinking. She tipped her chin up again. "I was marrying him for duty, a duty I chose to uphold."

"For duty? Or a need to prove yourself worthy to your family?" he asked.

She narrowed her eyes, tipping her head to the side. "And why do ye stay on a rock in the sea, alone? For duty? Or to prove yourself worthy of being the laird of Barra?"

Knock. Knock. "Mairi? Da?" Weylyn's voice came through the door.

Without breaking her stare, Mairi called out. "Aye, come in."

Alec's son pushed inward with Artemis rushing past his

legs to circle them before the hearth.

"Did ye give Mairi her signal?" Weylyn asked Alec, making Mairi finally break the stare between them.

"Signal?" she asked.

Weylyn pointed to the whistle tied about Alec's neck. "The whistle. I'm two short blasts. Cinnia is two long blasts, and yours is to be one short and one long blast."

Ballocks. Alec released a long breath as he waited.

Mairi tipped her gaze upward, moving from Weylyn's innocent face to the ceiling and back down, in an arc, to land on Alec. "And what is your father's signal?"

"There's only one whistle," Weylyn explained, his young face pinching in confusion. "It belongs to the chief, so he doesn't have a signal."

Her eyes cut into Alec, for the space of a heartbeat, then she threw her hands up in the air. "Out! Everybody out," she yelled. "Except Daisy."

"But— " Weylyn started.

"Out, and I will have no signal." She pointed at the door and took a deep breath to center a look on Weylyn. "And neither will ye or your sister, Weylyn," Mairi said. She glared at Alec. "We are not dogs."

"But it will be easier to hear when he needs one of us," Weylyn demanded, his shock turning to belligerent loyalty.

"He has a voice and a pair of legs," Mairi fumed. "Now both of ye, out." She pointed to the door where Daniel, one of the four seamen who knew of Mairi on Kisimul, stood. They'd come back with him earlier in case Mairi's brother tried to dock.

"And who the bloody hell are ye?" she asked, her temper still high.

"Daniel MacNeil," he answered, but his gaze shifted to Alec and darkened.

Alec immediately reached for his sword. "What's amiss?"

"A ship is docking on the back side of Kisimul."

• • •

Mairi raced after Alec as he strode down the steps into the great hall where two other men, whom she recognized from the journey over to Barra, stood, swords in hand. Alec's massive wolfhounds took up station on either side of him.

"I said for ye to stay in your room," Alec said, looking back at her. He pointed to Cinnia and Weylyn. "Ye two also, with Mairi up in her room. Now."

The children grabbed Mairi's hands, tugging her back toward the steps above. "I told ye they'd come for me," she said.

The red-haired man, Ian, jogged in through the door from the courtyard. "'Tis Angus Cameron," he said, catching his breath. "He's here on George Macrae's ship. He landed with five men and...his sister."

Mairi's hope drained out of her like water through sand. Neither the Camerons, nor the Macraes, knew or cared who she was. Fergus MacInnes had disliked the Camerons, and they had threatened him with sending the English to Kilchoan. If they knew her identity, they'd likely applaud Alec's efforts or try to take her themselves. *Mo chreach.*

Alec cursed low but sheathed his sword. He looked back toward her. "Take the children above. Angus Cameron is a childhood friend and will not carry ye away from Kisimul on a Macrae ship." She narrowed her eyes silently. "Take the children and yourself above...please."

It was the please that moved her. Had the word tasted bitter on his tongue, having to use it before his men? Cinnia and Weylyn tugged again, and she followed stiffly. They made it up to the landing when a man's voice boomed out.

"Lo, MacNeil. I've brought ye a prize to fix all your

bloody problems."

Mairi followed the children into her room and gently shut the door. "Who is Angus Cameron?"

"One of Da's old friends from the mainland," Cinnia said, picking up the fire poker to push the burned peat around inside the hearth. "There was a festival with the Macdonnell clan when Da was a lad, and his father would take him there to compete." She frowned at the fire that licked up anew.

"Ye don't like him?" Mairi asked. She could hear the man's voice from below but not the words.

"He's loud," Cinnia said. "And big, like a bear. And he smells."

"He's a warrior, Cin. Of course, he smells," Weylyn said, as if she were the silliest creature he'd met. He turned to look at Mairi, excitement on his face. "He's also funny, and whenever he comes, things happen."

Cinnia rolled her eyes. "I don't think Da likes things happening when Angus is here."

Alec surely wouldn't like disruption to his routine. Maybe she would like Angus Cameron. For no reason other than he messed up Alec MacNeil's carefully laid plans.

"And George Macrae?" she asked.

Weylyn shrugged. "He's been here a few times to discuss trade, but that's all I know."

"I wonder why Angus brought his sister," Cinnia said.

"Do ye like her?" Mairi asked.

Cinnia shrugged. "I've only met her once. Bessy Cameron. She's pretty, in a breakable kind of way."

"Aye," Weylyn said, scrunching his face. "With a brother so big and gruff, it's strange she's tiny and thin. Like her folks gave all her food to Angus instead of her. And I don't remember her saying much."

Pretty, obedient, and quiet. Alec was sure to like Bessy Cameron. Mairi's jaw felt tight, and she rubbed just under her ears to ease the tension. Alec had touched her there when he kissed her, barely ten minutes ago. She dropped her arms. It would be a blessing if Alec liked another woman. Maybe he'd give up his foolish plan to wed her.

Mairi moved to the door. "Your father won't tell us anything. If we want to know why they've come, we need to listen." She cracked the door, and, using the hand signal she'd seen Alec use with the dogs, she looked at Daisy. "Stay," she whispered.

"'Tis terrible," Angus said, his voice easily heard. "Her death. Revenge, my friend, will help ease the pain."

"Shut the door," Cinnia whispered.

Weylyn crept up to the crack with Mairi. Cinnia threw her arms out wide, looking to Heaven, and paced over to the fire.

Where Angus's voice was a tempest of blasts and booms, Alec's answers were strong, constant, and even.

"The bastard responsible is dead," Alec said.

Angus snorted loudly. "Most likely by one of his own, on the way back, after his foulness killing a woman. Bloody cod."

"And he curses all the time," Cinnia said from the hearth.

Another voice came from the stairs. "The Macraes stand behind ye, Alec. I know ye have two of your own ships, but mine is available if ye intend to attack the MacInnes."

"Aye," Angus boomed. "The Camerons stand behind ye, of course. In fact, I'm here to offer ye a new wife. My sister."

Mairi lost her balance, falling against the door. It shut hard with a loud crack.

"Shhhh," Cinnia hissed, eyes wide.

Weylyn crossed his arms. "They're bound to have heard that."

Damnation. She opened the door again.

"Ghosts perhaps?" Angus said and laughed. "To add to the curse of the place."

"More likely my children. Without their mother looking

after them, they don't follow orders very well," Alec's voice rose as if he were talking directly to Mairi. She scrunched her face like an angry child.

"Another reason Bessy should become your wife as soon as possible. There's a priest on Barra. It is summer with plenty of honey ale about and wildflowers that Bessy is fond of. Wait until ye see the sandy beaches on the west side of Barra, Bessy. And the land here is extremely fertile."

"Aye, MacNeil," George Macrae said. "I'd like to take a look at this soil Angus raves about. I would like—"

Alec's voice cut through. "I won't be taking her to wife; no offense, Bessy."

The whisper of her response barely made it up the short set of stairs. The woman was a mouse. What would Alec do with a mouse? Whistle for her? Send her scurrying with different blast patterns on that damn little rod?

"Why the bloody hell not?" Angus roared, sounding like a beast on a battlefield. "Ah… Someone in the village warming your bed?" Angus chuckled, his good humor restored. "I'm sure Bessy could overlook a lass or two. She's quite the obedient and forgiving woman."

Overlook? Change of mind. Mairi did not like Angus Cameron. At. All.

Weylyn looked at Mairi with raised eyebrows. "That's absolutely not appropriate, nor honorable," Mairi whispered to him. God forbid the boy grew up thinking he could tup other women after he wed. Did he even know what happened between a man and woman yet? She'd have to make sure Alec talked with him. The boy certainly didn't need to gain his information from a man like Angus Cameron.

"I appreciate your generous offer, but I decline," Alec said, his voice lower, making Mairi open the door wider to hear.

As if she'd been called to run a race, Daisy flew through

the room and scooted out the door. Mairi caught Weylyn's arm as he made to run after her, because it was too late. The dog ran down the steps and into the hall.

Bessy cried out and Angus cursed while Daisy barked. The high-pitched whistle broke through the voices. "Daisy," Alec called. "Artemis, come." The dog stopped barking. "We have quite a few dogs about," Alec said. "I apologize for the surprise. She was supposed to stay abovestairs with the children."

"Are there more?" Bessy asked.

"Aye," Alec said. "Lots. I train them to help people in the village and guard our shores."

"She'll grow used to the beasts," Angus said. "Now back to the wedding plans."

Mairi was beginning to feel an itch to kick Angus Cameron in the shins. Alec said something, but it was low, so Mairi stepped quietly into the hallway. Even though she motioned for Weylyn to stay behind, he followed, making an exaggerated effort to be as silent as the shadows around them.

"Decline, decline," Angus said, his voice riding even higher. "What plans are better than creating an alliance with the Camerons? With England infiltrating the mainland of Scotland like a ravenous beast, we both need alliances to keep a strong Scotland. Yet ye refuse my sister? Why?"

The sound of a sword being drawn brought on the scrape of many blades unleashing.

"Ballocks," Weylyn whispered, his eyes wide.

Ballocks was right. Was there about to be a bloodbath in Kisimul's great hall? Children above, Daisy below, along with an apparently very breakable woman. Intercession was needed.

Grabbing her skirts with one hand, Mairi ran down the steps. "Stop," she called, the scene much like she'd imagined. Kilted men stood opposite one another, crowding the room with Alec in the middle, sword out. Before him, a short, burly man with a full beard and narrowed eyes held his own sword high. Another man with graying hair stood beside Angus, sword drawn, point toward Alec. Dodging behind the Camerons was a petite woman, terror squeezing her face.

Alec looked fierce, his features darkened to a lethal glare. Strength and power radiated from his stance, as if he stood on a hill about to charge down over a doomed enemy. Mairi ran to the table, hiked her skirts and stepped up to stand above everyone. Angus looked her way, surprise muting the look of brutality in his stance.

"*Stad*, stop," she called again.

"Who in fiery damnation are *ye*?" Angus asked.

Alec glanced her way but kept his eyes on Angus. One step forward and war would break out on Kisimul.

Mairi took a big breath in. "I am Alec MacNeil's betrothed."

Chapter Nine

Mairi looked like an avenging angel atop the table, hair spread out in golden disarray, arms wide in proclamation. Betrothed? He didn't think for a second that she meant it. She'd obviously been eavesdropping and sought to stop the spilling of blood.

With two strides, Alec positioned himself before her, his hounds growling and snapping while Mairi's ill-trained dog barked and scampered about the legs of Cameron's men. Alec's blood pumped as he waited for his childhood acquaintance—turned adversary—to make a move.

Angus had been a tyrannous bastard while they were lads, and his penchant for blustery orders and self-abiding nature made him difficult to like. Alec was the only lad who'd stood up to him, and, after one particular pounding that he'd given Angus, he'd gained the boy's respect. Any friendship between them was owed to distance and irregular meetings.

Offering help was different from demanding Alec marry his sister, and Alec wasn't about to let someone threaten him in his own hall. "I think it is time ye leave Kisimul," Alec said slowly. "And Barra."

"Betrothed?" Angus drew out the word. His eyebrows caved even farther toward his scrunched nose. "Already. Ye made no mention of it when I wrote to ye about my sorrow over Joyce." Slowly the man lowered his sword. Macrae followed, as did his men.

"Who are ye, lass?" Angus asked.

Alec's men kept their swords drawn, and would continue to until he lowered his own. With Mairi exposed behind him, he wasn't going to. "She is—"

"I am Mairi...Sinclair, from the far north. My father was called home before the wedding could occur, but left me with his wishes. We will wed after the harvest. I need time to plan."

"Sinclair? John Sinclair is the chief," Angus said.

"I am a cousin's daughter," Mairi went on.

Alec felt her hand land on his shoulder as if it was the most natural occurrence. The feel of it brought back the sensation of her clinging to him during their kiss. She climbed down onto a chair, finally finding the floor, releasing her hold.

Angus met Alec's gaze. "Well, that changes things," he said. "Put down your damn sword, MacNeil. If ye'd just said ye were already engaged, I wouldn't have had to defend my sister's honor."

Bessy's honor was in danger only from her crass brother. "I hope, Bessy, ye did not take offense." Alec lowered his sword but did not sheath it. Bessy came a bit closer, her gaze closing in on Mairi. "Since I cannot take your generous offer, Angus, ye may leave Kisimul now."

"Now?" The large man's face relaxed in a wide grin. "The Wolf of Kisimul isn't given to neighborly hospitality, are ye? 'Tis dark, and the voyage back to the mainland, long."

"Certainly, we can let them stay the night," Mairi said, as if she were already the woman of the keep. Moving out from behind Alec, she strode over to Bessy and tipped her head, linking her arm through hers. "Welcome to Kisimul,

Lady Bessy. The children and I will find ye a room in which to refresh yourself. Although we do not currently have a cook, Cinnia made some lovely tarts earlier today, which I will send up." As if moving around armed, hardened men were nothing to worry over, Mairi wove Bessy and herself through them toward Alec.

"Thank ye," Bessy said. Relief lay heavy across her narrow shoulders. Was it relief at Mairi's rescue or the fact she wouldn't be forced to marry him? The woman was as timid as a beaten dog. The thought piqued at Alec's already thin control around her overbearing brother. The ladies continued up the steps to the second level.

Angus scratched the back of his large head. "She's a right bossy piece of fleece." He grinned at Alec. "Ye'll have your hands full bringing her to heel."

With Mairi out of the room, Alec sheathed his sword. He looked to Kenneth. "The soldiers' barracks along the wall has an extra room for Angus?"

"Aye," Kenneth said, his usual grin gone.

Alec turned back to the man. "Ye may stay on Kisimul since Bessy is here." His gaze moved to Macrae. "Ye and Angus's men can sleep on ship. There will be bannocks and ham in the morning." Macrae nodded.

"Ah now," Angus said, coming closer, his arm extended to thump Alec's shoulder. "Let us celebrate your upcoming alliance with the Sinclairs." Angus crooked his head with his smile. "Might ye have a barrel of whisky about?"

Alec kept his curse inside. It was going to be a long night.

• • •

Fog, grayish white, wafted before Mairi as she picked her way across the rocks, Daisy at her feet. She drew the shawl around her to block the moist chill that clung to the earth as dawn broke. The tide was low, exposing a wide beach of barnacle-covered boulders around the outside wall of the castle. Mairi looked toward where the village should be, but could see only the swirls of fog lit from the east as the rising sun fought to burn through it. She knew George Macrae's ship was moored somewhere nearby, but the thick gray blocked its bulk. She shivered slightly as the fog drifted by, almost like a snake encircling her.

Daisy picked her way over the slick boulders, covered with dark seaweed, slipping a few times where her nails couldn't dig in. "If ye fall in the rot, ye'll have to endure a cold bath before I let ye back in my bed," she warned.

"I will keep that in mind," came a voice, making Mairi gasp the wet air as she turned. Alec's large frame emerged from the thick fog toward her, his boots planting firmly on the exposed areas. "'Tis not much of a threat since I already wash in frigid water daily."

The lines of his hair and face grew crisp as he stepped closer, the fog seeming to part for its master. Plaid wrapped around his waist, the end slung up over his shoulder, white linen shirt against tanned skin, his sword sheathed against his hip, he looked like a Highland warrior crossing a moor toward battle.

"I was speaking of the dog," she replied.

Daisy sniffed at Alec's boots and then leaped to chase a small crab amongst the rocks. Alec perused the swirling gray. "Looking for an escape?"

"I wouldn't be much of a prisoner if I wasn't." Truthfully, Mairi just longed to feel the breeze and listen to the water after the long night of readying a room and visiting with the sulky Bessy Cameron. The woman barely spoke, but looked so forlorn that Mairi hadn't wanted to leave her until she was ready to sleep.

Mairi stood on an elevated boulder. With sure footing,

Alec stepped before her onto the sand, made of crushed shells, to bring his gaze level with hers. The fog encased them, making it seem as if they stood together in a small space instead of outside. "The Camerons are allies of the MacNeils," he said, his voice low. "But I do not know the breadth of their honor, Mairi. And I do not know much about George Macrae. It would be unwise for ye to approach them alone."

She raised one eyebrow. "Even if they think I belong to the ruthless Wolf of Kisimul?" She tilted her head to the side in question.

His mouth turned up at the corners. "If ye were to ask for passage away from Kisimul, they would know the betrothal is false. Without my formal claim, ye might have a bigger problem than me keeping ye comfortable in my castle." He stared intently into her eyes. "The walls of Kisimul protect ye."

"The walls of Kisimul imprison me," she whispered back. Mairi sighed and rolled her eyes, breaking the connection. "I'm not trying to jump on the Macrae's boat, Alec." She turned toward the billows of mist and stepped off her perch to stand at the water's edge. "Just needed some freedom from walls. Ye get to journey off Kisimul whenever ye want. Those of us *kept comfortable* at Kisimul are not afforded the same liberty."

Mairi lowered her shawl to let the mist feather across her cheeks and breathed in the sea air. The tang of tide reminded her of Aros. Home. A crunch of shells made Mairi hold her breath, her senses straining to detect just how close Alec had come without turning toward him.

"I will take ye across to Barra," he said directly behind her.

She didn't turn, continuing to follow the ribbons of mist before her. "When I agree to wed ye, I know."

"Mairi," he said as his hand covered her shoulder. It was

warm and heavy, a tether in the fog. He turned her toward him. "I will take ye once the fog clears and Angus leaves."

She frowned up at him. "Why so generous?"

"I would have ye see the beauty that is Barra. The isle may be small compared to Mull, but its white, sandy beaches and blue-water shallows flanked by wildflowers are quite bonny. Cinnia especially loves to pick bunches to weave into crowns." He encircled the top of her hair with one finger. The soft touch caused a ticklish chill to coat Mairi, making her body come alive. How could such a light touch feel…intimate and luring? She blinked as she searched his darkly handsome features, feeling his strength like the fortress jutting up behind him. What would it be like to have him touch her body like that? Such gentle power in his fingers?

"I…" She tore her gaze from his and looked down, clearing her throat slightly. "I would like that. I made many wildflower crowns as a lass on Mull. I challenge Barra to provide as breathtaking bounty of flowers as I'm accustomed." She looked back into his face.

He chuckled, and merriment lit his features. Her heart thumped harder at the transformation. The Wolf of Kisimul could smile, and when he did, he made her want to… Mairi's smile faded at her treasonous desires. She turned from him, looking outward where the body of the Macrae's large vessel was a bulky shape, a hundred yards out in the bay. The fog was beginning to lose the battle against the sun.

"Shall we return before the children worry ye've fallen down the well?" Alec asked, extending his arm.

Mairi took one more breath of mist and nodded. "I'm holding ye to your offer, though."

He raised his eyebrows. "The offer of marriage?"

She smacked him in the chest, feeling the hard muscle underneath the linen shirt. "Nay. The offer to tour Barra and see your paltry wildflowers."

"Ah yes," he said, taking her arm to help her over the boulders. "Artemis," he called.

"Daisy," she called with a treasonous scrunch of her nose at Alec.

She didn't know which name beckoned her dog, but the sweet pup bounded and skittered over the rocks to follow them back up to the castle.

• • •

"'Tis a bonny day, MacNeil," Angus bellowed in the courtyard. The sun was high, and all traces of the thick fog were gone, once more exposing Kisimul to whoever studied it on shore.

"A good day for sailing," Alec answered, about ready to throw the onerous man into the bay. Angus had drunk half his barrel of whisky the night before, snored enough to drive Kenneth and Ian to sleep in the hall instead of in beds in the barracks, and was now acting like he was an invited guest.

Angus laughed. "Throwing me off Kisimul?"

"Aye," Alec said, walking to the door in the thick wall encircling the keep and bailey. He'd been watching the fog lift and Tor Maclean's ship depart all morning. The weather had cooperated perfectly to keep Mairi shrouded, and her searchers should be gone for at least a week while they visited the northern isles.

He'd told Angus the ship was a northern trader, and the man barely looked at it. With Alec's two large sailing vessels, moored in the bay, one more ship moving about hadn't elicited questions from Mairi, and now she was safely tucked behind the walls of Kisimul as her brother sailed away. Alec ignored the twist of guilt in his gut.

"Then let us go to Barra," Angus said, pulling Alec's thoughts. "I've wanted to show Bessy your beaches. The land on Barra is exceedingly fertile. 'Twould be a good place to have a home. She may wish to stay even if ye don't wed her."

Alec narrowed his eyes. "Ye would abandon your sister here without family or husband?"

Angus stuck his finger in his ear, scratching at it. "That sounds quite ignoble, MacNeil. I was thinking she hasn't been happy at home and might wish to stay, maybe meet another MacNeil." He gestured toward Kenneth, who worked with the two male dogs Alec hoped to give Millie. "Like your cousin there. Young, handsome, strong enough to handle a wife." He laughed as if the thought of anyone needing strength to handle his obedient sister was absurd.

"Bessy is welcome to stay on Barra if she wishes it, but I cannot keep an eye on her for ye. And as the raid last fall shows, it is not safe for a woman alone, even on a distant island in the sea."

Angus flapped his hand as if shooing a fly. "Bessy would be fine, but I'd have her see the isle first."

The man just wanted to be rid of his sister. *Damnation.* "I plan to take Mairi and the children for a trip on the far side of Barra today. Bessy can come if she likes."

Angus clapped his hands together, making the dogs spin toward him, barking, tails between their legs. "Excellent, I will tell Bessy to be ready for me to take her." He strode off while a tightness curled in the muscles of Alec's gut. He'd invited Bessy, not Angus, but it would be strategically foolish to alienate the Camerons just because their chief was a crass, wheedling annoyance.

He strode over to Kenneth, who was using gentle words to remind the new dogs that they were safe. Kenneth hid a yawn behind a fist. "Does the man ever stay quiet?" he asked.

Alec could hear Angus Cameron yelling for Bessy inside the hall. "If he's silent, he's either dead or up to something."

Chapter Ten

Shades of pink, orange, yellow, even purple. The flowers bobbed atop tall green stems, bowing and swaying like waves in the sea breeze. Shimmery dragonflies hovered over a sea of color, zipping about in the sun. "Aren't they lovely," Cinnia said as she skipped through the field toward the white sand. The wide swath of dancing flowers grew right up to the beach, marking the border between the open ocean and Barra Isle.

"They are," Mairi said, only too aware that Alec could hear her admission. "One locked up on Kisimul would never know Barra could be so beautiful in the sun."

"A rare beauty. Even blown about by fury," Alec said, and she looked toward him. But instead of his gaze taking in the flowers or blue sea, he stared at Mairi as if talking about her.

She swallowed against the little thrill his words caused and looked away, perturbed at her response. He was her captor, not some handsome suitor with dark promises in his gaze. *Mo chreach*, he was muddling her resolve to hate him.

"MacNeil," Angus called from down the slope. He stood with George Macrae and held soil in his hand, letting the wind take it. "Ye could grow right up to the beaches, though the flowers would need to go." Even in the wind he sounded too loud, blasting through the peace of the small, breaking waves.

Alec walked with Mairi down the slope. She watched Weylyn throw a rock into the sea and run back from froth brought in on waves. Cinnia sat in a clump of pink flowers, picking low on their stems as she talked up to Bessy. Angus's sister wrapped herself in a wool shawl as if cold, but she smiled, probably happy that the wind muted her brother's booming diatribe.

"I think that's the first smile I've seen on her," Mairi said. "And she's not even a prisoner."

Alec ignored her stab. "It seems he wants to be rid of her."

Mairi looked up at him. "Leave her on Barra?"

"Aye."

"Humph… I like him even less. Didn't know that was possible."

Alec chuckled. "His men seem loyal enough, and as far as I've heard, the Cameron clan eats well and keeps their borders, therefore he must be a good chief. He's apparently made an alliance with the Macraes of Ardnamurchan. It will take a strong woman to curb Angus into any type of reflective man."

She looked at Alec. "Cinnia said ye were the only lad to best him in battle as a child, that he respects your strength."

"Strength is the only thing that men like Angus Cameron respect."

They walked side by side through the flowers, her steps weaving in between colorful clumps. "And what does the Wolf of Kisimul respect?" she asked, tucking a stray strand of hair behind her ear.

He didn't answer right away, just looked out where Weylyn dodged more waves. "Courage," he said, glancing toward her. "And…"

"Obedience?"

"I was going to say loyalty, but aye, in a hound and in my men, I depend on their obedience. But I think loyalty is better as it requires the animal or man to choose to obey. Choose to stay."

"They have freedom to decide," she said softly. "Unlike a prisoner."

He didn't respond, and she exhaled long. She could easily ruin this outing with sulking and sarcasm, but that would ruin it for her, too. "Ye must have hoped that your wife's people would have remained at Kisimul after she died," Mairi said.

He inhaled and released it slowly. "Everyone on Kisimul leaves."

"Ye haven't."

He turned to meet her gaze. "Nay, I have not. The chiefdom and the castle have my loyalty."

There was more behind his words, a loneliness. Pain. So, the great Wolf of Kisimul suffered. Mairi turned back to the sea. "Ye were good to give them the freedom to choose."

The heels of Mairi's boots sunk into the sand as they walked closer to the water's foamy edge. "I would have thought they would stay for the children."

"Not much courage in them." Alec bent, standing to skip a stone past the low waves breaking on the shoreline.

"They were afraid of ye?" she asked.

His lips hitched up into a wry grin. "They said it was the curse that chased them home. No one wanted to risk being the lady of Kisimul and dying early."

"Ah, but ye would risk the widow of your enemy," Mairi said, turning back to the surf.

Alec caught her wrist, halting her. "I don't believe in curses," he said. "Else I'd have taken Cinnia away." He dropped her arm, but they continued to look at each other. "Ye don't seem the type to believe in them, either."

Mairi twisted her mouth into a sardonic smile. "I am not." She caught the hair that slapped against her forehead to tuck it behind her ears. "And not all the women die. Your mother is still alive," Mairi said, glancing where Cinnia set a wreath on top of her curls.

"After losing four newborn daughters, she demanded to birth me in the village. When I lived, she was convinced that Kisimul was the source of the evil and became overly cautious while I grew. Although she cloistered me within the walls of Kisimul, she spent as much time as she could off our little island and left as soon as possible."

Mairi swallowed her comment about a mother leaving her son defenseless. "And your father's mother died at Kisimul?" Mairi asked.

"Aye, and probably a few before her, too, but life is hard. I don't think it has to do with some evil surfacing through the freshwater well to stalk Kisimul."

Mairi looked at Alec's strong profile as he stared out at the blue sea, his short hair tousled in the wind. His nose was a perfect slope down to lips that she knew were warm and sinfully delicious. "And ye are certain ye aren't worried about Cinnia growing older, so ye brought a sacrificial woman to be the lady of Kisimul?" Mairi asked. She pursed her lips tight and surveyed the varying shades of blue and green in the sunlit sea.

"I do not want to wed ye to be the sacrificial lady of Kisimul," he said.

She turned to meet his intense gaze. Lashes framed his gray-blue eyes, a furrow between them, showing his loss of humor. She breathed in deeply. "Ye just want to wed me to punish a dead man and his clan." Before he could deny it or justify his actions, she turned, her heel digging a divot in the sand as she strode down the beach toward Cinnia, who held a wreath of flowers out to her.

"It's lovely," Mairi said, taking the ring of purple and pink flowers to set on her head.

Cinnia rocked up on her toes. "The colors are perfect in your golden hair. Ye look like one of the fairy folk." She picked up two strands of Mairi's loose hair, holding them out to the sides. Her happiness transferred to Mairi, momentarily pushing away the disappointing fact that she wasn't truly free to enjoy the day, not when an invisible tether chained her to a rocky fortress surrounded by sea.

Bessy walked over, wearing a similar crown of yellow and pink flowers. "It seems we are all crowned fairy princesses," she said with an authentic smile. The wind and sun had put some color back into the woman's cheeks.

"Indeed," Mairi said.

"I will make one for Da to take to Millie," Cinnia said and fled toward the bank of flowers, her bare feet leaving deep dashes in the drier sand.

"I think Cinnia has the best idea," Mairi said, leaning down to unlace the borrowed leather boots. They were a bit tight, and shucking them felt wonderful. With a quick pull of the laces on her garters, Mairi loosened her stockings, letting them fall down her legs. She plucked them from her toes and set her feet free on the moderately warm sand.

"Goodness," Bessy said with a small giggle. "Aren't ye cold?"

"'Tis a warm day. Ye are from inland where the sea breeze doesn't reach ye. I've grown up in the rush of wind," Mairi said and wiggled her toes down in the sand.

Weylyn waved Mairi over, and she turned toward him. Bessy touched her arm. "Mairi?"

"I think Weylyn wants to show me something."

"It's just," Bessy said, pausing. "Do ye think if I stay on Barra, that I could stay on Kisimul? Ye don't have a cook, and I rather liked helping our cook in the kitchens. The kitchens tend to always be warm with the fires going. I could mind the children, too, and any of your bairns after ye wed the wolf…I mean The MacNeil," she said, her words coming fast like a flustered whirlwind of dandelion seeds.

Mairi's mouth opened as she fought the urge to make promises to help the woman who'd rather stay on a cursed island than return with her brother or live alone in a strange village. "I will speak with Alec about it," she said and squeezed Bessy's cold hand. Even if Mairi couldn't do much to help herself, she could argue on behalf of Bessy. She leaned closer to her, although no one was near. "We lasses need to stick together."

Bessy smiled broadly, relief opening her features. "Thank ye."

"Let's go see what Weylyn has found," Mairi said.

"Ye go. I don't want to get wet."

Mairi left Bessy standing in the dry sand and stepped lightly down the slope to the water's undulating edge. "Did ye find something?"

Weylyn held up a triangular piece of glass. "Look, its purple, the rarest kind of sea glass," he said, setting it in her palm. "The glass starts off as white, but the sea washing it makes it turn purple." He bent over her hand, pointing to the indented top. "If ye hold it this way, it looks like a heart."

Mairi ran her finger along the smooth humps at the top, following it down to the point. "It does look like a heart. Hmmm… Now whose heart could it be?"

He screwed up his face in a funny frown. "If I were Kenneth, I'd likely say that it was mine, and I'm giving it to ye."

Mairi laughed. "Is Kenneth giving ye lessons on wooing the lasses?"

Weylyn snorted in disgust. "Aye. Says it will come in handy later on."

She laughed harder. Cinnia ran over to look, and a larger wave washed in, making Mairi lift her skirts and dash upland in time to keep her hem dry. "Cinnia, watch your skirts," she called, but the girl already stood in the surf, her skirts weighed down by seawater. "Too late," Mairi called and laughed again.

She looked around, feeling a heavy gaze, and saw Alec watching her. Warmth spread into her cheeks, and she turned to walk toward the children who were running back and forth with the waves, searching for more sea glass. Mairi realized she still held the glass heart.

"What did he find?" Alec walked up behind her, making her inhale stutter.

Traitorous breath, she chided herself and turned with her hand outstretched so he didn't have to come close to see.

"Sea glass, the rarest color, and it looks like a heart," she said, all at once.

Instead of taking it from her palm, he rested his hand under hers, bending closer to look at it. "Aye, it does look like a heart." His gaze lifted to hers without him straightening. "And my son gave it to ye?"

She couldn't help but join Alec in his small smile. "I expect him to retrieve it any moment. Young men are known to be fickle."

Alec's grin broadened. He straightened, his attention turning back to Cinnia and Weylyn near the edge of the water. "It is good to hear ye laugh," he said casually, the pinch between his brows at odds with his smile.

Mairi tipped her head to the side, touching the flower crown. "I blame it on the sun, fresh breeze, and warm sand."

"Barra has more of all three than the rest of Scotland," he said, sounding almost boastful, definitely proud. She watched the waves of his hair dance in the wind, a dark lock sliding along his tanned forehead.

"Not on Kisimul?" she said.

His smile faded back to his normal, serious survey of the land around him. "Nay," he agreed. "Not on Kisimul."

Weylyn waved again with round arm gestures. "I think he wants us to go to him," Mairi said, her smile returning at the boy's antics. Without waiting for Alec, she hiked up her skirts and jogged lightly over to him. He held up a shell.

"There's something inside," he said. "Just watch." He placed the pointed shell into the water. "He'll come out."

Mairi turned, her back to the sea to block the lowering sun, and bent at the hips to spy the little creature. Alec squatted down over the boy's hand. In the distance Cinnia called out, but Mairi wasn't fast enough.

A wave, stronger than the rest, broke, swamping them with foam and saltwater. Mairi gasped. Weylyn dropped the snail and jumped up, as did Alec, who reached out to grab Mairi as the surge caught her skirts, hitting hard against the backs of her knees. Alec held her hands, but her feet washed out from beneath her.

"Mo chreach," she gasped as she plunged backward into the swirl of water.

Chapter Eleven

Alec lifted Mairi's hands as she sat in a foot of surf water. With the slope of the shore, the water reached up her back to the ends of her long hair. Gently, so as not to wrench her shoulders, he dragged her up, catching her against the water gushing back, as if Poseidon sought to snatch her into the ocean. "Stand up," Alec said, unable to completely hide his grin. She looked caught between mirth and fury.

"Ugh," she cried. "Ye try to stand with sand beneath ye and skirts weighted with the sea."

"Ye kept your crown," Cinnia called out from higher on the shore.

Mairi finally found her feet and stood. She pulled her one fisted hand from his to hold up the sea glass. "And my heart."

"'Tis my heart," Weylyn called. But with a glance from Alec, he produced a dark pout. "But ye can have it, Mairi."

Alec held her arm as they walked up the sand. He didn't dare drop it, or she might flop back into the surf like a beached mermaid. Mairi stopped to bend at Weylyn's side. "Ah, but 'tis yours to give to some lucky lass when ye grow older," she said and placed it back in his palm. "She will be lucky to get it."

His eyes lit up, and he glanced at Alec. Alec gave a silent nod, and Weylyn smiled broadly, tucking it in his pocket. "Thank ye," he said with a bob before running off.

Bessy hurried over. "Ye're drenched," she said, offering Mairi her shawl. "Ye'll catch your death." Genuine concern muted her smile.

Angus followed with George Macrae. "Ye aren't even wed yet, and death is already trying to take her." Angus laughed, oblivious to the pallor growing in his sister's face.

"No worries," Mairi said, her voice strong. "I am hale and hearty." But she did accept the shawl, and Alec felt her shiver as he held her arm, marching up the sandy slope.

Ian strode over with Kenneth. "The sun is starting to go down, and the temperature will drop. Best to get Mairi back to Kisimul."

"Escort the Camerons back so they can prepare to depart," Alec said. "I will see Mairi dry before bringing her across the open water."

"I wanted to talk with ye before departing," Angus said. "Your lady said Bessy could stay on at Kisimul."

Alec felt Mairi's fingers clench into his arm. "I haven't had a chance to discuss it with him yet."

Angus waved her off. "I will wait for your return to Kisimul before we leave Barra." Angus was using any excuse to prolong his stay.

"Very well," Alec said. "Ian, make sure to pick up some bread from Ruth and fish from the docks before maneuvering the ferry over."

"I can cook," Bessy said, a flush coming to her cheeks as if she'd talked out of place.

"Thank ye," Mairi said to her. "The children need to eat after spending all day in the wind and sun."

"Aye," Angus boomed. "As do the men." He patted his

round gut that hung a bit over the top of his kilt.

Alec led Mairi through the wildflowers, passing Kenneth on the way to his horse, whom they'd brought over. "I'll leave Sköll on Barra for the night," he said to him. "Stay close to the Camerons and Macrae."

Kenneth called to the children as Alec continued to lead Mairi toward his horse. "Where are we going?" she asked, a slight chatter to her speech. The wind had turned cold with the slanting of late day shadows.

"Somewhere warm." He interlaced his fingers for her foot to step into. It was bare, small, and cold. Her wee toes curled against his palm. He wanted to cup the tiny foot in his hand until it warmed, but she pulled herself into the saddle. He climbed on behind her and brought Sköll around to face inland.

"Ye're cold," he said to justify pulling her completely into the shelter of his arms and chest. Unlike the ride from Kilchoan, she didn't fight it. They rode in silence, her eyes straight ahead, her glorious hair free and dancing in the breeze. "What are ye thinking?" he asked, close to her ear.

"That ye shouldn't marry Bessy Cameron," she said.

He frowned at the back of her head. "I have no intention of wedding her."

"Good. Ye scare her, I think, and she believes in the curse of Kisimul. Her brother's an inconsiderate oaf who thinks only to unload her or use her. Bloody cod."

Alec kept his chuckle back. "Tell me what ye really think of Angus."

She twisted in the seat and saw his grin. She snorted softly through her nose. "I don't like to see women used or parceled off."

Alec's mouth tightened. "Like being married to another clan to form an alliance?"

She turned to face front, her shoulders stiff. "That was my

choice."

"Perhaps coming to Kisimul was Bessy's choice," he said. "I've been told I attract my fair share of gazes from lasses."

Mairi *tsk*ed. "Handsome and exceedingly humble." She shook her head but continued to stare forward.

Handsome? It was the first kind word she'd given him. Alec clicked his tongue, feeling lighter, and Sköll broke into a smooth gallop. Together as one, they flew across the rolling meadow toward the cottage near the forest, with smoke curling up from the crooked chimney. Mairi laughed, leaning into the wind, her hair streaming out on either side of him. It was a beautiful sound.

Alec slowed Sköll as he neared. Millie, having felt the vibrations of the horse, peeked out the doorway, her face breaking into a curious grin.

"Where are we?" Mairi asked as he reined in, scattering chickens in the yard.

"Millie's cottage."

"Millie?" Her eyes opened wide as her hands went to her muddy, wet skirts. "The woman who raised ye when your mother left?"

"Aye."

"Ballocks, Alec," she whispered, making Alec grin. "I won't be making any grand impression on her."

"Just so ye know, she deciphers lip movements."

Millie stepped out, drying hands on her apron. She nodded to him and looked at Mairi, one gray eyebrow raised.

"Mairi Maclean," he said, moving his lips slowly. She nodded.

"Ye told her my name?" Mairi asked. "I thought I was a secret."

"I trust Millie with my life, and she'd figure it out within five minutes, anyway."

Millie beckoned them into her cottage. It smelled of

herbs and fresh bread, the warm fire heating the small space. She made signs asking what happened to Mairi.

"A wave snuck up on her at the beach. Do ye have anything dry and warm for her?"

She beckoned Mairi behind a screen. "I think she wants me to bathe," Mairi called out.

"There's time," he answered, rolling up his sleeves. He wouldn't be able to stay in such warmth for long. "I'll see to her animals." He walked out into the early evening. Millie had a cow that would have already been milked, but he made certain the stables were clean and secure. He corralled the chickens to keep them safe from eagles searching for an easy meal. He was the only wolf on Barra, but some of the puppies born to the dogs on the isle had grown feral, despite his efforts to train and find them good homes. The dogs he placed worked to herd livestock and protect their families. Some even helped the elderly who lost sight, and hopefully Millie would like the two male dogs he was training to be her ears.

Twenty minutes later, Alec carried in a stack of peat squares for the fire.

"'Tis a bit tight but quite lovely," Mairi said behind the screen. She laughed then. "Aye, I am not lacking there."

Alec stomped his feet hard on the floorboards. Millie stuck her head around the screen. "The livestock are in for the night," he said. She gave a brief bow, her hand touching her heart in thanks. "Did she find ye dry clothes?" he called.

"Aye," Mairi said, coming out from the screen. Her hair was wet and gathered to the side in a small drying sheet to lay over one shoulder. The muddy sand was scrubbed away from her face. She wore a yellow dress with flowers embroidered into the skirt. Its waist was quite tight and pushed the swell of her breasts high. "I think it was hers when she was younger."

Millie nodded, her eyes bright as she held out a hand to Mairi.

"Aye, it is a lovely dress," Alec said.

Millie shook her head, frowning, and flipped her hand from the top of Mairi's head to the tips of her toes, which peeked out the bottom. "And aye, Mairi cleans up nicely," he corrected. Millie plopped her hands on her hips and tapped her foot. "And," Alec continued, his gaze meeting Mairi's, "ye look lovely."

Millie nodded and strode to the hearth where she had a small pot hanging over the hot embers. She stirred it while motioning for them to sit.

"I don't want to take her food," Mairi said, a hand before her lips.

"She won't let us leave without eating."

"Don't eat very much," she told him.

"Then she'll think I'm ill and not let me leave," he said, taking the bowl Millie set before him. "Thank ye. Smells wonderful."

Millie nodded at Mairi as she set down her bowl. "Thank ye. Do I smell rosemary?" Mairi asked. Millie nodded again and smiled.

"She has a robust herb garden," Alec said.

Millie motioned to Alec and then mimicked shoveling. "Ye planted it for her?" Mairi asked.

"Under her knowledgeable direction," he answered, eating heartily of the good stew. Millie turned to the small oven she had in the corner with a wooden bread paddle.

"She won't come back to Kisimul?" Mairi asked.

"Only at Christmastide or when one of the children is sick."

"Does she fear the curse?"

He exhaled long. "She thinks curses are brought on by the people who believe them, therefore she refuses to do so."

"Wise."

"Aye. She says she wants her freedom and doesn't feel

like she can leave when she's there."

"Hmmm... I know the feeling," Mairi said casually and spooned more stew in between her lips as she held his gaze.

The bread was as light and flavorful as usual, and the butter fresh and sweet. "'Tis delicious," Mairi said and chewed slowly. He watched the way her lips and delicate jaw moved. Unguarded, she smiled, thanking Millie again and praising her cooking talents.

Millie wrapped up the other loaf to send back with them. She always baked two, knowing Alec would be along nearly every day to check on her.

"We need to return to Kisimul before Angus Cameron takes it over," Alec said, and Millie made a face.

Mairi pulled Bessy's shawl around her. "She knows him?"

"From my youth, and he came last year to visit Barra with a request to settle some of his warriors here," Alec said.

"Oh? That's odd, isn't it?"

"The English are encroaching into Cameron territory. I suspect Angus is searching for ways to expand. He's rather fond of the beaches and brings up our fertile soil whenever I see him. I think trying to marry off Bessy to me is just another way he's attempting to put a foothold on Barra."

"I think Bessy should stay. We could use a cook, and she seems willing," Mairi said.

Alec froze, watching Mairi. Did she realize how her statement sounded? "Aye," he said slowly. "We could use a cook on Kisimul."

She turned to Millie, who hugged her. Was Mairi starting to warm to the idea of Kisimul being her home? With him? The thought made his pulse pick up.

Millie looked past Mairi to him and began signing. *Love her?*

His brows lowered, and his face pinched. Love her? She'd only recently stopped shouting at him.

Millie waved her hands, erasing her question. She signed again. *Have you bedded her?*

"What was that signal?" Mairi asked, her eyes wide. "With her finger and hand?"

Millie ignored her and raised her eyebrows at Alec. He shook his head.

She tipped her head to Mairi with clear orders to bed her as soon as he could. If he wanted to keep her.

"Do I want to know what ye two are discussing?" Mairi asked.

"I would say naught," Alec answered, kissing Millie on the cheek. "I will be by in a day or so," he told her.

She stood in the lit doorway as Alec helped Mairi up on Sköll's back.

"Goodness," Mairi said low. "I'm nearly falling out of this bodice."

"I hadn't noticed," Alec said, climbing atop before her, and pulled her arms to wrap around his chest as they rode.

"Liar." Even though he couldn't see her, he could hear the teasing glare in her voice. She waved at Millie as he clicked his tongue to get Sköll trotting away into the dark meadow.

• • •

Mairi leaned forward, relaxing against Alec. With her arms wrapped around him, she felt secure and warm. She laid her cheek against his back where his heart beat through. Lord, Alec MacNeil was…complex. His strength was evident, yet he held it in check, never flaunting it or using it to frighten people or animals. He'd taken her without permission, yet he seemed to respect all breathing creatures, even Angus Cameron. He cared for Millie, never forcing her to come to Kisimul.

Everyone leaves Kisimul. The phrase, and the pain edging

the brittle words, squeezed her heart, just a bit. After all, he was still the man who had stolen her from…wedding Geoff, who was possibly the man who'd beaten Daisy.

Hell. Her thoughts and feelings were jumbled. She couldn't deny the pull she felt toward Alec. Physically, since their first kiss, but there was more to him than muscle, brilliant eyes, and an irresistible mouth. Her cheeks warmed as she thought about the hand signal Millie had given before they'd departed. The woman was brazen and direct. Mairi liked her.

She pressed one hand to the swell of her breasts above the lace-edged neckline and breathed deeply of the summer night air. The moon was only the thinnest of slivers in the star-speckled sky, making the shadows impenetrable. She turned her head to the side. "We aren't headed to the docks?"

"I have something else to show ye before we row back to Kisimul," he said.

She chuckled. "Ye really don't want to deal with Angus."

"Aye, 'tis the only reason I'd wish to ride through a summer night with a beautiful lass wrapped around me."

Mairi's heart felt light within her, but she pushed his flirtatious words down. Perhaps he'd decided to woo her, trick her with flattery to wed him. "Are ye sure the children are well without us?"

"Ian and Kenneth would light a signal if there were a problem." He pointed out to the bay on his right, where the dark bulk of Kisimul sat on its rock. "Bessy has probably fed everyone and has the children up in their bedroom. No doubt her brother will wait until morning to leave."

He stopped on a knoll and dismounted, lifting her to the dewy grass. Her toes curled into the dampness as she looked about at the dark. "What am I to see?"

"Look up. It's the best view in the world," he answered as he grabbed a wool blanket from the back of his horse and shook it open, laying it out.

"The stars?" Mairi asked.

"There's no moon to hide them, and the sky is clear. Come," he said, patting the blanket next to him.

She pulled Bessy's shawl around her shoulders and sat, but he had a second blanket and draped it over her legs. "Lie back," he said, lowering slowly. She looked around at the darkness shrouding them, her breaths turning shallow at his nearness. His horse had wandered off, its neck bent to the summer grass, leaving them completely alone. With slow control, she leaned back to lie beside him, their shoulders touching. "That is Cepheus and Cassiopeia," he said, pointing toward the north.

"Aye." She easily picked out the constellations she'd learned from her father and raised her own finger to point toward the southeast. "And there is the flying Pegasus. They are bright and clear tonight."

"Ye know star patterns?" he asked.

"My father used to take my brother and me out in a boat when we were little, when the moon was new and the clouds were gone. It was peaceful, and he'd point out the constellations."

"He was important to ye," Alec said, his voice low, intimate.

"Aye." She turned her head to the side to meet his gaze in the darkness. "Fathers are very important to children. They teach them many things. Did your da teach ye about the stars?"

"Nay," he said, turning again to stare up. "Millie did. My da died in battle when I was young."

She reached across her chest to lay her hand on his upper arm. "I am sorry for that."

He turned his face to hers. "Your da, he is dead?"

"Last year, just after I wed Fergus."

The shape of his face stood out from the darkness. "Ye'd

wed Fergus MacInnes for your father, and then he died."

She inhaled and exhaled long. "There was no other possible reason but duty."

"And Geoff MacInnes?" he asked. "Ye said your brother didn't ask ye to wed him?"

Even without the moon glowing down, Mairi could see the hardness of Alec's mouth. She shook her head, rubbing her hair on the blanket. "Tor said I didn't have to, that he'd never make me wed where I didn't love."

"Ye said that ye don't love Geoff MacInnes," he said, bringing up their argument from before. "That your brother didn't ask ye to wed and your father had died. Ye could have waited to meet another chief, seal an alliance with another clan. Something must have drawn ye to MacInnes."

Mairi twisted a lock of her hair. "Nay, I don't love him." She sighed. "But…he asked." She straightened again to follow the star patterns, picking out the swan constellation, Cygnus.

"I asked, and ye said nay."

She gave a wry laugh. "Ye told me, and then ye asked me as a prisoner. I was free when Geoff proposed." She huffed. "And well…'tis foolish, I know, but the man I'd set my heart on since I was a lass had just married someone else. Cullen was completely enraptured by his new wife, and when Geoff asked, I thought that at least I could help my family with an alliance to our north."

"Cullen Duffie?" Alec asked, his voice gruff, making her turn to him in the darkness.

"Aye, do ye know him?"

"I've met the man."

From his tone, she could tell Alec loathed Cullen. It sent a flame of anger through her, and she pushed up onto one elbow. "What have ye against the MacDonalds of Islay? Or is it just Cullen Duffie ye want to slaughter?"

He pushed up onto his own elbow. "So ye love Cullen

Duffie?" he asked, though it sounded like an accusation.

"Nay, he's married to someone else," she said, her brows lowering.

"But if he weren't, ye would want to marry him."

Mairi stared at Alec, her eyes opening wider. Was he jealous of Cullen? Why would he be jealous of someone she had loved?

A meek woman, trying to attract the ruggedly handsome man lying next to her under the stars, would have assured him that she'd never really loved Cullen. But Mairi was not, nor ever would be, that woman. She lay flat once more and crossed her one arm below the hoisted mounds of her breasts in Millie's snug dress.

"Well," she said slowly and flipped her other hand about. "I don't know. I mean…Cullen Duffie…" She made her voice almost purr over his name and left it hanging there as if his name alone answered what every sane woman would desire.

"That's not an answer," Alec said tightly.

She turned toward him, still raised up on his elbow. He looked tortured as he waited. She even saw the white glimmer of his teeth between his lips as if they were clenched. Aye, Alec MacNeil was jealous. Why?

"Ye would marry him if something happened to his wife and he asked ye," he said, his voice flattening out, the emotion gone. Without moving, she could feel him pulling away, and she didn't like it. In fact, she hated it.

"Alec," she said slowly. "I am an honest woman. I grew up thinking I would marry Cullen. If he'd asked, I would likely have said aye. But he's left broken hearts all over the Highlands, and I guard my heart well. I doubt he ever knew of my interest."

Alec's teeth came down for a second on his bottom lip. Did he even know the vulnerability that small movement showed? The disciplined man who never gave away his emotions? How could he have slipped so?

Before she could remind herself again of her prisoner status, she reached forward to place her hand on the side of his face, her fingers brushing down his cropped beard. He didn't move, just stared down at her. The day together had been wonderful and relaxing, and the pull she felt toward him was undeniably fierce. His jealousy over Cullen confirmed that he was feeling the same.

Mairi stroked a finger down his cheek again. "Why don't ye kiss me, Alec. Make me certain I would say no if he asked."

He stared at her, the darkness like a veil around them. Alec's face filled the space above her, and he lowered down, his kiss simple. He was still angry or jealous. The realization spurred Mairi to reach her hands behind his head, pulling him over her for a real kiss. Their mouths met fully, warm and perfectly matched. She turned to him, her body scooting to snug up against his hard, hot frame.

Fingers raked through her hair to cup her head as Alec took over. He slanted her face against his, and she opened her mouth, letting him in to taste her. Her hands roamed across his broad shoulders and back as she released the constraints she'd kept on her passion all day.

His arms framing her face, Alec kissed her like he wanted to brand her, and she kissed him back the same way. Heat coursed through Mairi until the only thing that existed on that dark knoll, under the stars, was just the two of them. She hugged him to her, rubbing her pelvis against the hardness she felt through his kilt.

"The bodice is tight," she said, breathing against his mouth. He rolled her halfway on top of him, until his fingers could reach the ties in the back, yanking them loose. When Mairi lay flat again, he looked down on her.

Reaching up, he raked her hair out around her head. "Ye are an angel," he said.

"Hmmm... Would an angel do this?" Mairi lifted her shoulders, one at a time, as she slid a hand down her neckline and under one breast. She pulled upward, spilling the breast up and out of the bodice. She did the same for the other, so they sat atop her in perfect, pale display.

"Och, lass," Alec breathed and reached to kiss her again, his palm cupping one breast, lifting its weight, his fingers coming up to gently pinch her nipple. The sensation tugged muscles deep within Mairi. She moaned softly against his mouth and shifted with restless energy.

Alec kissed a path down her neck, his lips like flames licking along her skin, making her pant. His mouth closed around one jutting nipple, and Mairi gasped, arching her back to press into his laving tongue. His hand sought the other breast, plumping it and pinching until she pressed the *V* of her legs into him, asking without words.

She was a widow, after all. Had been married for nearly a year. No matter that Fergus, despite his frustrated stroking, had never been able to mount an erection to enter her. An embarrassment she wasn't willing to disclose to anyone. She'd fought off Normond MacInnes and managed to keep her maidenhead, but she didn't want to keep it anymore. As a widow, no one expected her to be a virgin, so why continue the farce. She wanted to know the pleasure that other women knew, and she had no doubt that Alec MacNeil could deliver it.

"Alec," she whispered, her hands trailing down the planes of his stomach, tugging the shirt from his kilt, which sat low on his waist. She slid her hands underneath to the smooth, hot skin of his torso, running her fingers along the gentle ridges of muscle there. In a quick motion, Alec untied the shirt at his neck and pulled it off over his head, leaving his beautifully chiseled chest bare.

"God's teeth," Mairi said. "Ye make me pant." He sat

up over her and slowly cupped her bare breasts, teasing her nipples. His hands were incredibly warm against the chill of the night air.

"And ye make me harder than the walls of Kisimul," he growled, lowering his mouth again to catch a nipple between his lips.

Mairi arched in to him and closed her eyes as she gave in to the pleasure his skillful tongue ignited within her body. When he traveled back up her neck to kiss her mouth, Mairi's fingers edged up his kilt until her hand reached his jutting cod. Thick and long, hot and hard. She stroked up and down in a rhythm to match her own, and Alec groaned deeply. In the darkness, it sounded like a growl, sending a thrill of chill bumps all over Mairi.

"Take me, Alec," she whispered against his mouth. "Take me here under the stars."

He leaned back to look down into her face. Would he deny her? Make her promise to wed him first? What would she say?

He released a breath, bending close. "I will make ye fly apart, Mairi Maclean." He touched a knuckle to the hollow of her throat, and skimmed it slowly down between the tight valley of her breasts. He kissed under her ear. "I will make ye burn," he whispered.

She pressed against him, a ticklish chill along her skin warring with the hot passion flaring up through her body. "Aye, make me fly apart, Alec MacNeil." She tugged at the waist of his wrapped kilt. When she loosened it, he stood, sliding it down his legs to fall somewhere at the end of the blanket. There was just enough starlight to see his form. Muscles, narrow waist and hips, and a tall, proud erection. Want throbbed through her, making Mairi weak and strung tight with anticipation at the same time. She pushed up, feeling caught in the grips of the dress, and wiggled until the bodice parted more in the back. She pulled the front away from her, including the tied sleeves. He helped her stand, the dress pooling at her feet. The two of them faced each other in the darkness, exposed but hidden in shadow, viewed only by the distant stars.

Alec's arms encircled her, pulling her in, covering her quickly cooling flesh with his heat. "Ye're warm," she said, her cheek against his chest, aware of the heavy thickness against her stomach.

"And ye're freezing." He rubbed her back, stroking down over her backside, cupping and lifting.

She tipped her face up to his. "Set me on fire, Alec. Give me your heat."

His gaze was intense, as if a battle raged within him. "Ye are sure?"

Was she? Mairi had dreaded giving her virginity to a man older than her father, and when he couldn't take it, the reprieve had been welcome, yet burdensome. Now she could choose to whom to give it. And she chose Alec MacNeil.

"Aye," she said. "Make me burn."

Chapter Twelve

Alec stared down into the face of an angel, a wickedly delicious angel with smooth skin, full breasts, and curves that could make a man weep for want. And she wanted him. He'd given Mairi time to send him off aching, but she'd said the words, asking him. She was a widow, without a need to guard her virginity. He wanted to wed her, and her words had stripped away nearly all of his self-discipline. A bloody legion of English couldn't distract him now from the woman before him, standing gloriously bare under the stars.

She reached up on her toes to grasp his shoulders, pressing the *V* of her legs against his rigid cod. "I want ye, Alec."

His hands stroked down her gently arched spine, cupping her sweet arse, plumping each smooth globe and pressing her slightly up and down to stroke him with her stomach. He groaned, kissing her fully, tasting and plundering her sweet mouth as his fingers tangled through her damp hair. Slowly they lowered to the blanket. From his knees, he looked down at her, hair spread about a lovely face, making her look like a star fallen from the sky above. Her curves were milky white in the darkness, silky and sweet.

She moved restlessly. "Come here," she said, reaching down to wrap her chilled fingers around him, sliding up and down with perfect rhythm.

Barely coherent, Alec pulled the other blanket over them in case she was cold. Lying on his side along her, he caught her face in his hands, kissing her soft lips, which opened and slanted against him. He stroked down her side to her hip, grasping it in his hand. "So soft," he whispered at her ear as she arched her head back, giving him access to her long, slender neck. He warmed her with unhurried kisses on the edge of her jaw. "Mairi, lass," he whispered. "Ye are perfect."

She tipped her face to connect with his gaze, a grin on those full lips. "And feeling perfectly wicked right now."

With a soft growl, Alec swooped back down to her mouth, ravishing her as thoroughly as she kissed him back. Fast, fierce, and molten. He breathed her in, her honeyed kiss blocking out the rest of the world.

Below she pressed the *V* of her legs against his thigh and claimed his cod again, stroking, rubbing him enticingly against her skin. His blood rushed through him, his heart pounding as if he raged in battle. Sweet, perfect battle to bring out her cries. Curving over her, his mouth found her peaked nipple, sucking it into his mouth, his tongue swirling, his teeth teasing. Mairi arched her back, holding her other breast, which he followed with equal attention.

Mairi's bare toes curled and rubbed along his legs. She wrapped her arms around him, trying to pull him over on top of her. "Please, Alec," she murmured. But he wasn't through teasing her into bliss.

Alec held her shoulders gently as he sat back on his heels. "Relax, lass." He lowered his mouth to just below the curve of her full breasts. While his hands stroked her sides, he kissed down her flat stomach, nibbling. When he reached the juncture of her legs, she moaned. He looked up to see her massaging her breasts, her head thrown back. He breathed deeply, reaching for his discipline when his body demanded he just mount her, thrusting into her wet, willing body. But he wanted her thrashing before him first.

He lowered his mouth, parting her with his fingers. Her legs widened as if begging for his touch. And so he touched, easily finding her most sensitive spot, flicking it with his tongue and sucking along it while she pressed into his mouth. She was drenched, the womanly scent driving him mad. He grabbed his own member, stroking himself as he lapped at her, teasing her nub over and over again.

"Alec!" she yelled, and he pressed one finger inside her incredibly tight channel. "Good God, Alec," she yelled. Her body tensed, sucking along his finger as she moaned deeply with her release. She breathed hard, her pelvis following the press of his hand. "Alec, damnation, I want ye in me."

She looked down her body toward him, watching him stroke himself. "Aye, Mairi. I know." He pressed the tip of his cod against her swollen channel and nearly lost control at the hot moisture kissing him there. She bent her knees to the heavens as she pressed up, sucking the first inch of him inside.

He swallowed hard, his muscles contracting as he moved over her, still barely connected. Wet heat in the tightest channel he'd ever known. She grabbed his shoulders, her nails biting into him. He leaned over her, covering her mouth with his and thrust forward, burying himself in Mairi's glorious body. Bloody heaven!

Pulling back out, he rammed in once more before his mind caught up to his pounding pulse. He pushed up onto his hands, looking down at Mairi. Her eyes were squeezed tight, her lips open. "My God, ye're a virgin."

He lowered back down, breathing hard, a firm grip on his discipline. He was hurting her. Framing her face with his arms, he kissed her gently. First her eyelids, their long lashes against her cheeks. He kept still, buried within her body as he stroked her hair, brushing his lips against her cheeks, her nose, and finally her lips. Her mouth opened under his to return his kiss. He stroked her breast, down her side to her hips. "Och, Mairi. I hurt ye."

"'Tis better," she said, opening her eyes with a small smile. "I expected the sting."

"I bloody hell didn't."

Her hands came up to his arse, pressing him to her, as she pulled herself up to kiss him. "We'll talk about that later, MacNeil." Her hand slid down between their bodies to where they were joined to cup his stones. "Right now, I want to feel ye move."

His eyes fell shut on the pleasure-pain he endured while forcing himself to remain still within her hot core. He growled in the back of his throat and withdrew slowly.

"Aye," she crooned, urging him with her hands on his arse, and he pressed back down into her. "Oh God," she breathed, a look of open passion across her angel face. She began to rock forward and back against him while he rooted her to the ground, urging him to take up the rhythm. "Harder, like the first time," she breathed. "I won't break. I swear." The feel of her tightness sucking along his length caught his breath. Bloody sinful heaven.

He inhaled her warm scent near her ear and rose up to stare into her eyes. "Hold on, Mairi."

A wicked grin of anticipation curved her lips. "Tell me," she whispered.

He wet his lower lip. "Ye are soaked with heat, lass." His arms came up around her face as he leaned in, right before her gaze. "Hold on, because I'm riding ye hard."

"Aye," she said, the word a near whimper. Grabbing the back of his head, she pulled his face down to hers, kissing him with her wet, open lips. As if cutting the ties of restraint, Alec plunged back into her, catching her moan in his mouth. In and out, he rammed hard against her straining body. Joined together, hot slapping of skin, he tasted their combined passion on their tongues and lips. Her nails sliced down his back, the sting adding to the lust shooting through Alec's blood. Faster, they drove forward together, pushing the ache of passion in each other higher. Only she existed, her sweet, musky smell, her wet kisses, the silk of her hair clutched in his fingers, and the molten heat of her core.

"Alec," she screamed into his mouth as she pressed against him, clinging to his shoulders to rise up as her channel throbbed and clenched around him. He continued his thrusts, roaring as he burst within her. Eyes open and lips parted, their gazes locked as he rocked into her and out, teasing out the last tremors of their releases.

• • •

Mairi shivered in the cool summer breeze, and Alec pulled the second blanket over them. She nestled against his body and listened to his heavy breathing as it slowed back to normal. He stroked the side of her face and kissed her forehead. The scent of their loving still clung to them.

He raised onto his elbow and looked down at her. He stroked a thumb over her kiss-swollen bottom lip. "Ye were a virgin. But ye are a widow."

The tightness of embarrassment clutched at her breath. She'd never talked about her shame to anyone. After a moment, she drew in a deep inhale. "He was never able to consummate the marriage," she whispered. "He…tried. Had me do things…but he never grew hard."

"That was not your fault," he said, and she looked away. He leaned over her, catching her face in his hands, guiding her back. "Mairi."

She blinked back the tears that ached behind her eyelids, finally meeting his gaze when the silence stretched. She wet her lips and breathed in fully. "And once I knew that he wouldn't or couldn't…" She raised her chin slightly. "I swore to myself that I would choose who to give my maidenhead to, and I chose ye."

The words came firm and swift, but unease coiled within Mairi, waiting. Alec lowered his face, kissing her tender lips firmly. When he pulled back, he made certain she was watching as he spoke. "Ye honor me, Mairi Maclean. Thank ye."

As if the coil was sliced through by his words, she relaxed, her eyes closing momentarily. She inhaled, an impish smile blossoming, and she blinked open. "Thank ye for not stopping when ye realized."

His grin was downright wicked. "I don't think I could have, even if a horde of Englishmen were running up the slope."

She gave him another kiss, a feeling of lightness giving her energy. Tapping the tip of her finger to his nose, she slowly pushed up into a seated position. "We should make sure the children are well at Kisimul." She looked toward the dark shape in the bay. "Even with Ian and Kenneth there, I don't like leaving them alone with Angus Cameron."

"Aye," he said, the smile fading from his mouth, and helped her stand. The small biting ache Mairi felt between her legs was nothing compared to the openness in her heart. Alec MacNeil was bloody amazing. She helped him dress, giving him small kisses, especially on the raked lines she'd scratched in the skin of his back. His body was rock solid, a perfectly sculpted figure of a warrior with the golden heart of a kind, honorable man. He was the right man to give her maidenhead.

He cradled her against him as they rode down to the docks, he keeping his horse smooth to not jar her nether regions. Such chivalry. Mairi's smile remained while he handed Sköll off to one of his men in town, who would take the horse for the night. Mairi stayed in the shadows, since she looked completely ravished with her wild hair, bare feet, popping bosom, and satisfied grin.

Alec claimed her hand as they walked along the line of tethered rowboats. The water lapped at them, and several sailing vessels in the small harbor creaked. Otherwise no one was about.

"Do people have specific rowboats to use?" she asked as they walked past the first tethered boat.

"Aye." He pointed at the first one. "That was my da's boat. He took it across from Kisimul when he went to the battle that claimed his life."

She stopped, her smile fading as she noticed how beat up and weathered it looked, as if it hadn't been used for decades. It was a wonder it hadn't sunk to the bottom. "It just sits here?"

"It's considered bad luck to use the boat of a dead man." He pointed to the one next to it. "That was my mother's. She took it across when she left Kisimul to travel to Iona."

"Ye don't use that one, either?"

"Nay. Some of the fishermen do." He shrugged.

Mairi looked down the line of small boats. "Which one is Joyce's?"

He cleared his throat and pointed to a trim little vessel, whose paint was chipping away. "It won't be used, either," he said. "At some point, I should probably burn hers. No one will touch it." As they walked past the little boat, Mairi saw wildflowers, still somewhat fresh from the afternoon, scattered in the bottom, along with one of the wreaths Cinnia had made. She blinked past the press of tears for the children who'd lost their mother so young.

Mairi breathed evenly, staring at the line of little

abandoned rowboats, and felt her throat contract. Good Lord. They were memorials to people who had abandoned Alec.

She managed to swallow. "Who do these other boats belong to?" she asked softly, pointing farther down the line.

"This one is Millie's," he said, pointing to one painted red. "I keep it tied here in case she ever wants to come across. Not that she will." His voice was strong, but the words struck against Mairi's heart. Alec MacNeil, strong and powerful warrior, hurt. Her chest began to ache, and she rubbed against it with her fist.

"Here is mine," he said, escorting her to a well-kept, white boat with blue trim. The furry face of a wolf, teeth glistening, was painted on the wooden seat just inside the bow. A small mast stood straight with a sail rolled against it, and the oars stood ready.

"I don't think I'll sit on the wolf's face," Mairi said, stepping in and finding another seat on the side toward the center. "My arse could be in jeopardy," she said, hoping to lighten the heaviness she felt.

Alec chuckled as he untied and coiled the rope onto the floor of the boat. He stepped close, bending to kiss her lips. "I promise to just nibble." He sat at the oars right behind her. Within minutes they were gliding across the water with the powerful strokes of Alec's shoulders and arms.

Even with the jewel-like stars twinkling overhead, Mairi's gaze kept lowering to watch Alec row. He hadn't bothered to tie his shirt, and his muscles strained against the confines of his sleeves. Damnation, maybe she was wanton after all and not the cold fish Fergus had called her, blaming her for his lack of rigidness. She squashed the man from her mind and concentrated on the thrust of the boat moving forward through the water. Alec MacNeil, the Wolf of Kisimul. A deadly warrior, a passionate, giving lover, a father, and a man who'd been hurt deeply. Aye, he was complex.

Mairi listened to the boat cut through the dark water with each of Alec's strong, sure strokes. What would happen now? Would he expect her to bed him again? God's teeth, she certainly hoped so. But what would that mean? Their relationship was confusing. Captive or lover?

Alec trailed the oars in the water as he slowed them near the dock on the closest side of Kisimul. The wall looked like a mountain in the dark as they bumped up against the wooden platform. Instead of rising to tie them in, Alec set the oars in their grips and turned to Mairi, taking her hand.

"I was thinking," he said. He paused, glancing up at the stars.

"About what just happened between us?" she asked.

"Aye." He looked back to her. "Ye said I never asked ye properly, that I told ye or asked ye while ye were trapped within Kisimul's walls."

What was he talking about?

With an inhale, he cupped her hand in both of his. "Mairi Maclean, will ye marry me?"

Mairi's breath caught. He looked sincere and exposed there in the shadows. He'd taken her from Geoff to avenge the murder of his wife, but he'd never been cruel or sought to frighten her into submission. He was an honorable man. She opened her mouth.

"Lo there, MacNeil," boomed Angus Cameron as he strode out the door cut into Kisimul's wall.

"Bloody damnation," Alec swore as the man marched down and set his blazing torch in the holder. He grabbed the rope from the boat, tugging it to tie it to the dock.

"Is something amiss?" Mairi asked, turning to the frowning man.

"That depends," Angus answered. "I stopped in the village for supplies before heading back here. A crone named Ruth had quite a lot to say. Said she'd never heard that Mairi

Sinclair was here at all. She didn't believe me when I said I'd spent the day with her." His gaze bounced between the two of them.

"I have not announced the betrothal to the village," Alec said. He helped Mairi stand, leading her off the small boat and onto the dock.

Angus continued, grabbing up his torch. "The only Mairi she knew about was the one Tor Maclean was searching for when he landed the other day on Barra. Mairi Maclean MacInnes, his sister. Seems he and the MacDonald of Islay, Cullen Duffie, were questioning everyone in the village, even ye, from what Ruth said."

Mairi's breath froze as she watched Angus's smile grow in the painful brightness of the torch. His bushy eyebrows rose. "So, I'm thinking that the honorable Alec MacNeil might just be growing ballocks enough to seek his rightful vengeance against the MacInnes." He bowed his head slightly to Mairi. "And ye are Mairi Maclean, war prize of Kisimul."

Chapter Thirteen

If he'd had his sword drawn, Alec might have skewered Angus Cameron where he stood, his triumphant smile slashed across his round, bushy face.

"Tor?" Mairi whispered, standing there, her hand on his arm. "Cullen? They were here? Just days ago." Her fingers curled into a tight fist and slid down to her side.

"Mairi—"

She held up a hand, silencing him. With her head high and the regal bearing of a queen, she grabbed the yellow skirts of Millie's dress and strode up the wooden dock toward the castle. Hair tumbling down around her stiff shoulders and bare feet made her look like a furious fairy marching off to war.

Angus made an appreciative grumble in his throat. "Now that's a fine lass for tupping." He chuckled. "Wondered what was taking ye so long. Seeking a bit of vengeance by fu—"

Alec's fist slammed into the bastard's jaw and nose, throwing him backward, arms flailing, to land on his arse. "Get the bloody hell off my island. Now." Alec ignored the warmth of his blood on his knuckles and stepped over Angus's thick legs to stride toward the castle.

Behind him, Angus spit. "Ye knocked out my bloody tooth."

"Ye have an hour to get your men off Kisimul," Alec turned and nodded to Ian who stood in the doorway. "Light the beacon." It would draw his men from shore, since at present there were more Camerons and Macraes on Kisimul than fighting MacNeils, and he wouldn't risk his children or Mairi. Ian ran off as Kenneth came out of the hall, sword drawn.

"Where's Mairi?" Alec asked.

"I don't think ye're going to like it," Kenneth said as they entered.

Only George Macrae stood inside, the other men hopefully on his ship. Alec pointed at him. "Angus Cameron has one hour to vacate Kisimul and Barra. Make sure he sees it happen."

George strode out the door, and Alec turned back to Kenneth. "Where is she?"

"I saw her heading down to the dungeon."

"Mo chreach," Alec murmured. "Guard the children," he ordered as he walked briskly toward the back of the keep.

He grabbed a lit torch, held in one of the iron wall sconces, and pushed through the heavy door. "Mairi," he called, his boots cracking against the cobblestone ramp as he descended underground.

She sat in the dark on the raised platform that had been her luxurious bed last week. Alec went to the door and shook the bars. She'd locked herself in with the key. "Dammit, Mairi. Ye knew they'd come look for ye. I wasn't about to start a war in my village when it could be avoided by ye marrying me first. It was just the two of them, and if they'd known ye were here, they'd have drawn their swords. I didn't want to kill your brother."

She kept her back to him, knees pulled up under her chin with her arms wrapped around them. It was cold down there. He rattled the bars. "*Mo chreach*, Mairi, open the door."

"Ye started a war the moment ye took me from Kilchoan," she said. "And if I am to remain a prisoner, I should be in the dungeon."

Alec's hands gripped the iron bars tightly, his cut knuckles dripping blood with the strain. "Your husband started a war the moment he came to Barra and slaughtered an innocent woman."

"If he never consummated the marriage, was he really my husband?" Mairi asked softly.

"I didn't know any of that," Alec said, frustration raking him. He slammed the heel of his palm on the bars and turned, pacing from one end of the short corridor to the other.

Mairi looked over her shoulder at him. "My family is worried about me. I was taken without any indication of why. They may think I'm dead. My mother... She must be tortured. What would ye do if Cinnia had been stolen away? With no word left or reassurance that she was even alive?"

Anger made one rash. Alec knew that, and yet the bloodlust for revenge at Joyce's brutal murder had been so fierce that he had reacted with hate in his heart. If Cinnia or Weylyn had been taken, he'd tear the world apart, finding them, and punish the bastard who'd taken them.

"I will write to your mother," he said, grabbing the back of his neck.

"Give me parchment and ink," Mairi said. "I will write in my own hand, so she knows I am well."

"Ye can write?" he asked.

"Aye," she said indignantly. "My father wanted *both* his children educated. I wrote all the missives Fergus sent out."

Alec froze. "Ye wrote for your hus—Fergus MacInnes?"

"I just said as much," she snapped.

Without a word, Alec strode up the ramp to the great hall. Angus stood there, a rag against his nose. "Ye bloody bastard," Angus boomed.

"Get the hell out of here," Alec yelled back, his voice just as loud.

"Bessy wants to stay," Angus said.

Alec pulled out a small lockbox on a shelf under the stairs, flipping it open to retrieve the letter he needed. "She's welcome. Ye are not."

"MacNeil," Angus said, his voice lower. "I meant no harm, out there." The apology in his voice brought Alec's head up. With his empty hand held up in surrender, Angus stared at Alec. Ian and Kenneth stood beside George and Angus, their swords drawn. "Ye are letting a lass work her way between us, friends since we were lads."

Why did the man think they were friends, just because he couldn't beat Alec in a fight? "If ye are trying to apologize, do it and then leave. Ye've worn out your welcome on Kisimul."

Angus's eyes narrowed. "Kisimul. A cursed rock in a bay away from your clan. Ye're all alone here, Alec MacNeil, abandoned by your kin."

"Shut your mouth," Ian said.

Angus grabbed his cod and swore at Ian before pivoting on his heel. He spit on the floor. "Cursed place. And if Bessy succumbs to the curse, consider yourself at war with the Camerons."

George Macrae gave Alec a brief nod. "I support the Camerons in this."

"Then ye need to get the bloody hell off my isle as well," Alec answered and motioned for Kenneth to follow them out. Voices outside showed that the men from the village had landed.

With the brittle parchment in hand, Alec tromped back

down to the dungeon where Mairi still sat on the bed, turned now toward the locked door of the cell. Alec grabbed the torch to bring it close to the bars and unfolded the letter. He flattened it up against the bars. "Did ye write this letter?"

Mairi's brows lowered as she squinted, stretching forward. She slid her bare feet off the bed and came over to the bars. "Is that…?"

"Blood? Aye," he answered. "Joyce's blood. Fergus MacInnes sliced her neck open and then left the letter, stabbed to her chest."

Mairi's lips opened, her eyes blinking at the horror she must be imagining. She inhaled and bent to look closer. She shook her head. "I didn't write this." She examined the bottom. "And neither did Fergus."

"What?" Alec held the letter up to the light, reading. "I, Fergus MacInnes, declare war on Clan MacNeil of Barra. We will kill ye off one at a time, starting with your women and children. Kisimul is cursed, and ye all will die." He held it back to her. "He signed it."

Mairi met his gaze. "Fergus couldn't write. I wrote all his letters, and even if he'd had someone else write that, he always insisted on signing a big FMI as his signature. I don't even think he knew how to spell MacInnes."

Alec stared at the words as his mind worked. "He was seen in Barra, he and his men. They were interested in the resources of the isle."

"But did anyone see him actually kill Joyce?" she asked softly.

"Nay."

• • •

Mairi woke.

Where am I? A musty smell tightened her nose, and she

pushed upward. *Oh, damp, dark Hell.* She exhaled long as she surveyed her cell. She'd refused to unlock the door, and Alec had brought her wool blankets and Daisy, who was curled on the hanging bed against her back. Mairi's faithful friend sat up and licked her.

"Ye're wondering how we got back down here, aren't ye?" she asked, scratching the dog's head, although Daisy seemed as blissfully happy as ever. Mairi cursed softly and glanced around the small cell. If he was going to keep her a prisoner, she would act like a prisoner.

Mairi looked where Alec had stood for a long time while she had curled up with Daisy and tried to ignore him. Had he waited until she'd fallen asleep? Lying on the floor, just inside the bars, was a folded parchment, quill, and inkwell. He'd left them for her to write to her mother, knowing that he'd bring war to Barra if he sent it to Aros.

She stretched, rising to use the privy, and was thankful that they'd left the privacy screen in place. There was no water in the basin with which to wash, and she longed for a bath after she and Alec had…

She sighed. Their time under the stars had been the best adventure of her life. And he'd asked her to marry him. Was it to avert a war with Tor and Cullen and their powerful clans? Or for revenge? How could she trust her captor? A captor who hadn't left a single bruise on her skin or delivered a single threat. Even locking her in his dungeon, he'd ordered her fed and kept warm. "Bloody terrible jailer," she whispered and walked over to the table where the key and Alec's dagger sat.

She rubbed her hands over her face, pocketed them, and leaned against the bed. "I don't know what is real, Daisy." The dog licked her cheek, and Mairi realized one of her tears had broken free. Footsteps came down the ramp, and Cinnia appeared with a tray.

"Did Da lock ye up down here?" she asked, her face

desperate.

"Nay," Mairi said, walking to the bars. Daisy jumped down to follow and wiggled out, hopping around Weylyn on the ramp.

Mairi unlocked the barred door and ushered Cinnia inside to the table. "We had an argument," Mairi said. "And I was reminded that I am still truly a prisoner here."

Cinnia's brows drew close in earnest. "Not if ye marry him."

Mairi sighed. "It's more complicated than that."

"Adults tend to make simple things complicated," Weylyn said, throwing a short piece of rope up the ramp for Daisy to fetch. "Do ye like our da?"

Mairi felt her lips curve into a grin at his question. "Sometimes, and sometimes he makes me furious."

"Sometimes is a good start," Cinnia said, her voice lifting. "Do ye like us?"

"Always," Mairi answered without hesitation. Could she bring war to Kisimul when she'd grown to love these two children? She scooped up the blank parchment and writing materials, setting them on the table. Her smile faded. "But your father brought me here without permission. When others find out, my clan will war with the MacNeils."

"Not if ye wed him," Cinnia said, crossing her arms as if Mairi were just being stubborn. "People wed all the time to prevent wars."

Wasn't that what Mairi had agreed to do with Geoff MacInnes? She pursed her lips. "This is an issue between Alec and me, not ye two."

Weylyn kept throwing the rope, tugging it from Daisy's teeth and throwing it again. "Did ye send him to battle your clan then?"

Mairi looked between Cinnia and Weylyn. "Did Alec leave Kisimul?"

Weylyn stopped, staring intently at her. "Aye. He left Kenneth to guard us and Bessy. We watched from the roof as our two galleons sailed away and a group of twenty men rode north from the village, Da in the lead."

Weylyn squatted down, hugging Daisy to him. "He was armed for war."

• • •

Mairi stood on the upper walkway, the breeze catching in her hair. Five days. Alec had been gone five full days and nights, and Kenneth wouldn't say where he'd gone or when he'd be back, the loyal bastard.

She told herself she shouldn't care, that Alec was her enemy, that she hated him or at least disliked him. That if Kenneth wasn't there to guard her, she would flee without a second thought, that she'd never agree to wed him, her captor, her enemy…the man who'd looked vulnerable under the stars before she kissed him. The man who showed her the boats, tethered and unused, of all the people who had abandoned him. The man who'd given her his own dagger so she wouldn't feel helpless as his prisoner.

"Damnation," she said, for every time she thought of him, his eyes and his quiet strength, her fury dissolved. She looked up at the gray clouds. Their heaviness mirrored her mood ever since he'd left without a word. She'd written the letter to her mother, giving it to Kenneth to send with someone sailing off Barra for the mainland. Mairi had said she was well and not in danger but couldn't bring herself to say where she was or who was to blame for her abduction. She was turning out to be just as terrible at escaping as Alec was at imprisoning.

"Any sign?" Bessy asked as she walked up behind her, wrapped in a thick shawl.

"Nay." Mairi shrugged. At least she could pretend not to

care. "Are the children occupied?" Bessy had taken on some of the cooking and helped Mairi clean and keep up with the children. Together they'd managed to lift years of filth from the great hall and two bedrooms. Next, they would tackle the kitchens and small room housing the freshwater well.

"Weylyn is working with all six dogs in the courtyard, and Cinnia is finishing up a batch of tarts in the upper kitchen. We still need to properly clean the lower kitchen."

"Aye, we'll get to it." Mairi touched her thin arm. "Thank goodness ye're here to help." Joyce must not have cared much about Kisimul to allow it to become so neglected. Why had she left without saying anything to Alec? Leaving her children behind? Was she that unhappy? It was obvious, from the way Alec did not talk of her, that they weren't in love, but they had seemed to tolerate each other.

"I'm extremely happy I could stay on Kisimul," Bessy said.

Mairi looked at her troubled eyes. "Was it horrible with the Camerons?"

"It was loud. I was fairly unseen."

"Well, ye're unseen here, too, but not because it's loud," Mairi said. "It's because there's no one here to see ye."

She smiled. "I prefer it that way."

"I come from a big clan, lots of family coming and going. But everyone is kind for the most part." Her chest tightened with missing them.

"Ye are fortunate."

Mairi watched the smoke from the cook fires snaking up from the cottages in the village. In the distance, a chorus of dogs began to bark, and Daisy danced up on her back legs, trying to reach over the wall. Bessy gasped. Riders charged over the knoll, lots of riders. From the north.

Mairi held her breath, though her heart began to hammer.

"Is it them?" Bessy asked.

"I think so," Mairi said. Scanning the group, she spotted Alec atop his black charger, racing down the hill with the grace of a wolf loping over the moors. She blinked, unwilling to admit the relief she felt at seeing him alive. "I need to go," she said, turning from the wall and racing into the keep.

"Where are ye going?" Bessy called.

Mairi ran into the bedroom she'd taken over again as soon as Alec left Kisimul. She grabbed her warm cloak, blanket, and pillow. Stopping in the middle of the room, she breathed deeply. She had time, for they had to row across the bay. What would she bring down with her to the dungeon?

She glanced in the polished glass mirror and frowned. She'd been helping to clean the root cellar. Dirt smudged her face, and the day dress she wore was threadbare at the elbows.

"I will be like a bird in a cage," she whispered and pulled the laces loose on the dirty bodice, shimmying out of the drab costume. She pulled out a blue dress that she and Cinnia had lengthened and re-stitched.

Knock. Knock. "Oh," Bessy said as she peeked around the door. She rushed over, grabbing up Mairi's brush, apparently catching on. Bessy smiled at her in the mirror. "We lasses must stick together."

Bessy helped her tighten the clean bodice as Mairi tossed her hair to make her soft curls bounce around her face.

"I'll go find the children," Bessy said.

"Thank ye." Mairi grabbed her supplies, including the key to the cell. She stepped lightly down the stairs, ran across the empty hall, and pushed through the heavy door that led underground. If she was going to spend more time down there, Bessy and she would need to give the dungeon a thorough cleaning.

Mairi hid her things on a table behind the privacy screen. Swirling around, she ran back to the gate, locking it from inside. Pocketing the key, she scooted up onto the bed, kicking off her slippers.

She pressed back against the rock wall, her chest rising rapidly. She fluffed her hair again and settled the blankets around her. *There. Locked away. A bonny bird in a cage.* Mairi frowned. Would he come down? She squirmed on the bed, crossing her arms under her bosom. Her breasts raised up, pressing a swell above the square, lace-bordered neckline. *Aye, that would help.*

The door to the dungeon opened at the top of the ramp. She relaxed her face into a look of boredom, as if she didn't care how long he'd been gone. Kenneth would report she'd been out, although the children had made it seem to him that she spent most of her time in her cell.

Heavy footsteps pounded down the slope. "Mairi?" The voice was deep and familiar, but not Alec. She turned, staring open-mouthed, as her brother, Tor, ran down before the cell, Cullen on his heels. "Mairi," Tor yelled.

"Are ye well, lass?" Cullen asked. They grabbed the iron bars of the cell, rattling the lock.

"I…I am well," she said, her eyes rising above them to Alec, who stood at the bottom of the ramp.

He had a swollen eye and a slash across his forehead. Mairi leaped up. "What's happened?" She noticed then that both Tor and Cullen looked beaten, their faces bruised, slashes along their arms, a bandage around Cullen's calf. "What the bloody hell happened?" she repeated.

Tor turned to Alec. "Open the damn door, MacNeil."

Alec took two steps forward, his gaze locked on Mairi. "I cannot," Alec said.

"Why the ballocks not?" Cullen demanded.

"Because," Mairi said, her voice soft. "I have the key."

Chapter Fourteen

Alec took in the sight of Mairi like a long haul off a cold ale after hours of hard swordplay. She was still here on Kisimul. Hadn't stolen Kenneth's boat or persuaded Cinnia and Weylyn to build her a raft to ferry her over to Barra. The tight coil of tension slowly relaxed across his shoulders as he saw she looked clean, warm, and healthy.

Every day he'd been gone, following her kin to South Uist, he'd tried to convince himself that if she had left Kisimul he would not follow her. That he had no right to seek revenge on the MacInnes if he couldn't prove Fergus MacInnes killed Joyce. That she might be better off not living on Kisimul, feeling trapped or tied to a curse. But as he'd docked the ferry, asking Kenneth about Mairi's whereabouts, waiting for the answer that would bring familiar pain or hope, he'd known his arguments with himself were for naught. Whether she was still on Kisimul or had fled, the two of them were not done.

"Ye have the key?" Tor asked slowly and glanced toward Alec. "Ye're a bloody terrible jailor to give your captive the key to her cell."

"He gave me his *singh dubh,* too," she said, slipping the black-handled dagger out from a strap under her blue skirt.

"How generous," Cullen mumbled with obvious mockery, and Alec considered slashing his other leg as well.

"Open the door, Mairi," Tor said.

"First, tell me what happened," she said, narrowing her eyes. "Why do ye all look like hell?" Her gaze slid along them, resting on Alec.

Alec braced his feet like he stood on the deck of a swaying ship, arms crossed. "Your brother and…friend responded poorly when I told them I had ye here on Kisimul."

"I would have been here sooner, Mairi," Tor said, his face pressed to the bars. "But the bastard needed to learn that he can't steal away innocent lasses."

"It looks like he might have taught ye and Cullen a few lessons, too," Mairi said, crossing her arms. "I think that cut needs to be stitched." She pointed to Tor's forehead.

"I told him that," Alec said.

"Pòg mo thòin," Tor said without looking at him.

"His man, Ian, is worse," Cullen said.

Mairi's eyes rounded. "Where is he?"

Alec glanced up the ramp. "The hall. He could use your help."

Mairi thrust the key through the bars. "Let me do it," she said as Tor tried to take it. Bending her wrist, she pushed it into the lock and turned. The door flew open. "All of ye need to be looked over. Taint could set in, and then where will ye be? Feverish, weak on the floor, and dead, that's where. Foolish boys, always looking to fight."

"It's what we're trained to do from the moment we can stand," Tor said defensively.

"Ye're also taught to use your mind and words."

Tor narrowed his eyes at Alec. "It feels better to slam a fist against a bastard's face than to have a chat."

"We'll see if it feels better when I stitch your face with needle and thread." She strode past them toward the ramp. "Come along."

"Not even a 'thank ye for coming to save me,'" Cullen murmured as he followed Tor Maclean up the ramp, Alec bringing up the rear.

Alec's gaze moved about the great hall as he walked in. Something was different. He looked up to see the chandelier brushed clear of cobwebs and new candles in the holders. The hearth was swept, as was the floor. An arrangement of candles and flowers sat in the middle of the long table. Had Bessy Cameron done all this?

Ian lay on a blanket by the hearth, his leg swollen and purple. "'Tis broken," Mairi said, touching the leg gingerly. Ian's face was pale, but he kept his complaints to himself. "It will need to be set." She glared at Ian. "What did ye do to break your leg?"

"He fell off his horse," Tor said.

"He was pushed off his horse," Alec said. "Fell wrong." He looked to his oarsman, Daniel. "Go to Adam at the smithy. Ask him for those iron braces he made when my da broke his leg. Chances are he's kept them. And then bring back Millie. Tell her we need her cures."

The man took off without question, and Alec met Mairi's gaze. "Millie can help ye, and she'll bring medicines in case the wounds become tainted."

Mairi surveyed the dozen men in the room, assessing their condition. They were dirty, but most were unharmed since Maclean and Duffie had been traveling with only a small party.

"First," she said. "Ye will all get clean and changed. Then those who have any wounds will report back to this hall to be patched up. Are any of ye bleeding right now?"

No one said anything. "Broken limbs, like Ian?"

Heads shook. "Good." Mairi flapped her hands, and the men filed out as if she were already the lady of Kisimul. Mairi peered past Alec. "Bessy, can ye heat fresh water in the kitchen? We will need it."

Bessy ran toward the well room while Mairi grumbled about the foolishness of men. Kenneth brought a cup of whisky to Ian and helped him sit up to drink. "Ye'll be needing some of this to help the setting," Kenneth said. He looked at Alec. "Looks like I missed all the fun."

Mairi pointed at her brother. "Go wash," Mairi said. "Broc." She nodded to Cullen's man. "Ye, too. I'm sure the MacNeils won't slit ye open here."

"I can handle myself just fine," Broc said with a grin, as if he didn't have a slash through his linen shirt and bruises along one side of his jaw.

Cullen snorted and waved Broc to follow him and Tor to the bailey. When Tor passed Alec, his brows were drawn as if puzzled. He glanced between him and Mairi and then stepped out into the late-day shadows.

Mairi's slippers whispered across the floor as she strode up to Alec. With a glance at Ian, who lay with his eyes closed, she tugged Alec to the alcove behind the stairs. In the flicker of a lit wall sconce, he watched the stern features of her face soften to concern. The pads of her fingers were cool as she touched his swollen eye. "Which one did this?" she asked, her voice soft.

"Your brother. I should have expected it."

He knew the white of his eye was bloody and the socket purple, yet she stared directly into it without flinching. "Ye told him I was here." She shook her head slightly. "Brought him back to Kisimul. Why?"

Alec looked up at the darkness hovering under the rafters. "Ye were right. Before. If Cinnia were taken, I'd tear this world apart to find her. Weylyn, too." He leveled his gaze back to hers. "Even believing that Fergus MacInnes killed Joyce, it was dishonorable to steal ye away. Ye had nothing to do with the crime." He paused. "Did ye send a letter to your mother?"

She nodded, breaking their gaze to look at her slippers. "But I didn't tell her where I was."

"Why not?"

She huffed. "I didn't want a horde of Macleans swarming to Kisimul with Cinnia, Weylyn, and Daisy in here. I just let her know I was safe and would write again soon."

The side of his mouth rose. "Ye aren't much of a prisoner."

Her lips tipped up at the corners. "We're bloody awful at this."

She grew serious as her gaze dropped to run along his arms and chest. Chill bumps spread across him as if her gaze were a caress, the memories of her touch along his skin still fresh. "Are ye hurt anywhere else?" she asked.

"Here and there, bruises, a few lucky slashes before I knocked the sword from your brother's hand."

"Where? Let me see how deep they are."

He pulled his shirt out of the waist of his kilt, lifting it to expose the worst of the cuts. Two purple bruises colored his ribs.

"Ballocks," she whispered, touching the six-inch scabbed slash across his middle. "It doesn't feel hot."

"I washed and bandaged it the first night."

"Maybe Millie has a poultice to keep it free of taint." She met his gaze. "Where else?"

Her eyes were beautiful, even in the shadows. Shaped perfectly and spiked with long lashes. And the arch of her brows communicated as much as her smiles and frowns. They lowered at his silence. "I asked—"

"I missed ye," he said, cutting her off. "And that stung more than any of my paltry cuts." The words were rough, coming from somewhere deep within him, and he frowned darkly at the weapon he'd just handed her.

Her lips closed and then opened. She stared up into his face. "I…I can mend that, too," she whispered and took a step toward him.

The closeness of her was like heat washing over icy skin. His arms came up around her, tugging her effortlessly into his embrace. Her soft form fit against him as if she'd been fashioned to match his hard frame.

Alec inhaled her sweet scent and bent to kiss her lush mouth. She slanted immediately to deepen the kiss. Warmth flamed into molten desire as her hands whisked down his shoulders and back to his arse. She squeezed it through his kilt. His cod responded, growing between them, begging for attention. With two steps, Alec backed her against the wall and explored the curves he'd dreamed about these past nights, sleeping under the stars. He raked fingers through her loose, wavy hair, the silk of it spreading about her shoulders. Breaking the kiss, he nuzzled his face in it, breathing hard.

"I will take ye right here in the hall if we keep this up," he whispered against her ear and reveled in the fact that she was panting as much as he.

"It seems ye are already quite up," she teased breathlessly.

He pulled the edge of her ear lobe into his mouth and felt her shiver. "And I would wager ye are drenched and open for me," he said, his voice husky. Bloody hell, he wanted her.

Her exhale seemed to tremble, and she clung to him. "We should talk," she said. "About the other night."

"Alec?" Kenneth called from the great hall. "Where are ye?"

The other night? Which part of it? The hot, carnal part, the part where he asked her to marry him, or the part where Angus had ruined everything?

"Damnation," Mairi whispered.

Alec couldn't agree more. He stepped back, leaving her to lean against the wall. He ran a hand over his erection, adjusting it as best he could. Her gaze lay heavy on it.

"Alec?" Kenneth called again.

"What?" Alec yelled, stepping around the wall.

"Millie began preparing to come to Kisimul when she saw the horses ride by. She and Father Lassiter are rowing over now," Kenneth said. His gaze dropped to Alec's kilt, and his eyebrows rose. He glanced behind Alec, but Mairi remained hidden in the alcove. "Did I interrupt something?"

Cinnia and Weylyn ran down the steps with Bessy chasing them. Daisy barked, running around him in tight circles. "Da," Cinnia called. "Millie is rowing over. We saw her from the walkway."

The sight of his children was like a frigid dip to his lust, helping immensely. "Aye, she's come to help heal the injured."

"Are ye injured?" Weylyn asked, his eyes wide.

"Not badly," Alec said. "Come, let us meet them at the dock." He caught Cinnia's arm and hugged her shoulders. She hugged back, and Weylyn smiled, running ahead. His chest contracted. Aye, he'd tear the world apart to find them. How could he blame Tor Maclean for caring as much for his sister?

"Is Mairi still in the dungeon?" Cinnia asked, frowning.

"Nay," Alec said.

"I think she might be fixing herself in the alcove there," Kenneth called as he dodged out through the doorway. Ian chuckled, his eyes still closed where he lay on the pallet by the hearth.

"Ballocks," Mairi cursed. She stomped out. "I'm coming."

• • •

Father Lassiter had thick brown hair with only a bit of gray at the temples. He walked with spry purpose through the arched gate in Kisimul's wall, heading toward Mairi. "Ye are Mairi Maclean?"

"Aye, Father." He'd apparently heard about her.

"Where are the badly injured?" he asked, wielding a rosary with a large cross dangling from the end. "I would give them last rites."

"I don't think there are any near death, Father," Mairi said. "Did Alec say there were?" She looked to the side where the soldiers' quarters ran the length of the interior wall.

"He wouldn't know for certain," the priest said, waving off her question. "Warriors often hide their injuries."

"Aye, they do," she said, though at least Tor, Cullen, and Alec seemed hearty. At the gate, Alec escorted Millie inside. Mairi smiled to her, nodding back in welcome.

The elderly woman held up a leather satchel. "Wonderful," Mairi said and beckoned her toward the great hall. "Alec," she threw over her shoulder. "Ye need to bathe, too. Then come see us. And send in the ironsmith when he arrives with Ian's splints."

They walked into the hall where Bessy stood, hand to her mouth over wide eyes as she stared at the spectacle before the hearth. Ian still lay on the pallet, but his eyes were open, arm straight in the air. His hand clenched around Father Lassiter's throat. "I'm not dying, ye idiot."

Chapter Fifteen

Mairi rushed over. "Ian, let go."

Ian's hand unclenched, and he let it drop back to his side. "Tell the man to stop trying to give me last rites. I'm not dying."

"I should hope not," Father Lassiter said, his voice sour. He rubbed a hand at his neck where his black shawl was askew. "For if ye die after attacking a man of God, ye're likely to go straight to a fiery inferno."

Ian's eyes closed. "Are there any other types of infernos?" he asked.

"Father," Mairi said. "Please take a seat." She turned to see Bessy's stricken face before she ran up the steps toward the bedrooms above. "I will get ye some wine."

"Make it a whisky," he said, frowning Ian's way.

Tor and Cullen strode in through the door, nodding toward the priest before returning to Mairi. Tor walked right up to her, grabbing her in a hug.

"Tor!" she yelled. "I'll spill Father Lassiter's whisky."

Cullen snatched the wooden cup from her hand, and Tor

continued to wrap her in a hug. "Let me hold ye a second, Mairi," he said. "I thought I'd never see ye again."

Mairi let her body relax in her brother's arms and hugged him back. She felt a press of tears behind her eyelids. He set her on her feet and rubbed his beard. She sniffed, grinning up at him. "'Tis good to see ye." She leaned around him to smile at Cullen. "And thank ye both for coming to find me."

"Well, now, that's better," Cullen said, walking up to swing her into his own arms. Before, Mairi's heart would have skipped a beat at being pressed against her brother's best friend. But now his embrace felt like that of another brother.

"Let her go." Alec's voice came from behind Mairi.

Instead of releasing her feet to the ground, Cullen continued to hold her to him. "And who are ye to tell me what to do?" Cullen asked.

Alec took steps toward them. "Ye aren't her kin, and ye have a wife of your own."

"She isn't your wife, either," Tor said. "Nor her captor anymore."

For several seconds, Mairi hung there. "Let me down, Cull." She hit the heel of her hand into his shoulder, and he lowered her until her toes found the floor. She turned out of his arms to face all three of them. Her eyes narrowed. "The battle is over. I am freed and safe, and there is still a killer loose if Fergus didn't kill Alec's wife. Instead of continuing to glare and threaten one another, I think ye should put your energy into figuring out who attacked the MacNeils."

The priest stood. "What's this? Fergus MacInnes killed Joyce MacNeil. He left a note stabbed to the woman's breast."

"'Twas not his signature," Mairi said.

"Why would someone put the blame on MacInnes?" Father Lassiter asked, but no one answered.

"I'm just interested in returning ye to Aros," Tor said. "Or to Kilchoan. Geoff's on the ship." He watched her closely, but she looked away, her stomach tight.

"Where is the ship?" she asked.

"My two galleons shot cannon holes through MacInnes's ship off the coast of South Uist," Alec said, stepping closer to her, his challenging gaze on Tor. "It's still afloat but is moored for repairs there before it is seaworthy."

"Ye could return us to Mull," Cullen said. "Since ye are the reason we left."

"And leave my clan open to another attack while I'm away?" Alec asked, crossing his arms. "Not likely." His biceps bulged.

Millie bustled around them, setting out little clay pots and long strips for covering wounds. Her gaze fell on their lips, reading the heated conversation. She stepped before Alec, tugging on his shirt. He held it for her while she worked a poultice into a thin strip of linen and placed it over the long slash.

"We will stay here until we can help Alec figure out who attacked and killed his wife," Mairi said. "At least until Geoff brings the ship down from South Uist."

Millie circled behind Alec, tying the linen behind him to keep the poultice in place. Letting his shirt fall, she pointed at Tor and made gestures for him to peel off his shirt.

"Check Cullen first," Tor said. "Take off your shirt," he said, and Cullen lifted his linen shirt over his broad shoulders and head. Several cuts lay barely closed; two of them looked red.

"Good God, Cull," Mairi said, stepping closer. "If ye die of taint, Rose will either fall into insanity or slice me open with that sword ye gave her on your wedding day." She reached to touch the three-inch gash when a hand coiled around her wrist.

Alec turned her away. Mairi's breath caught at the lethal glint in his gaze. "Let Millie take care of it. See to your brother's head."

Tor stood to the side watching, his hands stuck in his armpits. He released one to wave at Cullen. "My head can wait. Go ahead, Mairi, tend Cullen's cuts. He has many. There's one even on his arse."

"Ballocks," Cullen swore, giving Tor a sour look.

"There, too?" Tor said. "Mairi, he'll need his ballocks checked."

"She will not," Alec's voice boomed, the sound startling Bessy who'd just braved returning to the room. She pivoted, retreating upstairs again. Mairi went to Tor, frowning at the inquisitive smirk on his face.

"There's nothing wrong with my ballocks," Cullen said when Millie went to lift his kilt.

"Make sure she sees your lips move when ye say that," Mairi said. "She doesn't hear."

Cullen tapped her arm until she looked at him. "My ballocks are quite fine, thank ye. No need for fixing them." He looked at Tor. "That's not something I say every day."

Kenneth chuckled from the doorway. "I've got the men lined up out here in order of the most serious to Thomas, who has one hell of a splinter in his thumb. And the smithy dropped off the iron splints." He propped two long shafts inside.

Alec retrieved a needle and thread from the table and handed it to Mairi. "For your brother." His frown mellowed into a neutral line, but his eyes glinted with anger.

Mairi pushed Tor into a seat and washed the slash on his forehead with fresh well water. The ends of his flesh, still raw, gaped. Alec handed him a whisky, which Tor threw back as Mairi walked from the hearth with a heated needle. She made quick work, knowing that even her tough brother could withstand only so much pain. Alec handed him a second whisky when she tied off the thread. He gulped it down.

"'Twill give ye a roguish look," Mairi said. "Ava may like it."

Tor gave a satisfied snort and leaned back against the edge of the table. He crossed his ankles before him. "Aye, she does like a bit of wickedness and chase."

Mairi scrunched her nose at him. "Please brother, no more details."

Tor looked at Cullen and then Alec. "We will stay here until Geoff brings his ship around. In fact, with your priest here, we can finish what was rightfully started back on Kilchoan."

Mairi tensed. "What?"

Tor's mouth relaxed into a grin as he stared at Alec. "I've heard that Kisimul has a chapel, and we have a priest. I say we have a wedding."

Father Lassiter's eyes opened wide. "A wedding? It could be a blessing for this cursed castle."

"Kisimul is not cursed," Alec said, his face hard as he stared at Mairi's grinning brother like he was deciding which limb to tear off first.

"Or ye could wed outside," Tor said. "In the bailey."

The priest looked expectantly between them all. He finally rested on Alec. "If the lass here is wedding Geoff MacInnes, ye can wed Bessy Cameron."

"Who is Bessy Cameron?" Broc asked, looking around the room as he walked in to be tended.

Alec barely opened his mouth as he ground out his words. "I am not wedding Bessy Cameron."

"Is she the pretty mouse who's been scurrying in and out of here?" Cullen asked.

"She's been through a lot," Mairi said, frowning at Cullen.

Tor planted his feet on the floor with a thud and propped his hands on his knees. "When the heart decides who it wants, it can be a mouse or even a French woman."

"Or an English maid," Cullen returned with a pointed look at Tor.

"I am not marrying Bessy Cameron," Alec repeated, though neither of them looked at him.

"I would love Ava, sitting in slop, over a princess any day," Tor said, shrugging. "If he wants to wed a mouse, so be it." He stood, gesturing toward the priest. "Father, shall we go see about setting things up while Mairi tends these warriors?"

"Bloody, blazing hell," Alec swore. "I said, I am not wedding Bessy Cameron." His voice boomed loud enough to bring Geri and Freki running in from the crowded bailey. Growling, they turned to flank Alec.

Father Lassiter leaped back. "God's teeth," he cursed. He frowned and passed the sign of the cross before him, his eyes shifting to Alec. "Since I came all the way over here and can't deliver last rites to anyone," he said, glaring toward Ian, "I would like to wed someone. Now who will that be?"

Tor smiled wickedly. "Geoff and Mairi, once he brings the ship around."

Ooh, Mairi wanted to kick Tor. She glanced toward Alec who kept his face lethally neutral. The man had asked her to marry him the other night. Was the request just a response to their time under the stars on the knoll?

A pinch of worry sprouted anger inside Mairi. "This is no time to think of weddings when there are men to heal and a possible killer on Barra." She shook her head as she looked down at the poultice she was spreading for Millie to use. "Honestly, Tor, I thought ye could hold your whisky better than that."

"Ah, your brother deserves to loosen up, Mairi, what with worrying over ye these weeks." Broc grinned as he stood up to be inspected by the efficient Millie. His smile turned, though, when the old woman yanked up the back of his kilt, looking for injuries. "Just my legs," he said, turning quickly to pull the plaid from her hands.

Alec uncrossed his arms. "I can help," he said, walking

closer to Mairi. He leaned forward to pick up one of the vials, which Millie immediately took out of his hand and set back down with a small frown. Just the closeness of him made Mairi's stomach untwist and her cheeks warm.

Tor stood in the doorway, watching them. "MacNeil, we will talk now. Chief to chief." The seriousness of his tone made Mairi stiffen.

Alec looked to her brother. "*Now* ye wish to talk."

"Once all this talking is done, if someone wants to marry, I'll be in the chapel," Father Lassiter grumbled and walked out.

"This way," Alec said.

Tor held up his hand when Cullen made to follow. "It's more of a brother to bastard-who-stole-my-sister kind of talk," Tor said.

Alec snorted as if he were ready for anything that involved swords and daggers.

"Tor," Mairi said. "I just stitched ye up."

"Ye were the one who said we should talk instead of battle." Tor kissed the top of her head as he walked past.

Alec turned, his gaze resting on Mairi one more time before he headed up the stairs.

• • •

Alec's instincts yelled to prepare for a fight. His discipline kept him moving sedately forward across the wall walk that encircled Kisimul. He led Tor to the far end where he could see out toward the mainland. He turned, his hand ready to pull his sword or his dirk. Tor already had his out, but Alec wasn't going to take the bait. "What shall we talk about?" Alec asked, his tone bored.

Tor's fierce expression was a return of the look he'd given Alec when he'd told him Mairi's location. Tor spit on the stone. "What the bloody hell did ye do to my sister?"

"Nothing against her will, Maclean," Alec answered.

Tor stared hard at him, his lips curving in like he ate something sour. *"Mo chreach,"* he cursed and lowered his sword. He sheathed it. "Are ye going to marry her?"

Alec inhaled, focusing on the thin line of the horizon where a gray sky met a gray sea. "I already asked her."

"What did she say?" Tor stepped over to the same wall.

"Nothing."

"Then what did she do?"

Alec glanced at Tor. "She locked herself back into the dungeon."

Tor scratched his beard. "That doesn't sound promising. Though, I was sure—"

"Sure?" Alec asked, cutting him off.

Tor crossed his arms. "The way she's acting." He scratched his chin. "Her eyes follow ye about the room, and when Cullen took his shirt off, she barely looked."

Alec's fists clenched along with his jaw. "She usually looks at Duffie?"

"Oh, she's followed after him since she was small, like most of the other lasses, but she barely reacted to him down there. Makes me think her fondness has turned to someone else."

"Duffie's married now," Alec said.

"He was married a month ago when I caught Mairi spying on him bathing in the river at Aros."

Alec's teeth slid against one another as if he wanted to tear into Duffie's throat. He turned back to stare at the sea. "She already agreed to marry Geoff MacInnes to form an alliance for Aros," Alec said, steering them back to a topic that was less likely to make him slaughter a man today.

Tor cursed low. "I told her she didn't have to worry about an alliance with the MacInnes. I'd have her choose someone else."

Alec stared at Tor. "Ye've arranged to have them wed as soon as he arrives at Kisimul."

Tor grinned. "Ye may not have noticed, but my sister is a stubborn woman."

Alec would have laughed if bloodlust wasn't still pumping through his body. "Aye."

"I originally told her not to accept Geoff's offer to wed," Tor said. "She, of course, accepted, because she tends to do exactly what I tell her not to do, if she thinks it is right. I even convinced Geoff to send a pretty rogue to kiss her before the wedding, to tempt her into calling it off. When Mairi didn't arrive at the chapel, for a good half hour I thought perhaps she'd run away with him. Until we found the pretty rogue tied to a tree and tracks leading to the shore." Leaning back against the wall, Tor studied Alec.

"Ye suggested she marry MacInnes below, just now, to make her refuse?" Alec asked. Mairi's family was cunning or insane. He hadn't decided which.

Tor shrugged. "I wanted to see what she'd do. She got mad, which is typical, but then…" He paused, his eyes narrowing. "Then her cheeks turned rosy when ye came over to her."

"They did?"

"Aye, and that's when I knew for sure that she likes ye."

"She does?" Alec asked, uncrossing his arms.

"My sister doesn't blush even when she delivers a litany of curses before a priest, MacNeil."

Alec inhaled, and the air felt fresh with the droplets of mist coming in and something else. For the first time in days, since the night she'd turned away from him at Angus's accusation, Alec felt hope.

"So," Tor said. "What are ye going to do?"

Alec glanced at Mairi's brother, a wicked grin turning up his mouth. "Something her brother might not want to hear about."

Chapter Sixteen

Mairi arched her back, stretching, as Millie tied off the last bandage around one of Cullen's men. Considering the slashes on Alec and Tor, she'd expected worse injuries on the others, but apart from Ian's broken leg, the rest were mere scrapes and bruises.

"Thank ye," Mairi said to Millie, who nodded with a smile. She made a sign with her hands together, cradling her head. "A place to sleep? Aye." Where to put the woman who was closer to Alec than his own mother? Bessy and she hadn't tackled the airing of the two dusty spare bedrooms. Mairi touched her arm. "Ye can sleep in my room. The bed is large enough for us both."

They wrapped two meat pies, which Cinnia had baked for everyone, in some cloth to take above. The child had glowed over the compliments from the men as they gobbled them down. Weylyn then brought the dogs into the meadow and, from the laughing and applause, was entertaining the warriors with their tricks.

Maybe Alec was out there with them. She hadn't seen

him since he left to talk with Tor. Frowning, she chewed the seasoned venison wrapped in a golden crust. If either one of them had thrown the other over the castle wall, surely someone would have told her.

Mairi waved Millie to follow her. Night was falling and someone, probably Bessy, had lit the sconces in the hallway. Mairi led Millie to her room, pushing open the door. A warm fire sat in the grate and a tub waited before it. "God's teeth," Mairi said. "A bath?" She ran her fingers over the water and looked to Millie. "And it's warm."

Millie smiled broadly and motioned for her to get in the tub. Mairi gestured back that Millie could bathe, but the elderly woman frowned and motioned again for her to take advantage of the treat. "Well, I'll have to thank Bessy later." The poor woman seemed afraid to go anywhere near the men and had hidden away in the kitchens all day. Hopefully she hadn't heard what Cullen had said about her being a mouse.

Ducking behind a privacy screen, Mairi stripped free of the clinging weight of her clothes and wrapped herself loosely in a bath sheet to walk to the tub. It was large enough to sit in. Mairi dropped the sheet and stepped through the surface, letting the heat lick up her legs and higher as she lowered. She groaned at the heavenly sensation. A small dish attached to the tub held a bar of soap. It smelled of roses. Goodness. Bessy had thought of everything.

Millie nodded to her as she stood in her smock, having taken off her outer gown. She crawled into the bed and closed her eyes. The day must have been exhausting for someone of her age. Mairi washed her hair and the layers of worry, work, and grime from her body. When the water finally grew cold, she climbed out, wrapping herself in the bathing sheet.

The fire had burned low, and she stirred it up while clutching the sheet around herself.

Knock. Knock. A soft rap on the door made her stand,

turning toward it. She glanced at Millie, who breathed evenly, eyes closed and mouth open.

Mairi tread to the door. "Who is it?" she asked, without worrying about waking Millie, since she couldn't hear.

"Alec." One simple word sent her heart into a gallop.

Mairi glanced down at herself, naked and in a thin sheet. She shouldn't open the door, undone as she was, but her hand went to the handle anyway. She pulled it open enough to fit her face in the crack. "Aye?"

He held a candle in the darkness of the corridor. Voices and sporadic male laughter came up from the great hall below, reminding her that Kisimul was full to capacity with Tor's and Alec's warriors.

Alec's hair seemed darker, damp perhaps, and his face smooth from a fresh shave. If it were possible, she'd swear he was even handsomer than before. "Did ye enjoy the bath?" he asked.

Her eyebrow rose. "Ye ordered the bath?"

"Ye deserved it after today. Thank ye for helping my men."

Mairi's finger clutched the bathing sheet tighter as she resisted the urge to open the door and drop it. Everything about Alec called to her, but especially his kindness. Had anyone ever treated her so? "Thank ye," she said, opening the door farther.

His gaze dropped to the damp sheet and naked shoulders. When his eyes lifted back to hers, they were intense, and she knew without a word that he wanted to kiss her. Her breath quickened and she swallowed, taking a step backward into the room. Without breaking the invisible tether between them, he followed through the door, step for step, and closed it behind him.

"I…" He started and stopped, his gaze shifting to the bed.

Mairi turned her head to see Millie perched up on one

elbow, a grin on her very awake face. Mairi looked back to Alec. "She was exhausted, and I didn't know where to take her that was clean."

Alec nodded to Millie. "Oh, she's quite pleased about this," he said with a little snort. "I can leave ye to your rest."

Mairi doubted rest would come to her anytime soon with her heart running a race and her skin craving his touch. "If ye give me a minute, I can dress."

"Ye aren't tired?"

Not anymore. She shook her head. "I was thinking of looking at the stars."

A slow smile curved just the corners of Alec's sensuous mouth, feeding the sensations his gaze was conjuring within her already. "I will wait outside your door." He gave Millie one last nod and shut the door.

Mairi dodged behind the screen and threw on the clean smock she'd planned to wear to bed. It was a summer night and not too cool. She wrapped herself in a thick robe and shot her toes into her daytime slippers. Millie had turned onto her side away from the door, seemingly asleep, though Mairi knew better. When she opened the door, Alec was leaning against the wall. She was breathless, giddy as if she were sneaking out of the castle as a young lass.

Alec grasped her hand. His was warm, his strong fingers threading intimately between hers. He led her toward a back set of stairs. "Kisimul is overrun with eyes and ears."

"I think ye like living alone out here," she said, teasing him.

"Not completely alone." The words were innocent, but the look he gave was not. His tone told her he'd rather it be the two of them in this big fortress. Right now, she couldn't agree more.

She trailed him, still tethered by his hand, down three flights of stairs. His candle sputtered as a breeze penetrated the darkness.

He released her hand to unbar a door, and they stepped out into the clear night on the far side of Kisimul. The tide was high, giving them only a few feet of rock, which the sea licked at with gentle waves. "Careful," he said as he led her over flat boulders toward a small boat tied to a block of cement nestled amongst the natural rocks. Without a word, she let go of his hand and stepped into the boat while he untied the line.

The night shrouded them in shadows. Only the touch of oars to water whispered in the silence outside the walls of Kisimul. Mairi leaned back on her palms to view the familiar scattering of stars overhead. The moon had grown since their night on the hill. Clouds wisped across it. Mairi looked from Alec's back to the silhouette of the castle, glad to be free of it for a while. No matter what Alec called Kisimul, it would always be a prison to Mairi.

The small boat surged through the calm waters of Castle Bay toward the galleon on which Mairi had sailed to Barra. Without a veil of fury, she could appreciate the sleek lines of the large vessel, its naked masts pointing moonward.

Alec steadied the small boat against the galleon's side, and Mairi made her way past him to grab the rungs of a ladder, hoisting herself. Could he see her bare legs leading all the way up as she rose higher? The thought coiled tightly within her middle. At the top, she stepped over the gunwale to jump down onto the deck with a soft thud.

Mairi's inhale froze as Kenneth strode out of the shadows. "Thieving the *Sea Wolf* all on your own?" he asked with a grin. Without a hint of surprise at Alec climbing over the gunwale behind her, Mairi realized that Kenneth had seen them rowing over.

"The boat's tied lightly below," Alec said. "I'll take over watch."

Kenneth rubbed his beard. "Now I doubt ye'll be doing

much watching. Plenty of doing, not much watching," he said. He winked at Mairi, bowing slightly. "Milady, enjoy the Wolf." He chuckled at his insinuation and strode past Alec, giving him wide berth as Alec followed him, talking about security with Geoff MacInnes sailing back down from South Uist.

Mairi walked along the deck, blending into the shadows. Deserted, the boards creaked, the masts bending slightly with the wind and shifting waters below it. Without a crew, the ship seemed to wait, a giant ready to come alive to defend or attack. The sway was hardly noticeable, and she stared up at the sky where stars glittered.

"Ye are like a goddess with the moonlight on your face," Alec said from the shadows off to the side. His hushed words sent a thrill prickling through her body, and she lowered her view to search for him in the darkness. Alec's large frame broke from the shadow as he moved forward, his tread light on the deck boards.

She met his serious gaze and tried to keep her breaths even. "Are ye my mighty warrior, Orion, freed from the heavens?" she asked. The strength he possessed seemed to permeate the air between them, but instead of making her feel weak in comparison, it woke her fully.

A wry curve played about his lips, giving him a devilish look. "Ye have my fealty, goddess," he said, stepping to arm's length. "Command me how ye wish."

Her eyebrows rose with her grin, and she tapped her lip with a fingertip. Here, outside the castle walls, she felt free, her heart light. "Do ye dance?"

"Nay," he answered without pause.

"At all?"

"Who would I dance with? Kenneth?"

Reaching forward she placed a hand on his powerful shoulder. "He looks like he'd be quick on his feet."

Alec grunted, but pulled her closer, taking her hand.

"My father would twirl me around under the stars," she said and turned under their intertwined fingers. "Come now," she said when he didn't move. "I command ye to dance with me."

The pressure of Alec's hand on her waist sent a thrill through Mairi, and he pulled her around in a wide sweep along the deck. After a pass, she tripped over his boot. "I'm liable to lose a limb at this," she said, laughing.

His lips curved into a grin, making her heart speed. "Ye were warned that I've had no practice." He turned her twice more.

"Ye're quite good, actually. Must be all the training for battle ye do. Perhaps it would help your warriors to make them dance with one another."

He laughed out loud, warming Mairi's heart. "I like that sound," she said and met his gaze as they continued to sway.

He leaned forward, his lips close enough to her ear to bring chill bumps along her skin. "I like the sounds ye make, too."

Mairi placed her hands on his firm chest, and her pulse flew. She stroked down his hard, warm body to his narrow waist and edge of his kilt. "Mmmmm," she murmured.

"Aye, like that one," he answered.

With a tug, she freed the material from his kilt. Continuing the effort, Alec pulled the shirt up and off, his biceps flexing.

He was exquisite. His chest was broad and rippled with cut muscles, a fine sprinkling of hair and scars, silver in the moonlight. Standing before him, she slid her robe from her shoulders to pool at her feet. The light breeze puckered her nipples, making them sensitive against the rub of her smock.

"I command we play another game," she said, feeling giddy with anticipation. Without the heaviness of Kisimul pressing down on her, Mairi's mind churned with scandalous ideas. She had Alec alone and smiling. It was a night for miracles. Glancing at the cargo nets and cannons, she spied a set of stairs leading to the upper deck. "Have ye ever played All Hid?" she asked.

He studied her, his grin broadening. "Aye, as a child."

"Count to fifty," she whispered. "And then come find your goddess."

"Mairi—"

"Start with one," she instructed and turned on the toes of her slippers, wide eyes searching for a place to hide, or rather, a place to be found. Her smock raised, she flew silently toward the bow, which pointed out toward the open sea, and dodged around the large foremast to hide. She drew in deep breaths of fresh sea air as she waited, her back against the thick wood and ropes.

Her heart hammered. How long would it take him to track her down? And more importantly, what would he do when he found her? She ran her hands down her front, her body alive and sensitive under the thin fabric of her smock.

Lips open to exhale noiselessly, she strained to hear any clue as to where Alec moved. The wind tugged the ropes aloft, the lines like exposed skeletons without their sails covering them, and small waves lapped along the hull. But no footsteps. Perhaps he went belowdeck, thinking she'd prefer to be out of the summer breeze. Leaning carefully around the edge, Mairi peered into the darkness toward the steps and gasped.

Alec MacNeil, bare chested, his kilt slung low on his hips, leaned against the rail at the top of the steps. His boots were missing, explaining his stealth. When he met her gaze, he smiled. "I believe I've won your game," he said. "Now for the prize."

Chapter Seventeen

Alec leveled his stare on Mairi, letting her know there was no escape.

"How did ye find me?" she asked, disappearing behind the mast to peek around the other side.

He tipped his nose to the breeze. "Your scent. Roses mixed with heat." He stepped to the side, making her retreat, but he guessed her next move and dodged back as she attempted to run. He caught her lithe form, pulling her with him as he leaned back against the thick, unyielding mast.

Her seductive smile gave him all the permission he needed to stroke a path downward, the thin smock molding to her perfect curves. Her cool fingers rose up between them, sliding along his skin up his chest. The sensation shot lightning through his heated body. He hovered his mouth over hers, her breath touching his lips. "What prize do ye yield?" he asked.

A slip of her tongue plying the space between her lips nearly made him shake, his need huge and raw. "Ye tasted me," she whispered. "On the hill under the stars."

Just the memory of her musky sweetness thrummed

another strike of need through him. "Aye," he said, his voice almost a growl.

"I want to taste ye," she said.

His breath stopped as her palms flattened on his chest, her thin fingers raking softly down his body as she lowered, her white gown pooling around her on the deck. When she reached his stomach, she tipped her face up to smile wickedly at him and then at the obviousness of his arousal tenting out his kilt. She slid her hands up his legs as he braced them. When she encircled his length, he groaned. He yanked up his kilt, exposing her hand wrapped around his cod in the moonlight. She stroked, and he watched, leaning back against the mast. Reaching forward, he raked gently through her hair, the waves catching in the night breeze.

Holding him, she lowered her mouth. Wet heat surrounded him, and Alec's eyes closed as he relied on the mast to hold him upright. "Sweet Lord," he murmured, his voice thick as she worked along his length. As if realizing her power, Mairi grew bolder, stroking him with her tongue and fondling his stones. She pulled up until the coolness of the air broke along his skin. He opened his eyes to stare down at his sinful angel. Hair spread around her shoulders, a view of her ripe breasts spilling up out of her undone smock, her lips poised on the end of him. And then she descended, taking him fully inside her mouth.

Alec growled a fierce cry and reached down to haul Mairi up. He'd lose himself in that honeyed mouth if he didn't stop her. His lips covered hers as ravenous hunger rose up like a molten wave between them. Slanting, they melded completely against each other, tasting and giving in to their frantic kiss. Her hands reached behind him under his kilt to his bare arse. Breasts like soft twin moons pressed up between them as her smock fell to her waist. He palmed one as he kissed her, trailing his lips along her graceful neck on his way down to suck one nipple into his mouth.

"Och," she whispered and clung to him, reaching up on her toes to rub against his hardness.

With a tug on his belt, it loosened, and his kilt thudded to the deck. Mairi threw her head back as he bent over her breasts, loving them with his tongue and hot mouth, pinching and rolling her nipples. She grabbed his rigid heat, stroking and pressing his tip against her mound. His fingers followed, finding her sensitive nub. She hissed as he rubbed across it. He slipped lower as she ground against his hand.

He kissed back up to her ear as he pressed two fingers into her supple body. "Och, lass," he whispered. "Ye are drenched and so bloody hot."

"Alec, please..." She moaned as he rubbed and worked her flesh, reveling in her reactions to each touch. He withdrew his fingers. "Nay," she said, but he turned her around to face the mast.

Leaning against her bare back, he tugged her smock up around her hips. His hands covered her stomach under it, stroking lower, playing again with her as she arched her smooth back, thrusting her arse up higher and spreading her legs. She was ready, hot, and soaking. He nibbled against her ear. "Hold on, lass."

Her fingers curled into the ropes encircling the mast as he reached in front of her, spreading her, opening her wet woman's lips. He found the entrance easily from behind. Poised there at the opening, his hands rose to cup her full breasts.

"Alec," she pleaded, pushing back against him.

Bending over her, he groaned as he plunged forward, thrusting into her. Mairi's answering moan joined his to rise into the darkness. He clasped her hips, pumping into her from behind. Reaching forward to her nub, he strummed it quickly, making her thrash backward and then forward into his fingers.

"So hard," she said, panting. "So good. Harder."

Alec thrust deeper, lifting her onto the tips of her toes as she clasped the ropes around the mast. He felt her all around him, her hot wet channel sucking tightly as he rammed forward and up, filling her completely over and over again. Heat poured through him to the point he imagined steam rising from his skin into the night sky. Their rhythm increased, building as he used every part of his body to tease and pleasure Mairi.

"My God," she cried out. "Alec." Shaking with pleasure, her channel convulsed, gripping him until he felt himself shatter, too. Alec's fingers dug into her hips as he thrust, his oath roaring out of him. "Ye are mine," he yelled as he shot himself inside her quivering, molten body.

• • •

"We can go below," Alec said as he tucked the blanket around Mairi, cocooning them together on the floor of the upper deck. "There's a decent sized bed in the captain's quarters where I found this blanket."

Mairi snuggled against Alec, enjoying the feel of their naked bodies draped intimately together. No wonder Tor and his wife, Ava, spent so much time alone together. "I prefer the night sky overhead to wooden beams," she said and rolled onto her back to see the familiar constellations.

Now that her body had cooled somewhat, rational thought crept back in. What had he meant when he'd yelled that she was his? His powerful words had cut through her like a binding oath, like what she thought wedding vows should feel like.

"What are ye thinking?" he asked, his gaze still straight above him.

"A rather high number of things," she said.

She could see his mouth turn up at the corners. "'Tis hard to enjoy the stars with crowded thoughts."

That was the absolute truth. Mairi raised up on one elbow, letting her gaze wander the moonlit landscape of Alec's ruggedly handsome face. Perfectly sloped nose, angular cheeks leading to a strong jaw. He could be a painter's inspiration for masculine beauty. "What did ye mean? Before…when ye said that I am yours?"

He turned his gaze to hers. "I asked ye to wed with me that night in the boat."

"I didn't answer," she said.

"Nay, and I nearly slit Angus Cameron's throat." His face grew serious, and he reached up to pull her down for a kiss, his warm lips moving intimately against hers until she nearly forgot what they were discussing.

When he broke the kiss, she blinked as he touched her bottom lip with his thumb, sliding it gently along the edge. His voice was firm yet soft. "When I said ye were mine, I gave ye my oath. It is up to ye to accept it."

"An oath made before no one?" she whispered. Everything about Alec was strong, yet the vulnerability in his explanation drew her heart.

"An oath made before the only ones who matter: ye, me, the stars, and God."

The center of her stomach tightened and fluttered. "Ye mean, if I swear in kind, then…we are wed?"

His eyes searched hers. "For the sake of your kin, I would repeat it before a priest. But formal words before the church are not the oath. They are only ceremony and words, and people spout them without thought or heart." His face tightened, and she knew he must be thinking of those who had left him. His father to battle and death, his mother to her religion, Joyce to her secrets and murder, even Millie for her independence.

"A vow before the stars means more to ye?" Mairi asked, reaching out to touch his hair where it curled around one ear.

"Aye, if it comes from the heart."

Mairi's mind raced as she met his gaze. Could she commit with her whole heart to the man who'd stolen her, imprisoned her, and had hidden her away from her family when they came searching? Could she turn away from the man who had been gentle with her in her fury? Who showed kindness to animals, children, old women, and her? Could she walk away from the man she'd given her body to, trusting him to respect and love it, bringing her utter fulfillment without holding back? Could she commit to giving up her freedom to live on Kisimul?

Alec waited, and with each second passing she felt him draw away as his face hardened. He expected more pain. She touched his face, feeling the roughness of his shaved cheek, and leaned down to kiss him gently on his warm lips. "Alec…" She backed up slightly. "Ye are mine, and I am yours."

His lips parted, and she held a finger across them. "But," she continued. "I am not part of Kisimul."

He pushed up onto his elbow to be level with her and took her hand from his mouth. "I am The MacNeil of Barra Isle. Kisimul is my home."

"Kisimul is the home of the Wolf of Barra," Mairi said. "The lone wolf, away from his people." She shook her head. "A chief should sit among his people, not walled off on his own island." Mairi pushed up farther to sit, crossing her legs under her and pulling the edge of the blanket around her naked shoulders.

Alec followed her until they sat facing each other. "It is how it has always been," he said, his voice unwavering.

Mairi pursed her lips. "And there has always been a row of boats on the shore of Barra, unused and rotting, standing as silent memorials to all those who cannot or will not return to Kisimul. I would rather not have one representing me."

"The walls of Kisimul protect," Alec said. "No enemy has ever been able to breach the MacNeil seat."

"Alec," she said, leaning forward, her hand on his arm. "The walls that protect can also imprison." Mairi had learned that lesson the hard way while hiding from her stepson at Kilchoan. She shook her head. "I cannot live feeling like I'm imprisoned."

"Ye would have a way to leave whenever ye desire. A boat…" His words trailed off, and he looked away into the darkness of the night around them. The ship moved gently with the water underneath, and the ropes creaked with their tension strung above.

Mairi shivered from the breeze and distance from Alec. "Alec, I pledge myself to ye, but I cannot commit myself to Kisimul, and I have no idea what that means for us." Her words softened until the last sounds were mere whispers in the wind.

"There is no curse," he said, his gaze snapping back to her.

"Curses are created by fear and discontent." She exhaled slowly, closing and opening her eyes, willing him to see her heart. "If I stay on Kisimul, behind the massive walls between us and the world, won't discontent grow, won't I begin to fear that I am trapped? And won't that create a curse like the one that's been playing out on Kisimul over centuries?"

"I will be there with ye," he countered. "How could ye feel imprisoned?"

"I've lived as if in a cage before, at Kilchoan," Mairi said, shaking her head slowly. "I won't… I can't live that way again. It will smother my soul until I have nothing left to give to ye."

Alec stood up, the blanket falling from his lean, muscular body. He picked up his kilt from its pile near her abandoned smock and stepped into it, cinching it around his waist. He walked to the bow of the ship.

Unshed tears ached in her eyes as she stared at his back

under the moonlight. She should just agree to live with Alec wherever he dwelled. But how could she, when she knew what would happen? Mairi blinked as one tear broke free to slip over her bottom lid, a streak, cooling on its path down her cheek.

The silence lay heavy, and she fought to keep her breath even as she dropped her gaze to her hands. Voices broke through the silence of night. "There's a ship coming in, with all its lanterns doused," Alec said, glancing back at her from the rail. "Your betrothed, no doubt." His voice sounded hard, as if she'd said nay to him. Had she? She'd said nay to his way of life, to his home, to his heritage. Another tear followed the first, and she reached for her smock.

Mairi threw it over her head as the hushed voices grew, the sound of a large hull cutting through the bay near them. Would Geoff fire upon the empty vessel? Revenge for his damages? Or try to take it? Why else would he come up like this in the night without any lights?

She gasped as fire flared up behind her and spun on her toes toward Kisimul. Kisimul's warriors stood silhouetted against a growing row of beacon fires along the upper walls, watching and waiting. The silent display of strength and impenetrable power sent a chill down Mairi, and she wished to be behind those stone walls instead of standing barefoot on the deck of Geoff's target in nothing but her smock.

Shouts rang out on the incoming ship, and Mairi ran to stand beside Alec. If Geoff fired and hit them...she wanted to be beside Alec. "Go below," he said.

"He won't fire if he sees me standing here." Her voice sounded much firmer than her tear-streaked face looked.

"Ye may not give the impression of a waiting-to-be-rescued damsel, standing next to me alone, looking ravished." His words were hard as if he were switching from lover to warrior before her. The sound of oars in the water alongside the *Sea Wolf* made Mairi look over the rail. At least six smaller boats of men from Kisimul were halfway across to the ship.

"Damnation," she cursed and raked her fingers through the tangles in her hair. No matter what she did to make herself look less wanton, she still stood in her night clothes on an abandoned ship with a near naked Alec MacNeil.

Geoff's ship had swung around to aim its cannons at the bow of the *Sea Wolf* where they stood. He was close enough to be able to hear and see her now.

Mairi stepped up onto the forecastle cannon, balancing. "Geoff MacInnes!" Mairi yelled, cupping her hands around her mouth. "Stand down."

"Get off the cannon," Alec ordered.

Mairi planted her hands on her hips and looked down at him. "I won't be responsible for the death of your men or ye, Alec MacNeil." Several lanterns flickered to life on Geoff's ship. "Stand down, Geoff," she called. "All is well."

Next to her, Alec snorted, as if her statement was ludicrous. Did he welcome a battle? Brows drawn low and fist tight around the hilt of his mighty sword, he certainly looked like he craved the spill of blood. "Ye're going to want to get off that cannon before I fire it," he said.

"All is well?" Geoff MacInnes called back, pulling Mairi's gaze back across the narrow patch of dark water between the boats. "Ye are standing in your smock next to my undressed enemy."

Behind her, Mairi heard MacNeil warriors climbing along the decks. The clang of cannonballs being loaded cracked the ominous quiet of the night, making her heart race. She gasped lightly as Alec grabbed her around the waist, pulling her down to the deck. The warmth and strength in his hold felt like a brand, but she shook it off to look down on the men moving in disciplined order between the cannons. "Don't fire," she called.

"Mairi?" Tor's voice came from below, and she saw both he and Cullen charge toward her.

"Shite," she said. Could the night get worse?

"If ye want to take a swim this night, MacInnes," Alec yelled across the water. "By all means, fire upon us. Kisimul and its warriors are invincible."

Apparently, it *could* get worse.

Chapter Eighteen

Tor reached the top of the steps. "Mairi, go below."

"What are ye even doing over here?" Cullen asked, his gaze taking in her clothes and Alec's naked chest. "Damnation, MacNeil!" he yelled. "What are ye doing to Mairi?" He drew his sword, and for a moment Mairi thought he'd attack Alec from behind while Geoff threatened from the front.

She threw her arms wide, standing at Alec's back. She brushed against him, fighting the pull to lean in to him. "He was loving me under the stars, Cullen Duffie, not that it's any of your business."

Her words stopped Cullen in mid stride, his lethal gaze dropping to her. "Tor?" he asked, one brow rising as he turned to look for her brother.

Tor stood beside Alec, looking out at Geoff's ship. "Don't ask her to divulge any details," he said. "She's liable to tell ye, and I'll be too ill to defend this ship."

Mairi smacked her brother's arm. Alec's voice boomed out into the night. "Sneaking up through the shadows to fire upon a vacant ship is cowardly, MacInnes. I already showed ye the power of the *Sea Wolf* and *Sea Rose* along South Uist. If ye wish to war against me, meet me on the ground with swords."

"Alec," Mairi said, grabbing his arm, but he didn't budge.

"I will have my revenge, MacNeil," Geoff called across. "First for my ship, and second for my woman."

"God's ballocks, Geoff. I'm second to your bloody ship?" Mairi yelled back. She rubbed a hand down the side of her face. Aye, she was out of her mind to have considered wedding him. She leaned forward over the rail. "And I'm not your woman."

"Stand down, Geoff," Tor called across. "MacNeil was tricked into thinking the MacInnes were responsible for his wife's death. We discussed this at South Uist."

"Ye discussed it!" Geoff yelled back. "I was busy salvaging my ship."

A man from Geoff's ship yelled from the other side, drawing everyone's attention to the mountainous form of a second ship cutting through the water. "That would be Kenneth at the helm," Alec said.

Tor cupped his hands around his mouth to call out. "If ye wish to bring war to Kilchoan, in your first months as chief, by firing upon the heads of clan Maclean and MacDonald, ye're a bigger fool than Fergus MacInnes *and* his son combined. Especially when MacNeil's other ship is bearing down on ye."

In the spill of lantern light, Mairi could see Geoff's lips move on a curse, and he gripped the rail with both hands. She'd thought him fairly handsome just a month ago, but now she saw only a bitter coward who hadn't even disembarked on Barra to look for her. And the way he'd allowed his dogs to be treated was a good indication of his heart. Mairi reached around Alec to her brother, punching his arm. "How could ye let me almost marry him?"

Tor rubbed his abused bicep without taking his gaze off

the other ship. "I believe," he said through gritted teeth, "that I told ye I didn't think it was a good idea, little sister. But ye are as stubborn as the winter is long."

"Aye, MacNeil, ye're going to have your hands full with that lass," Cullen said with a side glance. "Maybe ye can teach her to obey that whistle ye use on the dogs."

"If there weren't cannons aimed at us right now, Cullen Duffie, I'd kick ye hard enough that Rose would have to wait at least three years to get with your child," Mairi said.

"It looks like Geoff's backing down," Tor said. He finally looked away from the MacInnes vessel. "No death and dismemberment right before your wedding." He nodded at them both.

"Actually," Alec said, turning to take in both Tor and Cullen. "Mairi did not say aye."

His words cut straight through Mairi, as if a cannon had indeed fired, splintering the world around them, sending a pointed spear straight through her. She almost doubled over without breath.

"What?" Tor asked, his arms dropping from their normal fold over his chest. "Mairi, ye've slept with the man. How could ye not take him as husband?"

"She is a widow, Tor," Cullen said, though his face was just as hard as her brother's. "We've known a number of merry widows who have not remarried."

"My sister," Tor snapped. "Will not be one of *those* merry widows."

"That's a bit hypocritical," Cullen said.

"I don't bloody care," Tor volleyed back, staring at Mairi.

For several seconds, she couldn't speak as she struggled for breath. The railing behind her kept her on her feet. "I…I didn't say no, either." She looked toward Alec, who had turned back to the bow, watching Geoff's sails raise to catch the breeze in the bay.

"Leave her be," Alec said without turning back. "I did not give her good reason to wed."

"What the hell does that mean?" Tor asked. "She said ye loved her well."

"He means," Mairi said, her words low. "I will not live on Kisimul." And he apparently wasn't willing to abandon the castle for her. With a quivering sob that she kept inside, Mairi turned, and, dashing down the steps to the mid deck, she grabbed her robe and ran toward Broc near the rope ladder.

"Mairi?" he asked, his eyes taking in her attire.

"Can ye row me back to Kisimul?"

"Aye," he said, looking past her. He shrugged. "Looks like we won't be having another battle tonight."

Then why did Mairi feel like she'd been shot through the most vital organ to life, her heart?

• • •

Alec strode across the bailey toward the soldiers' barracks without talking to any of the warriors. Hands fisted, it took every ounce of discipline he possessed not to run into the keep where he guessed Mairi had returned, most likely to tell his children she'd be leaving with Tor. He glanced toward the upper windows where candles lit the paned glass. He could stride up there, haul her against him, swear to her that he would never let her go, and entrap her with him here on Kisimul forever.

His hand caught the edge of the doorframe, his fingers curling into a fist around the wood. *Bloody damnation.* He couldn't force her to stay, imprisoning her just like she feared. Had his own mother left because she felt captive on Kisimul? Had Joyce? Was resentment the curse of Kisimul?

Curses are born of fear and discontent. Mairi's words echoed in his head until it began to throb.

"Ballocks." He pushed into the dark room where Ian rested, his broken leg lifted upon a short tower of pillows.

"I was wondering if ye were ever going to come in," Ian said, his tone surly, probably from not being able to accompany the men out on the bay.

"MacInnes decided that he was still outgunned," Alec said, throwing himself into a chair next to Ian before the hearth. Voices moved past the door outside in the courtyard, but no one entered.

"He's a coward," Ian said, pushing up higher into his seat. "But that's not what ye're in here for, is it?"

"How do ye—"

"Kenneth told me ye and Mairi were alone on the *Sea Wolf*, and now ye're here frowning like someone's slain your favorite dog."

Alec slumped forward, resting his elbows on his knees as he hung his head. He gripped his skull, rubbing hard through his hair. "She won't stay on Kisimul," he said.

"Ye asked her to marry ye?" Ian asked.

Alec nodded without looking up. "She said aye to that, but nay to living at Kisimul."

"And…?"

Alec raised his head to meet Ian's dark gaze. "I am the Wolf of Barra, the chief of Clan MacNeil, and the seat of the chief is Kisimul Castle. She may have said aye to me but has refused my home and all that I have been raised to be."

Ian rubbed his short beard and tipped his gaze to the dark rafters. He nodded as if churning Alec's words in his mind. After a moment, Ian leveled his stare at him. "Ye were raised, watching your father leave often and finally not return. Ye were raised, watching your mother wave as she sailed away and then Millie when ye wed. It seems ye are familiar with people ye care about, leaving." His one brow rose.

"That has nothing to do with my duty to keep Kisimul,"

Alec said, rising to pace to the hearth where he kicked at a block of half burned peat in the grate.

"Are ye letting Mairi leave Kisimul before she can leave ye?" Ian asked.

"Bloody ridiculous, Ian," Alec said, crossing his arms to stare down his best friend.

Ian shrugged. "Perhaps, but considering ye are the one in charge, as The MacNeil of Barra, I think ye can decide where ye live. Your people may like having their chief where they could stop in to strategize over a cup of ale. Cinnia and Weylyn would get to see the village children more than once or twice a year."

Alec kept his solid stance. "And what would happen to Kisimul?"

"We would keep it up for times of war. Use it as a place for formal gatherings, meetings with other clans."

Alec didn't respond. He looked off into the dark shadows of the small barracks. Soon it would fill with men.

"Alec," Ian said, bringing his gaze back to him. "Marry the lass."

"Says the man who's never deemed it necessary to stay with one lass for more than a month."

"Aye, but I don't look at those lasses the way I see ye look at Mairi Maclean. Bloody hell, Alec, I haven't heard ye laugh like ye did when ye took her to the shore since ye were a lad, before your da died. Ye can spend your life rowing and riding back and forth from this fortress because ye think it's your duty, or ye can choose something different. Maybe that will break the curse of Kisimul."

"There is no curse," Alec grumbled, but the words didn't sound as solid as they had before.

Ian sucked in a large inhale and leaned back in his seat. "Think about it, but not too long. Else we'll have to go all the way to the Isle of Mull to steal her again, when ye come to your bloody senses."

Alec stared at his best friend who gave him a slow, knowing nod. Had he already decided that he must deal with the pain of losing someone again? He'd half expected Mairi to be gone when he'd returned from tracking down her brother. He'd been ready for the pain then, but being here to watch her sail away with her kin… He didn't think he could do it.

"Thank ye," he said, heading for the door.

Ian huffed loudly. "If I can't help save the ships from the bloody MacInnes, at least I can help save us all from your grumpy rage if ye let her go."

Alec strode into the bailey where Kenneth waved him over. Alec's gaze circled the dark bailey, looking for Tor and Cullen. "Where are Maclean and Duffie?"

"Not sure," Kenneth said.

"I think checking on the Maclean lass," Daniel said from near the wall.

Damnation. Would they take her away tonight?

Alec turned toward the great hall where Father Lassiter stood, following him inside. "Now that the MacInnes have been scared off, since everyone is here, it seems we could have a celebration," the priest said. "A wedding perhaps?" His eyebrows rose.

His words stopped Alec at the table. In his mind, he'd already wed Mairi. It needed to be officiated before the church. Then she couldn't leave, and they'd figure out where they would live later. "Aye, Father, we should have a wedding tonight."

Father Lassiter looked shocked, and blinked several times. "Why that's bloody wonderful. I will tell Bessy right away."

Could the priest be that dense? "I am not marrying Bessy Cameron."

"But her brother wills it. He left a dowry with me for when

ye came around. A chest of gold plates, rolls of rich fabric—"

"I'm wedding Mairi Maclean."

"She doesn't even have a dowry," the middle-aged man said, his face growing tight with anger. "And she was betrothed to that MacInnes bastard. She's spoken for. 'Twould be a sin to take another man's wife."

Had the priest taken payment from Angus to make sure Alec wed his sister? He knew many priests were corrupt, but the ones that ventured to the outer Scottish isles were usually more about gathering souls than gathering gold.

Alec took a step toward the man. "Mairi Maclean is my wife already, in the eyes of God. If ye have a problem with making it official with the church, ye may leave Barra, and we will find another priest to sign the book."

Just as Alec turned, the blast of a cannon exploded, its impact on Kisimul's outer wall sending a vibration through the keep. "What the hell," Alec yelled, running out into the bailey.

"To arms," Kenneth called and looked to Alec, who signaled for the beacons around the wall to be relit.

Bam! A cascade of rocks could be heard on the outer wall as another cannon slammed into it.

"Signal the men who stayed back on the ships to come around and engage," Alec said as a bombardment of three cannonballs blasted into the wall.

"Fire!" the lookout on top of the wall yelled. Alec snapped his gaze up to see him pointing toward the village.

Tor and Cullen ran in the gate from the far outer wall. "Your village is on fire, MacNeil," Cullen yelled. "Ye need men back there."

"I have six men here who can row across," Tor said.

"Daniel," Alec called to his lead oarsman. "Kenneth is readying the ships to attack. Organize the rest of the men to row back to the village. Kisimul can withstand cannon."

Daniel ran, waving his hands for attention. Ian hobbled out of the soldiers' barracks with his leg wrapped tightly to the iron braces. Another cannon hit the back of Kisimul.

"MacInnes has a death wish," Ian said. He had his sword strapped to his good leg.

"Ye should be resting," Alec said, taking mental note of the men moving in their designated groupings.

"With cannons trying to blast into Kisimul? Not likely," he said. "I can help put out fires in the village."

"Find out who lit them," Alec said as he turned back to the keep where Mairi and his children were.

Kisimul will hold. It's held for centuries.

"Mairi!" he yelled as he tore into the keep.

He ran to the stairs and stopped at the bottom. Mairi stood at the top, looking every bit the angel in her white smock and robe. Her face looked pale, her eyes red. She'd been crying.

"Mairi."

She held up a hand to stop him from approaching. "I'll get the children," she said, her voice strong. "And Millie. We're safe here. Kisimul will never fall."

"The village is on fire," he said.

"Go," she said, waving him toward the door.

"We will talk when I return," he said, looking up at her, wanting to run up to touch her, hold her. "Don't leave."

She held the wooden railing at the top with both hands. "Make certain ye return," she said. "I don't want to add your boat to the line at the dock."

Another cannon blast hit the outer wall. "It will hold," Mairi said. "Go."

With one last look, he turned, running out to join his men.

Chapter Nineteen

Mairi ran into Cinnia's room. Both children stood at the windows, staring through the glass into the night. "Mairi," Cinnia yelled and ran across the room, throwing herself into Mairi's arms.

Mairi stroked her head. "Kisimul is stronger than cannonballs."

"That's what I told her," Weylyn said, but his face looked as white as a bleached sheet. Daisy whined, her ears perked high on her head as she sat on the bed beside Weylyn's dog.

"Let us get dressed," Mairi said and smiled. "If we are going to be under siege, we shouldn't do it in our bedclothes." She led Cinnia over to the privacy screen where her day dress hung. "I need to find my own and check on Millie. Meet me in my chamber." The children began helping each other into their clothes, and Mairi flew out the door, running down the hall.

She opened the door to find Millie already dressed. The woman pointed to the window and formed an *O* with her lips. Who? Mairi came closer, so Millie could see her lips move in the dim light. "Geoff MacInnes. He's angry about his ship being crippled off South Uist and me being taken from Kilchoan." Although he'd seemed much more infuriated about his bloody ship. With both Cullen and Tor here, as well as the MacNeil warriors, Geoff was a fool to attack.

Cinnia and Weylyn barged into the room, Daisy and Ares on their heels. Mairi ran behind her changing screen and threw on a new smock and her day gown. When she stepped out, Millie was hugging both children in to her.

"No worries, ye two," Mairi said with forced cheerfulness. "Kisimul has never fallen to attack. Cannonballs may mar the outer walls, but they will never break through to us."

"Where is Bessy?" Cinnia asked.

"I haven't seen her," Mairi said. With all the noise from the cannon fire, she surely would have come running.

"Maybe she's hiding," Weylyn said. "She's not very brave."

"Weylyn, run to her room and see if she's in there," Mairi said. "Meet us on the landing." Ares ran off with him.

Mairi bent to stroke Daisy, who stepped up on her bent knee to lick her cheek. She scratched behind the dog's ears. "Don't worry. Kisimul protects dogs as well." She kissed her smooth head.

Straightening, Mairi waved to Millie to follow with Cinnia out into the corridor. Mairi and Millie both held candles to light their way. Weylyn's boots cracked on the floorboards as he and Ares ran up, both panting.

"She's not in her room, and her fire's out, like she hasn't been there all night," he said.

"Maybe she is still in the kitchens," Mairi said. "We'll check, but let's stay out of the way of the warriors." She took hold of Weylyn's small hand and felt him shaking. He would become a mountain of strength like his father, but right now he was still a child of seven.

Mairi bent before him. "I need ye to keep an eye on

Ares and Daisy and any other hounds about. Ye have a way with them, and they're bound to be frightened." As if she understood, Daisy nuzzled into the boy and whined.

A look of pride replaced some of the fear in Weylyn's face. He stroked Daisy. "It will be fine," he said to her. "Kisimul never falls."

Cinnia took Millie's arm, and Mairi walked behind them to keep an eye on everyone in their small group. Behind them, the bailey emptied as men left the small island to fight. Geoff was an idiot if he thought he could win this. "What is he thinking?" Mairi whispered and ducked into the lower kitchen. The other two dogs from Kilchoan ran across the bailey to join them.

"Da must have taken Geri and Freki across with him," Weylyn said. "They are trained for battle."

Cinnia raced up the steps to the upper kitchen and then back down. "She's not up there," Cinnia yelled, holding her skirt as she leaped back down the steps.

The four of them, Ares, Daisy, and her two brothers ducked into the center bailey. It was empty except for Father Lassiter who stood by the chapel door. He waved them over with a broad smile as if he'd just spotted them in a crowd at a festival. They ran over, Daisy barking at him until Weylyn bent down and wrapped her in a hug.

"Glad to see ye," Father Lassiter said, breathing heavily. He wiped a dusty arm across his forehead, which was smudged with black. He was covered in dirt, bits of hay sticking to his dark coat. Had he been cleaning the chapel? "I thought I'd been completely abandoned when everyone left for the ships and village."

"Ye are safer here," Cinnia assured him.

"Have ye seen Bessy Cameron, Father?" Mairi asked.

Father Lassiter pointed across the bailey where Bessy stood in a corner of the inner wall. Eyes wide, she looked close to all-out panic. Mairi turned to go to her, but Father Lassiter's hand on her arm stopped her. "'Tis my calling to help those afraid for their mortal lives. I will coax her to join us." He went toward her like a man approaching a frightened foal, while the four of them waited.

Cannon blasts made Bessy jump, and she clasped her hands in the folds of her skirts while the priest spoke to her. His lips moved quickly, and Bessy shook her head. Was she too frightened to follow him?

Millie stood next to Mairi, watching the negotiation. She tugged on Mairi's sleeve, pulling her gaze. Millie's brows wrinkled inward, her eyes narrowed as if watching closely. She shook met Mairi's eyes before quickly swinging her gaze back to the priest and girl. "What is it?" Mairi asked.

Millie shook her head again, pinching her lips. She tapped her own throat roughly as if frustrated, obviously wanting to tell Mairi something. "Something is wrong?" Mairi asked.

Millie nodded, looking back to the two of them. Father Lassiter looked angry as Bessy spoke, a pleading look on her face. If she was afraid to move, then he should leave her there. She'd be safe hiding there in the corner.

Millie yanked on Mairi's sleeve, her hands moving in signals that Mairi couldn't understand.

"I think he gave up," Cinnia said, as Father Lassiter came back across the bailey. They stood beside the door into the great hall. Millie yanked the children inside with her. The four dogs and Mairi followed. Once inside, Millie lifted the bar to slide across the door as Father Lassiter pushed against it.

"Millie, let him in," Mairi said, even though the woman couldn't hear her.

"Blast it, woman, let me in," the priest said and pushed harder, forcing it wide open. Daisy barked and showed her teeth. The other dogs came up on Daisy's sides, growling.

Millie grabbed Mairi's arm, yanking her behind her.

"The woman is daft," Father Lassiter yelled over Daisy's barking and ran a hand over his head. His face was red, and his eyes narrowed. "Shut your yap," he snapped at the dog, kicking out at her with a boot.

"Don't kick her," Weylyn shouted back, leaping forward to drag Daisy away. "She's just anxious from the attack. They all are. Dogs pick up on danger."

As Father Lassiter stepped closer, Millie dodged in front of Mairi. Her hand rose up, and Mairi blinked. Good Lord, the woman held a *singh dubh*, its lethal point trained on the priest. Millie thought Father Lassiter was the danger. Before anyone could move, the old woman lunged toward him, planting her dagger into his arm as if she'd been aiming for his heart.

"Bloody bitch," Father Lassiter roared and swung his fist around, striking her in the jaw. Her body pitched to the side with the force, and she slammed to the floor. Cinnia screamed.

"Stop," Bessy yelled from the doorway. "Ye can't do this."

Mairi dove for Millie who lay on the floorboards, unmoving. Was she even breathing? She stared back at the priest. "Ye struck an old woman? Father, ye are a man of God."

"She is insane, and she surprised me," Father Lassiter said, yanking the blade out of his arm and wrapping it with a holy sash he'd pulled from around his neck. "Get water. In the well room. Go," he said.

"Nay," Bessy yelled, but Cinnia and Weylyn had already run into the well room. Ares and Daisy barked at Father Lassiter as the other two dogs stood over Millie on the ground as if guarding her. Bessy tried to grab the priest's shoulder, but he shook her off, banging her into the wall.

"Who are ye?" Mairi asked, but there was no time for him to answer or even for her to draw her own dagger as he lunged across the hall. He barreled into her, shoving her into the well room. She fell to the floor at the feet of the children. But instead of falling on stone, she was cushioned by hay. Mounds of hay. It filled the room, along with wooden seats Mairi recognized from the chapel.

Weylyn ran at him, but the man caught the boy easily with his good arm and threw him back in. He ducked out through the door where Daisy bit at his feet. "Damn dog," he hissed, kicking at her as he grabbed a lit torch stuck in a sconce on the side of the doorway.

Mairi glanced around her at the crisp, dry hay. *Oh God. Oh, Sweet Lord, save us.* She pushed up, running toward the open door, but didn't make it there before he brandished the torch into the room, touching the flames to the hay on both sides of the doorway. "Nay," Mairi yelled, hitting his arm, but he threw the torch to the back of the stuffed well room. Mairi gripped the door but couldn't wrench it free from his hand. Even with one arm injured, he was still stronger than her. Faces close together in the doorway, he slowly forced it closed, even as she leveraged her boot on the stone wall next to it. Cinnia ran up to help, and Weylyn, but they couldn't grip the door, their hands sliding off a black substance.

"Who are ye? Lucifer disguised as a priest?" Mairi spat. She would know who to damn with her last breath.

His face tightened into a sneer as his lips pulled back, showing little yellow teeth. All traces of a godly man had vanished. "Ye will die, not like Joyce by my blade, but by flame. Long live Angus Cameron, chief of Barra Isle and Kisimul Castle."

The door slammed shut, sealing them inside. Mairi spun around to see Weylyn and Cinnia wiping their black hands on their clothes, and she realized it was pitch. It was painted all over the walls and door. She dashed forward, stomping at the fire, and the children joined in, but the straw caught on fire faster than they could put it out. The smoke billowed up, filling the tiny room.

Mairi coughed, covering her mouth with a sleeve. "Water." She leaned over the rectangular stone well, but the bucket was missing. Only the chain hung in the middle, coiled to the top over the gaping black hole. He'd set this all up. Millie must have seen him say something to Bessy, and Bessy had pushed past her fear to try to save them. Had she known all along that the priest was a Cameron? That her brother was plotting to take over Barra? Was Alec battling him now in the village?

Alec. Could he withstand the hell of losing his children in a fiery blaze, the self-condemnation that would beat him bloody for leaving them on Kisimul to be murdered?

"Nay," she yelled against the crackling inferno building in the room. She couldn't allow it. Running to the door, Mairi beat on it. "Let us out!" Behind her Cinnia and Weylyn coughed, hacking against the black smoke. "Get down low," Mairi yelled, and they sank to the straw-scattered floor. Fire licked up the walls, burning hot. The bloody traitor had created an oven inside the well room, an oven meant to bake them to a crisp.

Cinnia crawled over to Mairi, tears streaking down her face. "We're going to die," she wailed.

Weylyn threw himself into Mairi's arms. "The flames are too fast. Too hot."

Fire licked up the walls to the wooden ceiling. There were no windows. Only the barred door and the…

"Well," she said. Coughing, she began to drag the children with her toward the rectangular hole in the ground. Weylyn followed, but Cinnia needed to be tugged, her body wracked with coughs. Standing up to lean over, Mairi breathed in the cool, clean air that sat just down inside the stone lip. "Lean in. Breathe," she said. Weylyn followed her order, but she had to lift Cinnia under her arms, throwing her face over the hole. "Breathe. The air is good down there," she said into the girl's hair, and felt her inhale.

Heat singeing her back, Mairi grabbed the chain, throwing it down the dark hole. "What are ye doing?" Weylyn asked, his wide eyes red from the smoke. Ash spots marked his young face.

"It's the only safe place," she answered.

He looked between her and the hole and nodded. "Aye."

"Come on, Cinnia," Mairi called against the girl, and she stirred. Mairi lifted her to sit her on the edge of the well.

"Where are we going?" Cinnia's words were rough whispers as if her throat had been scorched already.

Mairi wiped the ashy sweat from the girl's face. "We're going down." Down into the heart of Kisimul.

Chapter Twenty

Where the bloody hell had all these MacInnes come from?

Alec leaped from the ferry that had brought him, his hounds, a score of men, and his horse over from Kisimul. Flames shot up through the thatching on at least three cottages. Screams tore through him as he turned to whistle for Sköll. The horse trotted over, weaving between the chaos, so he could mount.

His men ran into the village, swords drawn to meet those torching the homes and attacking. Women and children fled toward the hills beyond to escape the carnage and smoke. With the pressure of his heel, Sköll turned toward four men who were setting Ruth's bakery on fire as she tried to hit them with the heavy wood board she used to take bread out of the ovens.

"Run, Ruth," he yelled. As she took off in another direction, eyes wide, Alec's sword swung down in an arc, slicing through two of the men, taking one head and one arm. Turning, Sköll knocked the other two over with his hind quarters, delivering a kick to one that left him unconscious while the other ran off.

Alec jumped off Sköll to battle two more men who came at him, warding off their thrusts easily. One fell to his sword and the other lost his weapon. With a powerful stride, Alec grabbed the man around the throat with his hand, squeezing until the bastard's eyes bulged. "What the hell are ye doing?"

The man couldn't speak in Alec's grip, but he didn't have to. Beyond him stood another large, barrel-chested warrior. One Alec had known most of his life. And suddenly he knew exactly what was going on. With a surge of fury, Alec threw the man he held toward the flaming wall of the bakery but kept his gaze on his true enemy. Angus Cameron.

Fury burned as brightly within him as the doomed houses around the village square. Muscles taut and blood pumping fast, Alec strode toward the bastard. Angus Cameron was going to die.

Angus stared, a wide smile on his paunchy face. "I'd hoped to do this the easy way after I had my man lure Joyce away from Kisimul. It was easier for him to kill her off that rock fortress of yours."

Lured away?

"Timid thing," he said. "Hardly knew what was happening to her."

Alec's stomach clenched. Poor Joyce, sent to wed a chief hardly old enough to be called a man. She'd suffered in loneliness at Kisimul, dutifully giving him children despite her sadness. Only to have her throat slit, executed for doing her duty in staying with him. The woman hadn't abandoned Kisimul and her children after all.

Angus shook his head. "With her gone, ye were supposed to marry my sister before your untimely death, leaving her in the seat of the clan until I came to claim it. But with the Maclean lass about, I've decided to kill ye now and take Barra by force." With that, Angus charged, lifting his claymore high with one hand while holding his wooden targe with the other.

The heavy force with which Angus barreled toward Alec may have slaughtered a lesser warrior, but Alec was quicker than the Cameron chief. Muscles and sinew, honed from hours of swordplay and tactical practice, threw Alec into defensive action. He lowered, dodged the man's bulk, and knocked his sword away as he turned, but Angus held onto the weapon. Alec spun and raised his boot, kicking Angus in the back with his heel. The force threw the man to the ground. He grunted as his round chest hit. Alec lifted his sword to strike, but the barking of his two hounds signaled for him to turn, lifting his sword in a defensive pose just in time.

George Macrae brought his blade down in a vicious, silent arc meant to cleave Alec at his shoulder. Instead, steel met steel, clanging loudly to add to the shouting of men and crackling of fire. Alec let the Macrae chief's sword continue downward, controlling the impact. With a twist of his sword and bend of his arms, Alec brought the bastard close until they stared at each other between crossed blades.

Macrae's teeth were gritted as he snarled at Alec. "'Tis your day to die, MacNeil, ye and your kin. Barra will belong to the Camerons and Macraes."

His kin? Alec's inhale battled past the tightening of his stomach at the man's words. Behind him, Angus cursed as Alec's large wolfhounds surrounded the man, snapping, barking, and biting when given the chance. Taking turns, they crashed their massive frames into him as he tried to rise. "Bloody beasts," he yelled, but Alec was caught in a staring contest with Macrae. The bastard waited for him to glance at Kisimul, the place where he'd locked his only kin up safely.

"They're dying right now," Macrae said, his words seething out of his teeth like the hiss of a snake.

"Kisimul will never fall," Alec said, and the recitation gave him strength. He turned, letting the man's press fall forward past him, and spun to slice toward Macrae, but Macrae managed to get his sword up in time to block. Alec kept his feet locked in the sway of momentum, as if the ground tilted like a tossing ship. A lifetime of riding the waves gave him unbeatable balance.

"Kisimul will be ours, along with Barra," Macrae said.

"Impossible," Alec said as he parried back and forth with the obviously talented swordsman. "Kisimul is impenetrable."

Macrae's frown turned into an evil smile. "Kisimul is inescapable."

A deep emotion washed through Alec, one that he'd never felt fully before. Fear. It rolled through him like an icy poison, threatening to numb and weaken him. He wanted to look toward the fortress in the bay. Only his discipline kept him centered on his foe. Even the sound of his dogs finding flesh on Angus, making the man scream as they continued to rip into him, didn't pull Alec's attention.

"Macrae, get them off me," Angus yelled between curses, but his coconspirator ignored him, making it very clear that George Macrae aspired to control Barra by himself. Out of the corner of his eye, Alec saw Kenneth run up, his claymore bloody.

Macrae struck again, his sword ringing out and sliding down Alec's blade. Without breaking his stride, shoving Macrae backward, Alec whistled twice, high-pitched blasts to scatter his lethal hounds so that Kenneth could advance. One deep yell from his cousin, the whoosh of his blade through the air, and Angus Cameron's head thudded to the ground.

"Kisimul," Kenneth yelled, but still Alec battled George Macrae, knowing the man needed him unfocused to win, but Alec parried each thrust, and Kenneth took off toward the docks. Men ran everywhere, and the slip of Macrae's confident smile showed that the tide had turned.

With a growl born of might and fury, pushing past the fear that threatened to crumble his strength, Alec advanced, faster, harder, legs braced and arms burning with the heat of use. He slashed forward, practically chasing the bastard Macrae. *Look away, and you are finished.*

The man blinked, wiping an arm across his forehead as he blocked Alec's blade. Alec felt him falter under his strength and changed the direction of his next thrust at the last second. His mighty sword clanged hard against the very top of his foe's blade, sending it scattering across the rocks. "Camerons and Macraes are no more!" he yelled and lifted his sword high.

"And your family is no more," George Macrae yelled back, making a last effort to throw himself along the ground toward his sword, but Alec's blade caught him across the neck, slicing deep. He rolled to the side, his hands gripping the flowing wound. Only then did Alec look to Kisimul.

Fire. The very center of Kisimul glowed orange against the blackness of the night. Like when Cinnia had set the kitchen ablaze but a hundred times larger. Alec's gut sunk deep inside. "Nay," Alec yelled, his voice booming out in the destroyed village center. Fire still smoldered some of the houses, as well as many of the boats that had been tied at the dock, including the ferry. It was a conscious effort to prevent them from returning to Kisimul.

Alec ran, his hounds at his sides, as he searched the dock for a seaworthy vessel. "I need a boat," he called to the warriors standing there, watching fire spark up in the sky over Kisimul. "My children," he yelled. "Mairi." He scanned the men but didn't see Tor Maclean or Cullen Duffie. Out in the bay, the two MacNeil ships flanked two others, at least one of them belonging to George Macrae.

"The seaworthy ones have been burned," Kenneth said, running up to Alec.

Ian hobbled after him, his face grim. "I should have stayed back." His eyes reflected the flames.

Alec ran toward the far end of the dock where the broken

boats, ghosts of his past, sat tethered. The Camerons had burned Joyce's boat and his mother's, but the decades-old rowboat, which had belonged to his father, lay half wedged under the boards. He yanked at it, desperation empowering his muscles as he brought it forward. "Oars," he yelled, and Daniel ran up carrying some that were only partly singed. Behind him Kenneth was ordering boards to be nailed together. He'd have a boat built shortly, but Alec wasn't waiting.

He climbed into his father's rowboat, and Daniel pushed him off into the bay. Water immediately began to seep into the bottom, but Alec just rowed, putting every bit of his remaining strength into his back and shoulders, pushing forward with his feet braced. Gurgles came up from the wormholes in the sides and the cracks of neglected wood. Smoke on the light breeze gave a haze over the water, as if he moved through an otherworldly, ashy mist. Halfway across, he heard the frantic barking of a dog. He'd left four on Kisimul with Mairi, Cinnia, Weylyn, and Millie. And Bessy Cameron. His face swung around toward the horrible scene of fire spitting up over the turrets of Kisimul. Could Bessy Cameron have started the fire? Been part of her brother's plan to take over Barra Isle?

Seawater flooded the bottom of the boat, making it sluggish. At this rate, it wouldn't make it to shore. *"Mo chreach,"* Alec cursed and dropped the oars into the rusted holders on the sides. He grabbed his boot, tugging until it released. Dropping the second one, he stood in the foot of water in his father's doomed boat. Without a thought of anything but reaching Kisimul, Alec dove into the black sea.

• • •

"Use the iron bars," Weylyn called up to Mairi. "They're a ladder down." He'd been the first to venture into the dark, narrow hole of the freshwater well. Mairi kept Cinnia before her as they faced the damp wall. Their heads were just below the upper edge of the well, where the air didn't scorch her throat with every inhale as it had in the room. When she looked up, the glow of fire filled the rectangular opening, spurring her to slide Cinnia and herself down, her foot kicking, searching for the next rung.

"Hold on, Cinnia," Mairi said to the quietly weeping girl. "The well will keep us safe." The girl shook in Mairi's arms. Or was that Mairi shaking? Flashes of light appeared to the sides of Mairi's vision, and she realized her breathing was much too fast. And if she fainted, she'd drop Cinnia, and the two of them would fall into Weylyn, probably killing them all when they hit the bottom and drowned. The thought sped her pulse even higher, but she made herself count to four with her inhale and then to five with her exhale.

Mairi's foot caught the rung, and she and Cinnia lowered another head-length down into the hole.

"It's cool below and not smoky," Weylyn called, his voice small. He must be far below.

"Are ye to water yet?" Mairi called, her toes finding another rung. She pulled the two of them lower, kicking at her own skirts that bunched up around them. She guided Cinnia's foot to occupy the same iron rung, rooted to the wall, and slapped at both of their skirts that were lifted to expose their legs to the cool air filling the long, tight space.

She heard the echo of a plop as if Weylyn had dropped a pebble in. "Almost," he called up. "I'll stop here. Ballocks, it's dark."

Although his voice was naturally high since he was seven years old, the inflection reminded Mairi of his father. *Alec. Where are ye? Hurry. I'm trying.*

She felt the press of desperate tears and blinked. She inhaled against Cinnia's hair, the sweet scent of soap covered by the bitter tang of smoke. Shivering, her fingers curling around the cold, wet iron, and a small whimper broke from her lips.

"Are ye afraid?" Cinnia asked, her face toward the wall. They were far enough down now that the fire raging above didn't light the mossy walls. It was good to hear the girl speak.

"Kisimul will protect us," Mairi echoed the words she'd heard Alec say.

"Ye're shaking," Cinnia said.

Mairi lowered them another rung. "I don't do well in dark, small spaces."

"Why?"

Oh Good Lord. Mairi didn't talk about her time at Kilchoan, under siege by her absent husband's lecherous son, Normond MacInnes. She preferred to stuff the experience deep inside where it couldn't hurt her, but being trapped in the well, feeling her elbows touch the sides and her back brush the wall behind her… It was bringing the memories to the surface like air bubbles released under water.

"I was trapped once," Mairi said and took another inhale of cool air to feed her aching limbs. The two of them lowered as one to the next rung.

"Tell me," Cinnia said. "If he survived then perhaps we can, too." Her voice was faint against the sounds of flames eating away at the wood above them, and Mairi could hear the tears in her words.

She kissed the back of Cinnia's head. "Of course we will." She inhaled and exhaled a long breath. *God, please let us live through this.* Swallowing against the burning grit in her throat, she released the tight hold on her nightmares. "I hid inside a trunk once, to escape a bad man. He'd been certain to find me in my chambers and was quite surprised to see I'd eluded him. But I was still there, locked in a dark, small wooden trunk. Problem was, I couldn't get out. So, when he left, I had to sit in the trunk until someone noticed me."

The words resurrected the memories of being crunched down in the chest. They beat at Mairi, making her heart pound and her hands tingle. Hours crawled by, nearly a whole day, before one of the kitchen maids brought up her meal, and she pounded on the trunk before the woman left. Hours of praying, crying, aching.

"Ye're breathing really fast," Cinnia said. She reached her hand to lay on top of Mairi's. "Don't worry. We aren't trapped. Kisimul is protecting us with its walls."

We are safe. The top is open. We will get out. Mairi repeated the words in her head and concentrated on slowing her breath. Flames danced above, licking at the walls. Mairi could almost hear the click of teeth in the crackling, like the fire was a great beast biting the hay and the beams holding up the ceiling. She glanced above at the bright light of orange, swirling and undulating as if the fire were truly alive. The heat traveled down the well, prickling against her cheeks, their bodies the border between the cold underneath and the fiery burn above.

"We should sing," Weylyn called. "Da says it helps to keep one brave."

"Good idea," Mairi said, forcing her voice to sound cheerful as she watched the dark beam engulfed in flames directly above them. *Crack!*

Weylyn's young voice echoed up the well toward her as she watched the beam, her breath stuck in her wildly beating chest. *Crack!* The beam was going to give way, and if it hit the well, flaming wood could shoot right down the hole.

"Lower," Mairi yelled, already bending her knee, her toes searching for the next rung. "Cinnia, move, we need to go lower."

The girl gasped at the loud popping and groan above. The whole room was about to crash down on top of them. "Climb down past me," Mairi said. Perhaps she could block the flaming debris from going farther.

"I'm afraid to fall," Cinnia said, clinging to the iron rungs in the wall.

Mairi stepped down below her two rungs. "I'll catch ye if ye fall, but ye have to move. Now!"

Part of the beam fell across the mouth of the well, sending sparks showering down the tube to fall on their heads. "Cinnia!"

The girl stepped down, her sobs open now. Mairi stroked her leg and felt her shaking. She grabbed the girl's foot. "I'll guide ye to the lower rung." Together the two of them traveled farther down toward Weylyn. "Keep singing, Weylyn, so we know when we've caught up to ye."

His voice grew louder as he sang the words of a Christmastide carol. Mairi gasped as he grabbed her foot. "I'm right here," he said.

She looked back up at the blazing rectangle about twenty feet above them. It truly looked like the gateway to Hell. "Cinnia, climb down past me," Mairi said, pulling her one foot and hand off the rungs for her to pass. If falling wood made it down, hopefully she would block it from reaching Cinnia and Weylyn. If she were going to die tonight, she would do it trying to save the two children. *God, give me strength. Please. Shield us.*

As if reading her thoughts, Cinnia began to say a prayer in Latin. Her whispers added to the ominous sound of cracking and snapping above. The beam was totally consumed by flames, just a dark mass of char suspended above them. "Flatten against the wall," Mairi instructed, her breath coming in desperate pants. Her gaze fastened to the beam, half of it broken free so it hung like a flaming sword, pointed down the throat of the well. A resounding crack and snap sent lit wood down the shaft just seconds before the entire flaming ceiling fell on top of the well. The sound of their screams filled the core of Kisimul.

Chapter Twenty-One

Alec's toes dug into the rocks surrounding Kisimul as he hauled his frozen, sopping body onto the shore. Even in summer, the North Atlantic water was known to freeze men, drowning them with numbness. But when his limbs began to slack, he kept them cutting through the water, the bright glow of the fire inside Kisimul his constant beacon.

For an instant, Alec's hope flared. There, on the outside of the wall, leaning against it, were two women. Daisy and Weylyn's dog, Ares, barked at him, jumping into and then out of the water. The two other dogs barked next to the women. He drew himself up to standing and ran toward them. Millie, a bleeding cut on her forehead, and Bessy Cameron.

"What have ye done?" Alec asked, and Bessy clung to Millie. The old woman's eyes blinked open, and she shook her head, patting Bessy's back as the younger woman sobbed. Millie made the sign of the cross with two fingers and then the sign of the devil with horns on her head.

"The priest? Is the devil?" he asked.

Millie nodded and ran a finger across her throat, then

pointed to Bessy. Bessy had killed the priest? Maybe he wasn't understanding Millie's signals, but he didn't have time to waste. "Where are the others, the children and Mairi?"

Bessy wailed, her piercing voice reaching inside Alec to twist his heart. Millie's eyes were wet, and she slowly shook her head. A chill sparked inside him, running down his spine. "Nay," he yelled, turning from them to run to the gate. Daisy followed on his heels. He looked down at the dog. "Where are they? Where is your mistress?" Alec yanked off his sopping shirt and threw his arm to point into the smoke-filled bailey. "Find her!"

The dog ran in through the arch, and Alec followed, holding the wet shirt loosely over his nose and mouth. All the buildings seemed to be ablaze, with the worst coming from the great hall. He almost stumbled over the body of Father Lassiter where he lay, a knife sticking out of his throat, point forward. Bessy had stabbed him from behind. Was he responsible for the fire?

Daisy's barks cut through the suffocating haze. Alec crouched lower where the air was fresher. As a breeze cut down from the night sky, it cleared enough that he saw Daisy standing before the charred door of the great hall. "Nay," Alec whispered, his lips brushing the wet shirt before his face. "Nay. God, don't take them."

He'd left them on Kisimul because he'd thought them safe. Kisimul would never fall, but a traitor had imprisoned them inside to die. He used his wet shirt to beat against the flames, hitting the charred side of the door. The glowing wood collapsed to ash near his feet. The heat burned his nose, and the smoke wound down his throat, making him cough. "Nay," he yelled and hacked. Daisy kept trying to leap inside, but the flames wouldn't allow it. Inside was a furnace like he'd never seen before. How could he reach them? *How can they be alive?*

"MacNeil!" Tor Maclean ran into the bailey, arm over his mouth. "Mairi? Is she here?" Behind him Cullen Duffie, Kenneth, and Ian followed, all of them covering their faces with arms and shirts. As they gathered in the center, they crouched lower.

Wild desperation mixed with fury inside Alec. He shook his head. "I don't know. Mairi." He looked to Kenneth and Ian. "Cinnia and Weylyn. I…I don't know where they are." The words threatened to crack Alec wide open. If they died… he would die. "We have to reach them, and the dog thinks they are in there." He pointed to the gutted great hall, fire still eating up the wood inside like a ravaging beast.

"In there!" Tor shouted, standing.

Cullen grabbed his arm, stopping him from running inside. "Water. Form a bucket line. Buckets, MacNeil. Where are they?"

Alec looked at the flames. *Run inside*. Could he reach them before he died? How far would he get? Someone grabbed his shoulders, dragging him backward onto the ground from right before the door. "Alec," Ian yelled in his face. "Alec MacNeil." Alec finally moved his gaze to Ian. His best friend looked ravished with anger and bitter desperation. "They aren't dead until we see it. They are still alive right now. Let's get this fire out."

A man rushed past them and then another, carrying buckets. The ferry Kenneth had ordered built had brought over twenty men, and they were forming a bucket line from the bay, through the gate, and into the bailey. Rotating through the line while holding their breath, working blind, they were able to survive the smoke.

Alec leaped up next to Ian and helped him hobble on his broken leg. He left Ian to be part of the line and ran with Tor and Cullen and a few of their men to pull up more water from the bay. As if God himself was angered, lightning cracked across the sky, cleaving the clouds that had moved in.

"A bloody blessing," Kenneth called as rain started to fall in heavy drops. A cheer rose up along the line, invigorating the men.

Alec dumped a bucket of seawater into the blazing hall. It spit and sizzled in the smoke. He could see across to where flames shot out of the well room, the door completely burned away. What had made the fire burn so hot, so fast?

He grabbed the bucket from another man and threw it toward the small room off the hall. What was left of the walls burned with vicious, wavering flames, as if they were teased into a demonic frenzy. He'd seen this before on a raid long ago. Pitch—black, sticky pitch would burn with such wickedness.

Alec backed from the room with hacking coughs and looked up at the pelting rain. He wiped two hands down his wet face. Someone had coated the well room in pitch.

Ian ran awkwardly in from the gate. "The lass says the bastard priest wasn't a priest, and he locked them in the well room." Men abandoned their areas to converge on the great hall, buckets and axes in hand. Daisy dodged between their legs, rushing in and out, barking as if that helped. Alec took one more gulp of night air and led them inside the still-burning hall, a path of wet ash under his bare feet. Broken glass from the shattered windows stabbed at his soles, but he barely noticed.

He grabbed another bucket from a man, throwing the water inside the blackened well room. The rafters had fallen in, a forest of burned trees laying haphazardly, like a pyre, over the top of the well. The floor of the room above had collapsed with various pieces of furniture, a privacy screen, a broken chest with smoking contents spilled out over everything.

Alec turned in a tight circle as the men worked around him, throwing more water on the burned mess. "Mairi! Cinnia! Weylyn!" he yelled and coughed, spitting out the wet char on his tongue. Where were they? The mound of smoking debris was enormous. Could they be buried? *Nay, God.* Wrapping the sash of his plaid around his hands, Alec grabbed for a smoldering rafter, his muscles fueled by his desperate hope that he would find them somehow alive.

"Grab the other end!" Alec yelled to Tor, and the two of them lifted the massive beam, rolling it to the side to grab another. The little room filled with men, some throwing water, others lifting beams from the pile. One at a time, smoldering wood and splintered furniture were rolled off until the edge of the well was uncovered. A blue hood lay under it, and Alec snatched it up in his blackened fingers. Mairi's hood. His gaze met Tor's. "They are here. Somewhere, they are bloody here." His words were a snarl, and the two of them dove back into the pile, flipping crumbling wood over and off the edges of the well. With each lift, Alec prayed he wouldn't find a lifeless limb or dull eyes in a blackened face.

"Where are they?" Cullen asked.

Alec leaped over the moved boards, digging at the charred remains of clothing and burned, fallen plaster. Were they here? The more frantic he became, the faster he moved until he was throwing piles off the well, digging in the black ash and still-hot embers, singeing and blistering his hands.

"Alec," Ian said, and Kenneth grabbed his shoulders, causing him to stop.

"Maybe they got out," Kenneth said. "Maybe they are somewhere else in the castle, hiding, away from the flames."

"Ye said Bessy saw him lock them in here," Alec said, his gaze moving across the bared parts of the floor. "Pitch was painted on the walls and straw packed in here." His teeth ground together. "A bloody oven, the bastard trapped them in a God damned furnace." He held out the wrinkled blue hood that Mairi wore. Ash and water mottled it. "And this was here."

Ian looked at the gaping hole in the ceiling. "It could have fallen through."

But Alec's instincts were screaming at him that they were close. His gaze scanned the wreckage around them, smoking black walls, pools of seawater between charred wood and fallen plaster. *Damnation! Where are ye?*

Daisy barked, her front feet perching on the still-covered edge of the well. Her tail wagged, and she dropped to circle the low wall around it. "The well," Alec yelled. It went fifty feet down into the ground that held up the mighty castle. He met Tor as they both leaped toward it, ripping back the planks and plaster. Daisy barked, trying to jump onto the hole.

"Off," Alec said, pushing the dog to safety. He opened his mouth to call down the dark hole when a sound wafted upward. "Shut your mouths," he called, and his breath and heart held tight, waiting for the high-pitched whistle he thought he'd heard.

It came again, the dog whistle that he'd given Weylyn to train the new hounds.

"Weylyn? Cinnia? Mairi?" Alec yelled, his voice funneling downward.

"Da?" Weylyn's little voice hit him, cracking his tight chest open. Alec hung his head between his shoulders as he leaned on the well's edge, relief nearly crippling him.

"Aye," he called down. "We will get ye out. Are Cinnia and Mairi with ye?"

"Aye," Mairi's voice came up. "The three of us are here. The priest isn't a priest. He's a Cameron," she called up.

"He's dead," Tor yelled down. "Are ye all right, Mairi? The children?"

Kenneth helped Alec carefully pull off the last of the wood over the top.

"I think so," Mairi said, coughing. The haggard, weak sound pushed Alec over the edge of the well.

"I'm coming down to get ye," he said.

"Bloody good idea," Mairi whispered from below. "Someone should get blankets for the children."

Alec grasped the iron rungs built into the wall of the rectangular well, thankful it was large enough to let him pass. His bare toes curled around each rung as he lowered. "How far are ye down?"

"I don't know," Mairi answered. "When the roof began to fall, we went as far as we could."

"I'm just above the water," Weylyn said.

"Da?" Cinnia's whisper caught at Alec, and he nearly slipped in his haste to reach her.

"I'm coming, Cinnia," he said. "Hold on."

"I've got her," Mairi said. "Don't fall or we'll all end up in the water."

Her voice was still far below, but Alec concentrated on keeping hold of the slippery rungs. "Keep talking," he said.

"Ye were right," Mairi said. "About Kisimul."

"I think ye were right," he answered, listening for her words, a lifeline to everyone he loved. Aye, loved. "Kisimul is cursed."

"Not its heart," Mairi said, her voice beautifully close now.

"Its heart?" Alec asked, coming closer. Step after careful step. It was dark, but he could almost feel the life below his feet.

"Aye," Mairi said. "The well gave us a way to survive. It is the heart of Kisimul, and it saved us."

The pressure of gratefulness rose behind Alec's eyes, and his palm brushed against the damp well wall. Its strength and stability had protected them. He looked down into the blackness. "I think I've reached ye," he said.

"Cinnia first," Mairi said. "Come on, sweet. Your da is here to take ye up."

Cinnia's quiet sobs made Alec's fists clench around the iron. If Angus Cameron and his bloody priest weren't already dead, he'd cut them end to end. Letting go with one hand, he reached down. "Grab my hand, Cinnia." His fingers sifted through the dark air until they brushed against her little cool fingers. "That's it, climb up to me."

"Here's a rung," Mairi said below. She must be guiding his daughter's feet. Little by little he pulled her up until Cinnia was in his arms. She clung to him, and he reveled in the feel of her strength.

"I'll get her up, then I'll be back for ye two," Alec said. "Just hold on."

"Aye, Da," Weylyn said, and Alec lifted Cinnia up the ladder until the darkness opened up to torchlight and half a dozen faces leaning over the well. Kenneth reached in to lift Cinnia out. Dazed and pale, with smudges of ash over her face, she gave Alec a small nod, and he lowered back down.

"We've climbed up a bit," Mairi said. "Weylyn's above me now."

Alec reached down for his son, his little hand grasping tightly to his forearm. "Ye just hold on, Mairi. Don't try to climb. I don't want ye to fall."

"I'm not staying here," she said with a croaking edge of stubbornness. "Lead us up."

"Don't fall," he said.

"Not planning to."

He began to climb with Weylyn before him, slower this time. "Ye have a stubborn nature, lass," he said, waiting for her soft voice before he took another step higher. Weylyn didn't seem to be in a hurry as long as Alec had him against his chest.

"Ye are going to have to get used to it," she whispered.

Alec stopped, questions cluttering his head, but now was not the time. He needed them safe, out in the light, where he could check them over for injuries. "We are almost to the top," he said. The climb seemed longer as he stopped to listen for Mairi's movements. Every other step, he thought he heard her whimper. "Almost there. See the light?"

She didn't answer. "Mairi?" No answer. "Mairi?" he yelled.

"I can climb," Weylyn said. "Go get her." With that, his brave son pulled upward away from him, counting out loud each rung as he moved toward the men at the top.

Alec wanted to dive down the rungs, but he couldn't knock Mairi or chance pushing her into the deep pool below. "Mairi, answer me."

"Damnation," she whispered. "I…I can't feel my arms anymore." Her words were like the tiniest of breezes through the leaves of a tree. He felt them more than he heard them.

"Hold on," he said, using the same voice he used to push his warriors. "Don't ye dare let go."

"I love ye, Alec MacNeil," she whispered. It sounded like good-bye.

"Tell me to my face, Mairi Maclean." Panic surged through Alec's muscles as he felt frantically with his toes until they touched the top of her hair. "I'm here. Don't let go."

"I don't… Can't hold on."

"Your brother is above. He'll kill me if I let ye die down here."

A whispered laugh was right below him. How to get her without knocking her off the ladder? Alec pushed his back against the opposite wall to lower around her. He felt for her arms and realized she'd threaded them through the rungs, her hands limp and dangling. She'd worn herself out keeping his children alive.

He looped an arm around her waist, pulling her up against his chest, and felt her stiffen. "Ye're hurt," he said. She didn't answer. Slowly disentangling her arms from the rungs, he turned her in to him to set her arms over his shoulders.

"I've got ye. I'm not letting go. Never, Mairi. I'm never letting go of ye."

"Ye promise," she murmured, the brush of her lips against his bare chest, completely limp in his arms.

"With all my heart," he said, lifting her higher with each strong step.

"I see them," Tor called from above, his arms already reaching for his sister.

"Be careful," Alec said. "She's hurt. I'm not sure where or how badly." He loosened his hold for Tor to take her, but Mairi's arms wouldn't let go. "I'll bring her up," Alec said, stepping into the torchlight.

"Good God," Cullen said, and Tor held a blanket up to gently lower it over her shoulders. "Her back."

Alec stepped over the lip of the well, and a cheer flooded the tight room. Weylyn ran to hug his leg and Kenneth sat holding Cinnia. They seemed to be well. Dirty, exhausted, but smiles on their faces.

"She needs a healer," Tor said, his face grim, making Alec tuck Mairi against his shoulder. Through the rain, he carried her into the relatively untouched soldiers' quarters. Millie, her head bandaged, hurried over as Alec set Mairi on the bed Ian had occupied earlier. Slowly he turned her to face the mattress and lowered the blanket.

Anger and fear rose up in him like bile as he stared at the open gashes that had raked through her bodice. Charred and blistered, her flayed skin bled. Weylyn came in with Tor. "She made us climb below her, so when the ceiling caved in, anything that fell down the well would hit her first. She told Cinnia and me to press flat against the wall."

"Something fell down the hole?" Alec asked, his words gruff.

"Aye," Weylyn said, blinking back tears. "And it was on fire."

Chapter Twenty-Two

Mairi slept and, in the darkness, nightmares popped in and out. Burning rooms, a sneering priest who wasn't a priest at all, fire eating up her dress, scorching her back.

"Ye are safe." The deep whispers penetrated the pain, and in her dream she looked upward to see a bright light, Alec's face looking down. "I've got ye." And then he did have her, his warmth penetrating the cold that racked her, making her lungs burn and convulse with coughs. Even the pain ebbed when he held her. Clean water slid down her throat, making her wince and choke. Warm liquid followed when her coughing stopped. Sweet with honey, it coated the soreness.

She lay on something soft that smelled of flowers. The smell of smoke remained only in her fitful dreams. Mairi's neck ached, and she realized that she lay on her stomach. She blinked, the effort causing the shadows before her to bend and change. But she was too tired to follow them and relaxed back into dreams.

"Look at the stars." Alec smiled across from her in the boat as they glided under a night sky, clear and pierced with bright

constellations.

"I'd rather look at ye," she replied.

He rose, moving along the boat, which didn't even sway. She stood to face him as his lips came down to hers. His hands reached around to her back, sliding down her spine, and she gasped, rearing back. Alec's face shifted, concern heavy on his brows.

She blinked back tears, and the night scene shifted to daylight. The pain on her back ached and prickled at the same time, almost making her lapse back into darkness.

"*Stad*, her eyes are opening." Alec's voice called to her consciousness, and she fought to follow it. "Mairi, can ye hear me, love?"

Love? She was still asleep and let herself drift away again. Dreams flitted along with the churning chaos that comes with unconsciousness.

"Mairi, dear." Her mother whispered. "You will be fine. I'm here now." Her mother's strong voice faded into a scene of her childhood home, Aros, the blues and greens of the water offshore when the sun beat down. But then it turned into Kisimul, surrounded on all sides.

"I will lift her." Joan Maclean's voice was as strong as it always had been.

"I will," Alec answered her, stubbornness making his voice sharp and lethal.

"I am her mother."

"I am her husband."

Husband. Mairi clung to the word as water licked at her skin, making her shiver at the cold. *Fingers, numb and aching, curled along the edge of a small boat moored in the bay, one of the unused boats Alec had shown her. It began to sink, and she pushed away from it, swimming toward Kisimul to crawl upon the rocks where the sun could reach her. The sun beat harshly on her bare back, burning it, blistering it until she whimpered.*

"Ye are strong, Mairi." Alec's words calmed her, and she felt his warmth. His heat was different than the burning on her back. His was a gentle sun. "Drink," he said, and she opened her lips. It seemed that she was always drinking something. She relaxed back into oblivion.

Mairi blinked, her eyelids opening and closing slowly as if they were hinges that needed oil. She lay on her side, her face toward a low fire across the cottage room. This was Millie's cottage. Through the darkness, Mairi saw the woman lying on a pallet before the fire, breathing evenly.

Lips dry. Tongue stuck to the roof of her mouth. Mairi shifted in the bed, feeling the ache of unused limbs and a heavy binding across most of her back. A dampness clung to her body, as if she'd rested in morning dew. She needed to change her smock.

A shadow rose from the chair beside her, large and familiar. Alec moved silently to a washstand and wrung out a cloth, the water trickling back in. He bent before her and wiped the wet cloth along her lips. Jaw covered with an unkempt beard, eyes dark, lips tight. His haunted look reminded her of the warriors returning from a long series of battles. How long had she been asleep?

Warm fingers brushed some of her hair away from her forehead. She turned her face into his hand, looking up. Alec stilled. "Mairi?" he breathed and lay his palm against her forehead.

"Och, MacNeil," she whispered, her voice rough. "Ye've been battling."

Alec dropped the rag on the floor, bending over her, his hands wiping down her arms. "Your fever." He cradled her face in his hands, his mouth parted. "It's gone," he breathed out in a rush. "Thank God, it's gone."

She'd known she was hurt as she ran through her nightmares and dreams. "How long?" she asked and lifted her hand to grasp his wrist.

"Ye've been in and out of consciousness for nearly a fortnight."

Two weeks. Mairi let her hand fall back to the bed. "I am sorry," she said, feeling the press of tears in her eyes, but they didn't come. Did she not have enough water in her body to shed tears?

Alec ran his hand up one side of his face to pinch the bridge between his eyes. He blinked several times. "I am the one who is sorry. For leaving ye, for leaving my family there with a demented enemy. For leaving ye where ye were trapped on Kisimul."

She slid her hand across the blanket to his knee, resting it there, wanting the feel of contact. "Kisimul saved us." Her eyes opened wider as she realized the children weren't in the cottage. "Cinnia and Weylyn?"

"Well," he answered quickly, and a smile spread across his mouth. His eyes shut momentarily. "Because of ye, Mairi." He leaned closer, touching her face again as if to make sure she was still without fever. "Ye saved them, sacrificed yourself to keep them unharmed."

Tears did manage to form in her stinging eyes, one pearling out over her bottom lid. "I love them."

He caught the tear on his knuckle. His face serious. "Mairi, I—" but behind him someone pushed up to stand.

"Is she talking in her sleep again?" It was her mother.

"Nay," Alec said, his lips turning up as he kept the connection between their gazes. "The fever broke."

"What?" Mairi's mother jumped to her bedside. "Mairi," she cried, pushing past Alec with elbows and skirts. Her hands slid down Mairi's face, her lips puckering to press on her forehead, testing the temperature like she had when she was a child. Mairi inhaled the familiar scent of home that her mother carried with her.

"Thank the good Lord," Joan cried, wiping her hand down Mairi's arms and stomach. "Ye're soaked." She smiled widely. "Not a bit of fever."

The chill from her wet clothes made her shiver. "My back bloody hell hurts," Mairi said, her voice sounding caked in sand. "And my neck from lying here."

Another body rose from behind Alec. How many people were sleeping on the floor of Millie's cottage? "She's cursing. That's a good sign." Tor's face came into the glow of the candle flickering on the bedside table.

Alec lifted her slowly to sit. She cursed softly. "My back?" she asked. She met Alec's gaze. "From the fire."

"Aye," Alec said. "Ye have a bad burn, but it's healing."

"Millie started using snail slime on the burns immediately," Joan said with a nod toward the woman who had woken on some instinct. Millie brought over a cup of something steaming. "And feverfew and honey for your throat," Joan said, taking the cup with a smile and nod. Millie grinned down at Mairi and pressed her fingers against the pulse in Mairi's wrist. She nodded to Joan, her face seeming to relax as if great relief released all the tiny muscles amongst her wrinkles.

The brew wet Mairi's mouth and slid down her throat, clearing it.

"We need to change her smock and sheets," Joan said and flapped her hands to shoo Alec and Tor out of the room.

"I will be just outside," Alec said and bent to kiss her forehead, his lips lingering as if he, too, wanted to test the coolness of her skin.

Daisy's brothers followed Millie to where she had a folded pile of sheets near the hearth. "Millie likes the dogs?" Mairi asked, afraid to ask about her sweet Daisy. She blinked, her face pinching toward despair.

"They dragged her from the burning great hall when she was unconscious," Alec said from the doorway where he stopped, his gaze meeting hers. Such emotion sat in his eyes, yet he just smiled. "Daisy is sleeping with the children. She is fine."

• • •

"Mairi!" Weylyn yelled, running inside the cottage, Daisy on his heels. Bathed, dressed, combed, and fed, Mairi sat up on the low bed that had held her these past weeks. Weylyn and Daisy pushed past Mairi's mother to jump up onto the bed. The jarring pulled at Mairi's back, but she kept her smile.

"Careful," Joan scolded. Daisy licked furiously at Mairi's hand as Weylyn pulled her back.

Mairi laughed and felt tears press hard in her eyes. It seemed she cried easier now. "My sweet pup."

Weylyn smiled hugely. "She barked and ran to Da when he swam onshore. Then she barked at the well to tell everyone where we were." He scratched Daisy's head. "Such a smart girl."

Mairi looked at Alec who was walking in with a load of cut peat. "Ye swam? At night, in the North Atlantic."

"My da's rotting boat was the only one not burning, and it sank halfway across," Alec said, lowering his burden beside the hearth.

Weylyn jounced the bed with excitement, and Mairi winced slightly. "Did ye tell her about the mansion—?"

"Stop bouncing her," Alec said.

"Mairi, Mairi!" Cinnia ran inside, her hands clutching wildflowers. Their red, pink, and purple heads bobbed on stems. "Ye're awake!"

Mairi smiled broadly as Cinnia dropped the flowers in her lap and bent to gingerly hug her. She looked perfectly sound, just like Weylyn, and relief nearly reduced Mairi to a puddle of sobs.

"Ye're hurting her," Alec said, his hands reaching out to haul them back.

Mairi shook her head and sniffed. "I'm just relieved they are well."

"We are," Cinnia said. "Thanks to ye. I never would have gone down that well without ye coaxing me, showing me how brave ye were even after being locked in the trunk at Kilchoan." She looked at Alec. "She's the bravest lady I've ever met."

Mairi's breath stopped in her chest as she met Alec's hard gaze. She could read the lethal promise in his face. Cinnia must have told him her story about eluding her stepson while at Kilchoan. Normand MacInnes's days were few if he ever showed himself again.

Outside, Millie's chickens squawked, and Daisy ran out the door barking. Tor swung in through the doorway. "There are riders approaching."

Alec's face tightened in impatience. "It's becoming more crowded by the minute," he said.

Mairi flexed her toes where they sat on the wood floor. Everything felt stiff. "Ye're used to a huge, empty castle around ye." Millie handed her another cup of fragrant, heavily honeyed brew, and she took a sip. It soothed away any vestiges of sore throat.

Outside, horses clopped in the pebbled courtyard. "Where is she?" came a voice out front. "Mairi? Joan?" Ava Maclean, Tor's wife, rushed inside the door. She had her young babe strapped to her chest. Grace Ellington, her companion and half sister, followed. "Oh, thank the good Lord," Ava said and bent before Mairi to hug her, one hand supporting baby Hazel.

"Mind her back," Joan said. "It's badly burned."

"Absolutely horrible," Grace said and squeezed Mairi's other hand.

"What are ye two doing here? And the wee one?" Mairi asked.

Tor walked inside, pulling Ava in to him, his thumb brushing softly at Hazel's pink cheek as he leaned over both of them. His joy at seeing his wife warred with his grumpy expression. "Aye, what are ye doing here?"

"Two weeks is too long to go without a word," Ava retorted. "And don't start yelling at Gavin. Grace and I were going to leave with Hazel on our own. It was either lock us up—"

"Which he knew he couldn't do without getting a knife in his damned gut," Grace said, making a slashing motion with her hand. In the lovely riding habit and fine hood that she wore, the brandishing and swearing was comic. Mairi fought to keep her smile from bursting into laughter.

"Lock us up or come along with us," Ava said and punctuated her explanation with a sharp nod.

"He took six others with us to help keep Hazel safe," Grace added. "We were perfectly fine. Rose ordered some of Cullen's men to guard Aros, while you all were occupied up here. Thus, there's no need to be concerned about home." Her delicate English accent floated about them in humorous contrast to the homey cottage strewn with healing tinctures and poultice wraps.

Tor kissed Ava, bringing a rosy stain to her cheeks, and helped her unwrap Hazel to take his bairn into his arms.

"Ye didn't have to come all this way," Mairi said.

"Pish," Ava said, waving her hand. "We should have left with Joan when Cullen first came to collect her. We needed to make sure ye hadn't been killed in that terrible fire."

"It takes a lot to kill a Maclean," Joan said and sat on the bed next to Mairi. Her mother pulled her into a hug without hurting her back at all. How did mothers do that?

"My," Grace continued, studying Alec. "You must be

the ferocious Wolf of Kisimul." She let her gaze wander appreciatively over Alec's brawny arms and chest, making Mairi's smile tighten.

"Alec MacNeil, the chief of Barra Island and Kisimul," Mairi said for introduction. "And the man who rescued me from wedding Geoff MacInnes." *And my husband*, sat right on the tip of Mairi's tongue, but she kept it there. Alec had said he'd married her before the stars and that it was up to her to complete the union with her oath. But when she'd tried before…the pain of his rejection stung worse than her back. She swallowed and looked away from him. "And this is Millie," she introduced. "I've taken up her bed for the last two weeks."

Millie brushed off the gratitude with a smile and some signs with her hands.

"She says that ye would do the same for her," Alec said. "That ye are a hero for saving the children." He looked to Ava and Grace. "Millie doesn't hear. She reads lips and uses her hands to speak."

Ava smiled. "Saved the children? It sounds like there's quite a story to be told."

"It could be a whole ballad to the brave and beautiful Mairi Maclean," Cullen called from the open window as he grinned inside. "I think I'll write it." He winked at Mairi. Years ago, the gesture would have set Mairi's heart racing, but not now. She glanced to Alec, who wore a frown as he eyed Cullen. But then Rose, Cullen's new wife, appeared beside him in the window.

"*Mon dieu*, Cullen," Rose said, rolling her eyes at him before returning to smile broadly at Mairi. "'Tis so good to see you awake," she said in her French accent.

"Ye came all this way," Mairi said, shaking her head. "I didn't even know the MacDonalds and Duffies had a ship."

"We don't," Cullen said with a grin. "But a few choice

words from my fierce wife—"

"Along with the combined force of Gavin's men from Aros and Cullen's uncle's men from Dunyvaig," Grace added.

"Persuaded Geoff MacInnes that he needed to turn around and sail us back to Barra," Rose finished.

"Good God," Mairi whispered. "Ye have all been busy while I just slept."

"Sleep is healing," Ava said, drawing Grace closer to spy down the back of Mairi's loose dress. "The burn is extensive." Millie signed about the snail slime poultice she was using while Mairi and Alec translated.

"Wonderful," Ava said.

"Millie started it before I arrived," Joan said. "Working swiftly may have been what saved Mairi." Joan sniffed with her smile, nodding her head at Millie.

Millie pointed to a corner where she had a number of flat rocks stacked. "God's teeth," Grace said. "Look at all these snails." Millie beamed as she waved them toward the doorway, and they followed.

"She has more outside," Alec said, walking toward Mairi, his frown still in place. He bent before her and picked up a foot to place a slipper on it. Then the other.

"Are we going somewhere?" Mairi asked, a smile bright on her lips. Joan had barely let her stand, let alone venture outdoors.

"Somewhere not so damn crowded."

"A charred Kisimul is looking pretty good right now, isn't it?" Mairi asked as he helped her up to stretch her legs. Alec didn't say anything, his face grim. Mairi touched his cheek. "We will rebuild."

His gaze snapped down to hers. "We?"

"Mairi?" A timid voice pulled her attention to the door where Bessy stood. There were tears in her eyes, her fingers gripping the doorframe.

Mairi smiled at her, and Bessy ran inside, arms outstretched. "I am so sorry." Tears ran down her face as she pressed into Mairi, hugging without touching her back. "My brother threatened to kill me if I said anything about the priest being a Cameron. I didn't know their plans."

"Alec told me ye killed him," Mairi whispered against the side of Bessy's face. Bessy shook as if the memory was washing over her.

"He wouldn't let me pull Millie out of the hall that was on fire. Said she should die, too." Her gaze moved to Alec. "That she was like a mother to The MacNeil and needed to die with the rest of his family." She turned back to Mairi. "He dragged me out into the bailey, but he didn't expect me to be carrying a blade." She swallowed hard and wiped her face. "When I returned for Millie, the two dogs had pulled her free of the room, but I couldn't get through it to the well room door."

Mairi lay her palm on Bessy's cold hand. "I always knew ye were brave."

As if her kind words were the squeeze on sopping rags, tears welled over Bessy's lower lids to re-wet her cheeks. "But I was terribly frightened," she whispered.

"It's how we act that makes us brave." Mairi looked toward the open window where the babble of voices rose and fell with French, English, and Scots accents. "Have ye met my family yet?" What a beautifully tangled family she had. Bessy shook her head, her face paling. Mairi indicated the door. "They don't bite."

Alec caught Mairi's hand, bending his face down to her. "Ye said we."

"What?" she asked, looking up into his handsome face. He was frowning, but his eyes were alert, searching.

"Just a minute ago, about rebuilding Kisimul, ye said—"

"Mairi," Tor yelled inside. "Looks like Ava, Grace, and Rose frightened poor Geoff enough to make him give back your dowry."

Alec cursed under his breath and straightened up, crossing his arms over his chest to frown at Tor as he walked in. "Good, ye're up," he said and took her arm, leading her out into the sunshine where a cart was parked, her dowry trunk tied to the back.

"The ladies of Mull and Islay are a powerful force," Mairi said.

Cinnia ran up to her with a crown of wildflowers in her hands. "Here, for ye." Bluebells, daisies, and bright yellow trefoil flowers were intertwined into a ring. "In celebration of ye being well again."

"It's lovely," Mairi said, bending for her to place it on her loose hair, which her mother had brushed into gleaming after her morning bath. "Thank ye." When she stood up, Rose came to give her a gentle squeeze.

Alec took Mairi's arm. "We?" he said near her ear. "We need to talk. Ye said we." He led her around the cart where one of her brother's warriors from Aros helped Tor unload the dowry trunk.

"Mairi," Gavin said with a large grin. "Good to see ye up." His smile hardened, making his youth fade away to maturity. "Geoff sends his apologies," he said, his gaze moving to Alec with a nod. "Ye are free from your betrothal."

Alec snorted. "She was free the moment she left Kilchoan." He tried to lead her away, but Tor's second-in-command, Hamish, came to give her a kiss, and then Broc Duffie. With each person, Alec's face tightened until his glance was razor sharp. Mairi hid her grin. The man, used to his solitude, was ready to explode in all the commotion.

Mairi's mother walked over. "I think Mairi should go back inside out of the sun."

"The sun feels wonderful," Mairi said.

Alec's voice boomed. "And we are going for a ride."

"What? She's not up to it yet," Joan said. "She'll lose her seat."

"Not sitting before me." Alec continued to lead Mairi away from the clusters of people in Millie's courtyard. They walked slowly behind Millie's swayback, thatched barn where Sköll stood, looking quite out of place in the crude dwelling.

He left her to lean against the stone wall as he quickly saddled his horse. Mairi was tired from the activity, but watching Alec, the muscles of his arms and back flexing and moving, kicked up her pulse. Without a word, he led the horse and then Mairi outside, lifting her into the large saddle. He swung up behind, pulling her intimately against his inner thighs. His kilt rode up, giving her a beautiful view of his tanned, powerful legs. Memories of those legs intertwined with her own rose up inside Mairi, making her cheeks warm. She touched her palm to one. When had she started to blush like a prim, innocent lass?

"Where are we going?" she asked.

His breath was warm on her ear, and her inhale caught. "Somewhere private." He set his horse into a rolling canter across the green grass of the meadow and uphill toward the knoll overlooking Kisimul, where they'd first made love under the stars. Despite the sun, the breeze was cool, and she shivered in Alec's arms. He bent back, slowing the horse, and whipped out a wool blanket to cover her, wrapping them together.

As they crested the knoll, Mairi's gaze turned to Kisimul, the proud fortress in the sea. It looked…cursed. The fire must have been fierce. Black painted the upper turrets behind the great hall where the fire had licked up to bring down the upper bedrooms. The gray stone stood solemn and still. The MacNeil Wolf flag didn't fly from the wall. The ferry wasn't docked. "It looks lonely," she said, her words caught in the breeze.

Alec dismounted and reached up to pull her off, setting

her down in the swaying grass, speckled with wild daisies. "No one is on Kisimul. It is cursed."

Mairi looked into his face. His expression was hard, tortured. "Kisimul isn't cursed," Mairi said. "It saved us, its walls too strong to fall in the fire."

He exhaled long. "I am so sorry."

"Ye didn't— "

"I left ye there, with a madman. Ye were locked inside."

"But Kisimul protected us in the end," she said.

He exhaled and looked at it, bulky and burned like a scorched carcass in the bay. "I was raised there, raised alone. It was all I knew. It stood for MacNeil strength."

"It still does," she said. "And we can rebuild it."

He turned to her, searching her eyes. "Ye said we."

Mairi took Alec's hands. "Aye." She met his gaze, suddenly unsure. "Ye said on the ship that night." She glanced down at her toes peeking from her skirts. "That ye had given me your oath. That I needed to give ye the oath back, and we'd be wed. I tried." She looked up to meet his eyes. They were such a beautiful stormy blue in the sunlight. "I will stay with ye, even on Kisimul. As long as I'm with ye, no matter where that is, I am yours. Before ye and God, I swear this."

Mairi blinked, realizing that tears sat in her eyes. Blushing and weeping; what had love done to her? *Love*. Aye, that was the squeeze she felt in her chest as she waited for Alec to respond.

He drew her in to him, his hand going to her hair to fix her flower crown. His fingers trailed down through her waves to her shoulder, and his sensuous mouth softened. "Ye swore."

She nodded. "I can't imagine leaving here." She swallowed. "Leaving ye. Even if we are on Kisimul."

"Curses are made of fear and discontent," he said, using her words. He shook his head. "I will give ye the freedom to leave, though know wherever ye go, I will follow. When I thought I'd lost ye, I knew…I knew for certain that I love ye, Mairi."

Mairi blinked against the tears swimming in her vision and stepped closer into his arms. "I love ye, too, Alec MacNeil. I'm not going anywhere."

Alec cupped her cheeks and lowered his mouth to hers as she wrapped her hands around the back of his neck. Their lips met urgently and completely, a continual oath to each other, sealing it with something stronger than words. The sun beat down, the fresh breeze blowing as God and all creation witnessed Mairi and Alec's union. Sealed completely with a kiss that was given and taken with absolute love.

"Ho there," came Kenneth's voice, making Alec slowly break the kiss. But his gaze remained connected to Mairi.

"Shall we make it official then?" Ian called.

Alec turned, pulling Mairi into his side. Lips still damp with their oath, Mairi stared out at the procession coming up onto the knoll. "Oh my," she breathed. A mass of people walked toward them, Weylyn and Cinnia, running in front with Daisy. Kenneth slapped Alec on the back.

"I take it she said aye," Ian said, working his still-bound leg under him, his arm propped on a crutch. He smiled at Mairi.

"I did," she said. "But…?" Her arm went out to the people trudging up the hill. Her family in the lead, but followed by Barra villagers, several ladies around Millie. One of the women shrieked as Millie's dogs flew past her to run up the hill with Daisy, Ares, and Alec's wolfhounds.

"They've come to see their chief wed," Ian said.

Kenneth looked out toward the large group. "Your priest from Mull came and has agreed to save our souls until another cleric can be found for Barra. He can bless ye and bless the ground as well."

"The ground?" Mairi asked, looking down at the grass

where the daisies waved up at her.

Alec pulled her around to face him. "We are building, but not on Kisimul. This hill is where our home will be."

"But Kisimul?" she asked.

"We will rebuild, but we will not live there. If Weylyn or Cinnia wish to return when they leave home, they can, but they will have the choice. Otherwise, Kisimul will be used for official functions and as a refuge if Barra is in danger."

Mairi looked out at the bay, remembering the view in the dark with stars overhead. "This meadow is our special place," she whispered and looked to Alec.

"Aye, lass." He bent close to her ear. "Where I will love ye under the stars." His words sent a sensual shiver down through Mairi, and she turned to kiss him again.

Someone cleared his throat. "I believe there are some oaths to take before the kiss." Father Kenan smiled, his bushy brows raised, and Mairi released her hold on Alec. By then the group of over a hundred people had made it up, filling their grassy hill. Children chased butterflies and dragonflies amongst the flowers. Dogs chased the children, making them laugh and tumble. And people clustered around, smiling and shushing one another.

It was the most beautiful of days, and Mairi tipped her face to the blue sky. With Father Kenan's words, they repeated their oaths for the crowd, and before the clergy could suggest it, Alec pulled her back into his arms.

"Ye are no longer the lone Wolf of Kisimul Castle," Mairi said, smiling into his face.

"And ye are no longer its captive," he said. "Ye are Mairi MacNeil, and I love ye."

"Come here," she said, tugging him down. "I love ye, too."

As their lips met, a cheer rose through the crowd, but Mairi lost herself in the power wrapping around her, protecting her and freeing her at the same time. The power of love.

Acknowledgments

Thank you, Braden, for all your loving support. Without you, I could not be the woman I am. You believed in me when I started writing, lifted me up when I faltered, literally carried me when I was too weak to walk, held me when I shook and hurt, and celebrated with me every time I won with a positive doctor's appointment. You are a fabulous father, an honorable man, and a brawny and powerful Highlander, who is always up for "loving me under the stars." I love you for always.

• • •

As at the end of each of my books, I please ask that you, my awesome readers, remind yourselves of the whispered symptoms of ovarian cancer. I am now a six-year survivor, one of the lucky ones. Please don't rely on luck. If you experience any of these symptoms, consistently for three weeks or more, go see your GYN.

Bloating

Eating less and feeling full faster

Abdominal pain

Trouble with your bladder

Other symptoms may include: indigestion, back pain, pain with intercourse, constipation, fatigue, and menstrual irregularities.

About the Author

Heather McCollum is an award-winning historical romance writer. She is a member of Romance Writers of America and the Ruby Slippered Sisterhood of 2009 Golden Heart finalists.

The ancient magic and lush beauty of Great Britain entrances Ms. McCollum's heart and imagination every time she visits. The country's history and landscape have been a backdrop for her writing ever since her first journey across the pond.

When she is not creating vibrant characters and magical adventures on the page, she is roaring her own battle cry in the war against ovarian cancer. Ms. McCollum recently slayed the cancer beast and resides with her very own Highland hero, rescued golden retriever, and three kids in the wilds of suburbia on the mid-Atlantic coast. For more information about Ms. McCollum, please visit www.HeatherMcCollum.com.

URL and Social Media links:

Website: HeatherMcCollum.com
Facebook: facebook.com/HeatherMcCollumAuthor
Twitter: twitter.com/HMcCollumAuthor
Pinterest: pinterest.com/hmccollumauthor/
Instagram: instagram.com/heathermccollumauthor/

Discover the Highland Isles series...

The Beast of Aros Castle

The Rogue of Islay Isle

The Devil of Dunakin Castle

Also by Heather McCollum

Highland Heart

Captured Heart

Tangled Hearts

Untamed Hearts

Crimson Heart

The Scottish Rogue

The Savage Highlander

The Wicked Viscount

The Highland Outlaw

Highland Conquest

Highland Warrior

Highland Justice

Highland Beast

Highland Surrender

The Highlander's Unexpected Proposal

The Highlander's Pirate Lass

The Highlander's Tudor Lass

The Highlander's Secret Avenger

Get Scandalous with these historical reads...

How to Marry a Marquess

a Wedded by Scandal novel by Stacy Reid

Lady Evie Chesterfield is a darling of the *ton* who refuses to become engaged. She's been desperately in love with her brother's friend, Richard Maitland, Marquess of Westfall, since forever. But the dark, dangerous marquess only sees her has a friend and refuses to marry any woman. When circumstances change and Evie has no choice but to take a husband, she decides to convince London's most notorious gentleman to marry her by seducing the scoundrel.

The Duke Meets His Match

an Infamous Somertons novel by Tina Gabrielle

Chloe Somerton grew up poor. Desperate to aid her sisters, she'd picked a pocket...or two. Now Chloe has a chance to marry a young, wealthy lord. Only his mentor—a dark, dangerous duke—stands in her way. The duke knows about her past, and she'll do anything to keep him from telling. What begins as a battle of wills soon escalates into a fierce attraction...

How to Lose a Highlander

a MacGregor Lairds novel by Michelle McLean

In this Highlander *Taming of the Shrew* meets *How to Lose a Guy in 10 Days* tale, Sorcha Campbell and Laird Malcolm MacGregor are determined to break the bonds of their forced matrimony. To do so, they'll have to keep their hands, and hearts, to themselves, or risk being permanently wed. But there's a thin line between love and hate, and even their feuding clans might not be enough to keep their passion at bay.

The Elusive Wife

a Marriage Mart Mayhem novel by Callie Hutton

Newly arrived from the country for the Season, Lady Olivia is appalled to discover that her own husband, Jason Cavendish, Lord Coventry, doesn't even recognize her. She's not about to tell the arrogant arse she's his wife. Instead, she flirts with him by night and has her modiste send her mounting bills to him by day. Hell hath no fury like a woman scorned...too bad this woman finds her husband nearly irresistible.